Seven Patients

by

Atul Kumar

TELEMACHUS PRESS

Seven Patients

The publisher does not have any control over and does not assume any responsibility for author or third-party websites or their content.

Cover art and design by Telemachus Press, LLC

Cover Art:
Copyright © Thinkstockphoto/100843778/Hemera
Copyright © Thinkstockphoto/104115210/iStockphoto
Copyright © Thinkstockphoto/104193660/iStockphoto
Copyright © Thinkstockphoto/98380835/iStockphoto

Published by Telemachus Press, LLC
http://www.telemachuspress.com

ISBN# 978-1-937387-63-1 (eBook)
ISBN# 978-1-937387-64-8 (paperback)

Version 2012.05.30

Printed in the United States of America
10 9 8 7 6 5 4 3 2 1

To Neeta Varshney.

*"The art of medicine consists in amusing the patient
while nature cures the disease."*

François-Marie Arouet (aka—Voltaire)

Seven Patients

Chapter One:
Shaken

WE WERE JUST about to start our team dinner at 11 p.m. when everyone's pager simultaneously went off. There was no need to check the message because the overhead intercom blared, "CODE BLUE, ER, ETA 2 min; CODE BLUE, ER, ETA 2 min."

Scarfing down whatever morsels of food we could stuff into our mouths, we all ran to the ER and took our positions near the large trauma doors ... awaiting whatever disaster was headed our way.

The atmosphere was one of tense anxiety, with everyone ready to leap to action but with nothing yet to do. Masks were donned and gloves snapped on as all ER personnel made their way towards the trauma doors; leaving the 20 ER patients who were in various states of agony and distress temporarily ignored.

All attention was focused on the two humongous double doors leading to the ambulance docking bay. The immediate team was two senior physicians, two residents, two interns, a respiratory therapist, a pharmacist, three nurses, and me, the omnipresent token medical student—harbinger of just enough knowledge to be dangerous.

After 20 seconds of uncertain stares and unnoticed tics, a faint siren was heard, getting louder and louder—there would be no

Doppler effect with this ambulance as it would stop just a few yards from where I stood.

As the siren was reaching an almost unbearable crescendo it suddenly died, tires screeched, gears crunched, and there was that moment of deafening silence before the trauma doors ferociously flung open. A team of paramedics rushed in and Dr. Peters began to get debriefed. The patient was surrounded by medical personnel so quickly that I never even got a glance.

"Cyanotic and apneic on arrival, unresponsive to pain, unable to intubate in the field, naso-tracheal tube placed without complication, responded to positive ventilation, heart rate 180 and weak at first, now strong, poor breath sounds on the right, normal on the left. No IV access. C-collar placed. Pupils dilated and unreactive. Initially flaccid, and unfortunately that hasn't changed much," the lead medic expelled in a single breath en route from the door to trauma bay #2, a total distance of about 20 feet.

All the while Dr. Peters made no comment and looked only at her patient, nodding once at the end of his report, a nod only found in the medical world, indicating he did a superb job and his superiors would be notified of his efforts. Understanding they were relieved, the medics quickly peeled off to complete their paperwork at the central work station.

"Get me an IV kit, hook up the EKG leads, and get CT ready STAT," barked Dr. Peters, with a confidence that comes only with years of experience and having seen everything before, at least twice. "Also call the OR and give them a heads up. You," pointing to one of the senior residents, "take off the remaining clothes and do a complete primary assessment while she scribes."

Having something to do, the crowd dispersed, each with their own specific task. I was finally able to nudge my way in and get a look at our focus of attention for this evening. It was strange— despite the number of people, the room seemed vacuous. Instead of the normal array of large life-sustaining machinery, everything was miniature. Four physicians and a respiratory therapist were huddled around a gurney. As I drew nearer I realized it wasn't a gurney at all; it was a crib.

Our patient was a mere ten pounds and barely two feet in size. This was a pediatric code!

No wonder the commotion was more intense than normal, children, and especially infants, always put medical personnel on edge. I'm not entirely sure why. I used to think it's because nobody wants to see a child sick, but I think the real reason is that pediatric care is so highly litigious that everything is scrutinized.

In an effort to make myself useful I quickly looked around the room. I must have repeated this gesture several times because a nurse came up to me and recommended perhaps I stand on a stool and observe instead of spinning around like a dreidel in everyone's way.

Withdrawn, I slouched down, found a stool, and silently took up position in the corner of the room and out of the way, the omnipresent but seldom noticed medical student. At least this time I had a nice bird's eye view.

"I got IV access, left foot," announced one of the residents.

"Leads in place, normal rhythm with tachycardia," announced another.

"Hand me the 3.5 French tube, the 4's too big for this lil' guy … and some cricothyroid pressure, gentle there … FUCK, he's in spasm. Get the fiber optic set here now! CT ready for us yet?" Dr. Peters was starting to get strained. She seldom didn't get things on the first try, and two failed intubation attempts was not going to set her in a good mood.

The fiber optic intubation set appeared out of nowhere, and the pediatric laryngoscope was so small it looked like a toy. Almost immediately a high resolution image appeared on the LCD monitor. On the screen was a wide field image of the trauma bay, followed by an image of a tongue, a pharynx, and soon, the trachea, a small dark opening leading right to the lungs. Next we saw the clear plastic tube fill in the gap and the picture went snowy as the scope was removed. The endotracheal tube's balloon was inflated and artificial ventilation initiated. Almost instantly the baby went from a bluish hue to a healthy pink color as both lungs began to rhythmically rise and fall with each pump of the tiny ventilator bag, no larger than the size of a small juice box. The whole process took about 10 seconds.

"CT is ready," hollered a voice from the hallway. As soon as the vital signs were confirmed to be present and relatively stable, the baby was ushered to the scanner by an entourage of no less than seven highly trained professionals with only one goal: keeping this stranger alive.

I saw them turn the corner and disappear, but not before I saw Dr. Peters shaking her head. The subtle gesture was for her and her alone, but having the bird's eye view, I caught it. She was kicking herself for requiring the video guided scope. Granted it makes intubations much easier, using it is an admission of failing to intubate the "real" way, sans technological assistance. It's analogous to the pre-GPS days when we had to stop the car and ask for directions. Nobody liked doing it, but sometimes it was just necessary.

As quickly as the trauma bay was populated, it vacated. Only I remained within the empty room. No longer organized and sanitary, instead it was deserted with medical detritus scattered everywhere. Miniature and futuristic looking machines littered the room. Most were still on and emitting various beeps and tones, just without the consistent undulations associated with a beating heart or other functioning organs.

I stepped off my pedestal and directly into a puddle of unknown fluid. It was more viscous than water, but relatively odorless, probably something used to lubricate tubes for intubation. As I started to wipe the goo off my shoes, I heard footsteps enter the room.

"Hey, are you one of the docs that took care of that kid that was just here? I'm Detective Higgs," boomed a baritone voice from above.

I looked up, and up some more, and there stood not a man, but a mobile mountain. He must have been at least 6 feet, 8 inches tall and 300 pounds. His tan uniform and bullet proof vest couldn't conceal that he spent a considerable amount of time in a gym. The well worn shoulder strap and rapid release holster had definitely seen some action. The confidence in his stance and steadiness of his voice indicated he was secure in his abilities and comfortable in the hospital setting.

"Hi Detective," I replied while standing on one foot with a gooey towel dripping who knew what in my hand. "I'm not sure that I'm going to be of much help to you. I'm just the medical student. I think the active players in this rescue are still down the hall in radiology."

He just stood there, taking everything in. I broke the silence, "I know the age of criminals has been decreasing, but the kid here couldn't have been more than five months, way too young to do much more than wet a diaper."

My attempt at humor was met with more silence.

He scanned the room, presumably looking for somebody else to talk to, but I was the only one in sight. I'm sure merely uttering 'medical student' had prompted his complete disinterest. Deciding his time would be better spent elsewhere, he turned and left without another word.

Being a medical student meant I was on the lowest rung of the medical hierarchy, staff and physicians paid more attention to volunteers. The next rung of the ladder was senior medical student, or Sub I (meaning a graduating student, or Sub-Intern), followed by intern (referring to the first year of one's residency), resident (senior resident generally means that 2 years remain until completion and chief resident refers to the final year of residency, which can vary from 3 to 7 years in length). One can either quit and start a career after residency or continue to train by way of fellowship, another 1 to 3 years of super-specialization. After all training is complete, a physician is known as an 'attending' in which they are fully board certified and the top of the totem pole.

After medical school is when the MD degree is bestowed, and one becomes a real 'doctor' and is no longer a student. But it's only after completion of internship that a doctor obtains an actual medical license and drug prescription privileges. But good luck practicing any medicine, which requires board certification; that is only granted after completion of residency or fellowship, depending on which field in medicine.

Given my tremendous immediate responsibilities of wiping goo off my shoe, I decided to follow him. Hell, if the goo could be used to intubate an infant, it wouldn't harm my kicks.

"Excuse me, Detective?" I called out as I chased him down the hallway to the center of the ER—the "command center" as we dubbed it. This was the central hub where all the computers and charts were located. Surrounding it were 12 rooms with clear Plexiglass doors. Off to the side were the two massive trauma bays and a third one that could be opened up if needed. Further down the hall was a similar setup, only smaller with eight rooms and no trauma area.

Man the guy could move! I had to jog to catch up to him, and he wasn't even walking fast. "Is there something I can help you with? I pretty much saw everything that happened."

He pondered the offer and replied, "Yeah, who's in charge today? Can you go get them for me? I'll be in the lounge."

Great, the only thing medical students are good for—getting stuff. Oh well, I had nothing better going on. "Sure, it's Dr. Peters. I'll find her for you. What do I tell her you want to talk about?"

"Peters, huh? Don't worry about it then. She's one of the few who'll find me when she has a chance. She knows where I'll be." He sauntered off into the physicians' lounge.

Figuring I probably shouldn't follow; I snuck into the lounge anyway, before the door closed behind him and locked me out. The detective must be a higher-up to have access to the coveted lounge. Only chief residents and attending physicians have the clearance required to enter.

In reality it's nothing more than a few padded chairs and tables, LCD televisions, a handful of computers, and a kitchen, but it provides a respite from the bustling ER. Not to mention free food—not the generic shrink-wrapped sandwiches and no-name colas. The kitchen is stocked with everything from double-shot Starbucks and Rockstar energy drinks to catered hot food from local restaurants.

The detective grabbed a Diet Coke from the fridge and took a seat in the back corner, like he'd done this a number of times before. Before he could grab the nearest magazine, I walked over and tried to start up a conversation. It couldn't hurt to have an ally in the police world.

"Detective Higgs, right?" He looked up, but said nothing. "Hi, I'm Rajen. Just started my third year of medical school here. I don't have much experience, but every time I've seen law enforcement in the ER it's usually restraining somebody with either a psychiatric or drug problem, or escorting the loser of a bar fight. Pediatric law enforcement is a new one for me. What brings you by today?"

"Well, I figure since you already saw the kid, it's not a huge secret. Did you see the couple of teens my partner had cuffed in the holding area?" I nodded, negative. "Well, those are supposedly the parents, if you can call 'em that. Don't even know if they're out of high school yet. It's just like that 'Baby Shaker' game people used to play on their phones before it was banned, only in real life."

"You mean the *parents* did this to her? It could've been an accident, right?"

"It wasn't no accident, that's for sure. I bet the parents did it, and more likely than not, on purpose. They just didn't anticipate getting caught. Everyone thinks they're smart enough to get away. I bet the kid will have perfectly round cigarette burns all over her arms (of course the parents are going to claim it's from rashes that she scratched), and then there will be numerous broken bones in various stages of healing (the parents will know nothing about those). The kicker is, and I'll bet you 10:1 on this, the story will be that the kid fell from a crib or table or something when nobody was around and they just found her down. They'll try to blame a nanny or something, but will provide no contact information or name of the alleged caregiver."

He took a break to take a pull from his Diet Coke, emptying the seemingly tiny can in his giant paw. He crumbled the can and slammed it into the garbage can with force. "It eats me alive that people do this to innocent little children …"

Just then Dr. Peters walked in. "Evening, Detective. I take it you're here for the shake-n-bake I just escorted to the OR?" The grisly way medical professionals refer to Shaken Baby Syndrome. She nodded in my direction, with a hint of recognition, but clearly not recalling my name.

"Yeah, how'd you guess? Parents keep getting younger. Figure the Mom is still in her teens and your guess is as good as mine on who the Pop is. One thing's for sure, it's not the dude with her now. He could give a rat's ass about the kid. Baby got the usual findings?"

"I think so, I definitely saw the characteristic cigarette burns and the CT showed a subdural hematoma which was compressing the brain and causing a significant midline shift. There were several bruises that I'm sure correspond to underlying broken bones. The neurosurgeon is on his way over to drain the hematoma now. I'd give her a 30% chance of making it, and if she does, she'll be just like the CP'ers and FLK's."

"CP'ers?" I tentatively asked as I introduced myself to the famed Dr. Peters, the number two in the university ER hierarchy and on the famed hospital board of directors. She could easily make or break a neophyte medical student's career.

"Ah, yes, you just started today, didn't you? I remember your application. You did very well, pleasure to meet you." She shook my hand as she poured herself a coffee, black. "Sorry your first major ER case has to be such a sad one. CP'ers is just more dark medical jargon; it's how we refer to kids with cerebral palsy, the ones who are institutionalized with self-destructive behaviors. You've undoubtedly seen them in public, wearing helmets and goggles 'cause they bang their heads and poke their eyes out. Some can talk, most just drool. They're a huge burden on the family and society."

Higgs got up and cracked his knuckles, startling me. I thought firecrackers just went off. He moved towards us with a glint in his eyes; something was about to happen. "Hey Doc," he whispered in an almost conspiratorial tone, "you up for a game of 'good cop, bad doc' like we used to play before you had kids and got soft?"

Peters chugged down half her coffee and winked at Higgs, "Oh, I'm in, just like in the good ol' days, when you had a six-pack and not a keg?"

"Touché. Let's bring med student along, and show him what medicine is really like." Turning to me he said, "Follow us kid, and keep your mouth *shut*."

~~~~

"Hey Doc, I ain't been to med school or anything, but last I checked you got to complete puberty to have a kid, right?"

"Well, you have to be at least part way through …" Peters did a double take before continuing, "Wait, are you seriously telling me *those* two are the culprits?"

I was rushing to keep up as we fast approached a couple of kids handcuffed in the corner of the ER. One would think they'd be scared and crying. Instead, she was kicking her 'Hello Kitty' backpack while yelling at the peach-fuzzed boy sitting on the steel bench. Whether he was sitting due to fatigue or because his pants were so baggy and that they couldn't resist gravity was anybody's guess.

The other officer stood erect as Higgs and Peters entered the small holding room and shut the door. I disappeared into the corner, remembering my only job was to keep quiet.

"What is the patient's name?" Questioned Dr. Peters, clearly directed to the pair of teens.

Nobody responded, or even acknowledged our presence in the small room for that matter. The girl kept questioning her boyfriend about how many blowjobs he'd received in the past month. He buried himself so far into his Raiders hoodie that I could barely see the bill of his oddly angled baseball cap.

WHAM! The sound of a thunderclap immediately got everybody's attention.

After a good long stare, Higgs broke the silence, "Listen you little rascals, the next item I punch is going to be one of you twerps if you don't show the good Doctor here some respect."

I don't know what kind of force it takes to dent a detaining room wall, but Higgs had it, and seemed to have used this technique before judging by the similar dents scattered about the back wall.

"The doctor politely asked you two the name of her *critically ill* patient. Either of you two able to provide this information?"

"It doesn't have a name yet," whispered the girl.

"Doesn't have a name? How old is she?"

"Six weeks."

"And ... why doesn't she have a name yet? Didn't you get a birth certificate?"

"Well, not exactly. I sorta left the hospital before the doctor discharged us. So I never got a certificate."

Peters and Higgs both rolled their eyes and the big man boomed, "Correct me if I'm wrong, Doc, but leaving the hospital with a baby against medical advice is kidnapping, isn't it?"

"Yup, you're right. Unless of course the mother gives a false name and bogus address, in which case it's just another Jane Doe and nothing can be proven." A self satisfied smirk appeared on the girl's face.

It was quickly erased as Dr. Peters continued, "Although it'd be easy enough to figure out given the age of the mother, time and date of delivery, age of the child, and blood type. They'd all match up with the Jane Doe and she'd no longer be an unknown individual, but guilty of kidnapping, child abuse, and whatever else you can throw at her."

Beads of sweat started appearing on our Jane Doe. John Doe was still buried in his clothing, like a ground hog that hadn't yet come up for spring.

Higgs again took the lead, "Are you the mother, Miss?"

Looking down at her backpack and fluttering her eyes, she whispered, "Yes."

"What's your name?"

"She doesn't have a name."

"Not her name, we can fill out the death certificate later. Your ..."

"She's DEAD?" Jane jumped up; the concerned look on her face was something even a seasoned actress couldn't fake. I think we just confirmed she was our patient's mother.

"She will be if you don't start answering my questions faster. I'm sure the doctor here needs to be saving her life and not wasting her

time on you two. But she can't be in two places at once, so I suggest
you be more cooperative."

"Juanita."

"And what's your name, *Dad?*" asked Higgs as he reached over
and threw off the kid's hoodie, revealing a baseball cap so low it covered his eyebrows and was rotated to provide shade to his left ear.

He leapt off the bench and stood up glaring at Higgs' collarbone
before tilting his head up and making eye contact. The detective had
at least three hands and eight stones on the wannabe gangbanger
trying to unsuccessfully stare him down. The staring match lasted 30
seconds, thankfully Dr. Peters intervened, or else I don't know if I
could have held in my laughter at the situation.

"So, what's your name? Are you the father?" asked Peters.

"I want my lawyer!"

Higgs shoved him down so he was again sitting on the bench.
Good move, or else his jeans might have settled around his ankles
instead of precariously dangling mid thigh around his two pairs of
boxers.

"You're not under arrest, Einstein; you're only being detained
seeing as how you were found at the scene of an unconscious six-
week old baby who was kidnapped from a hospital.

"Not to mention that lawyering up is as good as pleading guilty.
By the looks of it I don't think you're going to be springing for one
of those big firm partners with your lunch money. Hell, if it's even
your lunch money and not stolen."

He spit on the wall. "Fuck you, pig! I earn! I'm gonna get your
badge and you're gonna be out looking for work as a rent-a-cop. This
is harassment and police brutality." Higgs stepped back from the
alleged father and not so subtly placed his hand on his now unfas-
tened, but still holstered, revolver. John Doe took notice, "You ever
even fire your piece?"

I almost missed it, but in a flash of movement, Higgs had his gun drawn and the barrel shoved against the side of John's head, pushing him into the wall at an odd angle.

Peters nonchalantly entered the discussion seeing the distress beginning to form on John Doe's expression. "Don't worry, Detective, I saw the whole thing just now. He was aggravated and attempted to attack you. Go ahead and pull the trigger; I'll be your witness to self-defense. Kindly do me a favor and make sure it's lethal. The surgeons have their hands full with the baby at present, and we don't have another OR available."

"Wha ... wha ... you can't do that! You're a *doctor*," blathered our John Doe, no longer looking so tough with snot dripping from his nose.

Higgs shoved the gun a bit further and continued, "I believe the good Doctor asked you what your name was. Are you going to answer her questions or am I going to have to act in self defense as she suggested?"

He nodded. All questions were rapidly answered without any bravado or backtalk. A healthy number of tissues were consumed from the nearby box before Higgs and Peters left the room.

~~~~

"John and Juanita huh? Do you believe their story?"

Higgs and Peters were discussing the case just outside the interrogation room. John (turns out that was his real name) was more than happy to answer any and all questions once he realized that Higgs had indeed fired his piece before and Dr. Peters wasn't going to offer any more sympathy than the detective. In fact they both played the "bad" role pretty well.

The couple was still in the interrogation room while deciding what should be done next. Juanita cradled the head of her now sobbing man as he blew his nose and recanted the events of how he was almost killed, even though she was only two feet away when it all transpired.

As the minutes dragged by, Juanita seemed to be growing more distant from John, lacking the affection one would expect from an innocent couple. She stopped cradling his head; instead her arm was limp as he leaned on her shoulder. She was staring off in the distant, clearly thinking about something else.

"She's hiding something, Doc; I can see it in her eyes," Higgs said with complete confidence.

"I agree. He seems legit though, those sobs are the real deal. Whether they are from fear or pain from that lump you gave him on his right temple is anybody's guess. At least he didn't need any stitches! I really believe he did just walk in and find the kid unresponsive without having anything to do with the shaking or other abuse. Poor chap even thinks it's his kid."

I just watched in stunned silence. I couldn't believe that this was how medicine was practiced. Neither Peters nor Higgs were taking particular joy in what they had just done. Quite the contrary, they seemed very professional and detached from the situation, knowing this was an imperfect way to deal with a broken system. Medical passersby seemed to understand that something serious was going on and avoided the corridor which we occupied. The few staff that did enter for supplies in the adjacent storeroom did so rapidly, without lingering a second longer than needed. It was the proverbial hiding place in plain sight. If people knew that a minor had just been threatened at gunpoint *inside* a hospital with the attending physician watching, even condoning it … the media would have a field day.

But judging that Peters and Higgs were planning how best to continue their questioning and how they hadn't even flinched with the initial interrogation, this couldn't be an isolated occurrence in just this hospital. Babies were shaken by dysfunctional couples daily across the country. I wondered if this was how it was handled elsewhere. Unfortunately I couldn't bring it up with any of my friends. If word got out this occurred and that I was present and didn't try to stop it, I'd be just as liable. The inherent problem was unfortunately that if I had tried to stop it, I'd likely have been given poor marks on my rotation, completely unacceptable to any medical student.

Fantastic, accessory to police brutality and abuse of power charges, at the very minimum. Just what the Dean hoped we'd learn as part of our training.

I turned just as the door to the detaining room closed behind Peters with Higgs. John and Juanita both went rigid on the bench, trying their best to appear calm and collected. They failed.

I scooted up to the window to get a better look. Unfortunately, the reinforced double paned glass and concrete walls didn't allow me much in the way of audio. They were still doing the good guy, bad guy routine. Higgs slammed his palm onto the table like he meant it. No wonder there were so many dings and scrapes on everything in the room.

Words were exchanged and suddenly John jumped up and faced both Higgs and Peters. His expression completely changed as though faced with an impossible decision or undeniable truth. He went from teary eyed to enraged. His chest pushed forward, his eyes suddenly focused and intent upon revenge. He pulled back his arm looked like he was going to lash out against Higgs when he suddenly turned and bitch slapped Juanita.

Instead of intervening, Peters and Higgs just watched the events unfold. I was transfixed. I thought that I should perhaps intervene, but without hearing what happened, I didn't know which side to take.

John was now yelling so loud that spittle was flying out of his mouth like a snowstorm. His face was beet red and his eyes looked like they were going to bulge out of his head. His anger was focused solely on Juanita. Instead of cowering away, she accepted the onslaught with a downtrodden expression of guilt and remorse. Sitting while John stood, it was clear that he was the one in power and she the sinner.

John punched the wall and kicked the nearby chair. Turning towards the upturned chair his intentions were clear. He wanted revenge. Walking towards the chair, he hefted it and was about to hurl it at Juanita when Higgs intervened and slammed him against the wall, causing John to lose his grip and drop the chair. Higgs muscled John into taking a seat on the far end of the bench while Peters escorted Juanita out and into the adjacent holding cell, motioning to me that it was OK to follow her in.

After Higgs cuffed John, he joined Peters next door. "Juanita, you have one chance to confess, or you too are going to be cuffed and escorted to the police station." It was obvious Higgs wasn't joking given the no-nonsense tone of his voice and the too close for comfort location of his stance, well into her personal space.

Juanita broke down and started sobbing. She fell to her knees and was no longer the tough defiant rebel she was trying to portray earlier. Her true form revealed a vulnerable teenager lost in a world of mistakes and bad decisions.

She lay in fetal position by Higgs' boots, sobbing like the apocalypse was upon us … or at least upon her. Peters finally caved and bent down next to her, handing her some tissues and rubbing her back. She resembled a small child yearning for her mother. Peters' compassion and motherly instincts took over as she calmed Juanita down, proving that the 'bad doc' role was in fact just an act. Higgs and I stood mesmerized, just watching in a state of catatonia as the two women bonded over sobs and tears.

After several minutes and many tissues, Juanita's sobbing slowly subsided and she turned her petite form towards Higgs and almost inaudibly whispered, "John is innocent, I used to love him, but he …"

Higgs, not used to the warm and fuzzy role the situation required, deferred the questioning to Peters who gently coaxed Juanita to continue her story. "Go ahead, dear. We're on your side."

"He … he … just became so possessive of me. He thought the baby was his when I was pregnant. I tried to tell him it wasn't, but he didn't want to believe it. Once I actually gave birth, that's when the violence started." She lifted up her shirt to reveal several bruises. I could make out the impression of a ring and knuckles in the most recent bruise.

She took a few deep breaths and continued. "It became too much for me. I couldn't raise a baby with the person John had become. The violence was a side of John I didn't know about until after the baby was born. I knew I wanted him out of my life. When I told him I wanted him gone he went totally nuts. He'd never leave the baby alone. He was always at her side 24/7. He even carried her with him when he went to the bathroom. That's sorta why I never gave her a name, you know? To keep him detached until Daikens came back."

"You're doing just great, dear. Can you tell us who Daikens is?" Juanita was still lying on the floor, her head in Peters' lap, while the Doc was gently stroking her hair.

She again started sobbing anew. But after a bit she calmed down and continued her confessional, "Daikens is her real father. Him and I were together for a year before I got pregnant. He used to run with a bad crowd and once he realized he was going to be a father he wanted to do something good. See, Daikens was a dealer. But the day he knew he was becoming a father he went straight to the police and came clean. He even bargained with the cops to help them catch a bunch of dealers and higher-ups in the East LA drug scene.

"He didn't tell me any of this. I found out after he went to the slammer. He worked with the cops on some sting or something, I'm not sure what it's called, and they busted like 18 people that week because of Daikens' help … he really put himself at risk. Hell, he even got shot in the arm when it all went down. Part of the deal was that he'd only have to do one year of hard time and then some parole because of his help. That was six months ago.

"I was *pissed* at him for ditching me and wasn't sure what to do while he was in jail. That's when I met John. He was so sweet to me and helped me with the pregnancy and everything. I was thinking that things could really work out with John … well, until, you know, the violence started."

Peters continued stroking her hair as she recounted what she'd been through, asking, "Did you tell John he wasn't the father?"

"Oh sure, I mean I was already two months pregnant even before I even met him. But he didn't want to believe it wasn't his child. He kept saying that because he loved me so much the child developed faster than normal so we could bring it into the world early."

"What about Daikens?"

"When John started hitting me, I knew he was wrong for me. Daikens would always write me, so eventually I started writing back and then starting visiting him in jail. He was understanding of what I was going through. He blamed himself for all of it. He wanted to get back with me after he got out and he said we'd start a good life together. Plus he told me he had a lot of money put away that nobody knew about that we could use to get ourselves started."

I noticed Higgs taking notes while she spoke. Her confession was clearly on record.

Juanita continued, "Last week I told Daikens about the times John hit me. Daikens didn't take it well and got really mad. He even said he'd hurt John real bad. I was afraid he'd even kill John once he got out." She started sobbing again, "And then I'd be all alone forever."

A look of understanding passed between Peters and Higgs, they'd already put the whole story together. I was still confused by a couple things: how and why a seventeen year old thought it was a good idea to have a child, and why she'd think it was a good idea to raise it with a former drug dealer *after* she confessed to him that she was cheating on him while he was in jail. It didn't exactly strike me as a recipe for success.

Higgs piped in, "How did the baby get hurt if John was always at her side?"

Deep breaths and more sobs, but fortunately no tears to wait through this time as she continued, "I got in touch with one of Daikens' friends who owed Daikens a huge favor. I guess he saved his life or something back in his dealing days. We came up with a plan that we'd shake the baby, but just a little bit, and then when John saw that she was sick he'd call for help and they'd arrest him for abuse.

"So I faked a fall and pretended to sprain my ankle. He went to the store to get me a brace and ice packs. While he was gone "J" came over and shook the baby. But he's really big and I guess he shook her too hard, I told him to stop, but he said we had to make it look real. I started to get worried and just went into the shower.

"I guess he left after he shook her. A few minutes later John came home and freaked out! He yelled that the baby was blue and wasn't breathing. He ran into the shower and automatically blamed me. Then he punched me here." She pointed to the newest bruise she'd shown us earlier.

"You poor thing," Peters was a genuinely caring individual and now hugging Juanita. "Then what happened?"

"I fell after he hit me, but then I got up and came out of the shower and told him to call 911. I changed real quick and by then the ambulance was there … you know the rest."

"Juanita," Peters looked her straight in the eyes for a few seconds before continuing, "now you have to be honest with me here." She nodded that she would be. "When was the last time you actually saw or held your baby before today?"

She looked away as she tried to count the time, "Over three weeks. Like I said, John became scary possessive of her. He never ever let me see or hold her. When I'd try is when he'd hit me."

"Okay, dear, I believe you. I'm going to go outside for a while and make sure the ER is under control. I'll have a nurse bring you some food and juice. Would you like that?"

She perked up at the mention of food.

~~~~

We reconvened outside. Higgs was the first to speak, "You thinking what I am, Doc?"

"Yeah, John's got some serious problems. He'll need a psych eval, might even get away with everything."

"That's what I'm thinking. I've seen this before, but it's been the woman who gets attached to the child. I've never seen it happen with a guy before. Role reversal or something?"

I knew if I didn't ask now things were going to happen fast and I'd never get a chance, so I interrupted and asked them both what was going on. I thought I might get in trouble, but instead they were quite happy to bring me up to speed.

"I'll start," said Higgs. "See, John fell in love with Juanita. But nobody is so stupid that they can't figure out there's no way in bloody hell a normal healthy *term* child can be born within six months of meeting somebody. That explains his bullshit excuses about the child growing fast. But deep down inside, he's pissed that the kid isn't his, so in his head he blames Juanita for being unfaithful to him. He's angry at the child because he knows it's not his. Problem is he can't fully come to terms with the fact it ain't his kid."

Peters continued, "Over time he becomes more attached to the child. But then anger replaces the bond and he starts to abuse the child; hence the cigarette burns and broken bones. He doesn't want to kill the child, but when rage takes over he takes it out on both the baby and Juanita. As the beatings got more intense, he didn't want Juanita seeing the baby, else she might report him; thus, he prohibited her from interacting with the child."

I started to understand what Higgs and Peters figured out several minutes ago. "This should be a straightforward case. Just take John to jail, right?"

Laughter greeted my comment, followed by a whopping pat on the back from Higgs. "They're so innocent at this stage, aren't they?" he said to Peters.

"Unfortunately no, Raj." Huh, she remembered my name! "There'll be several lawyers involved. John will likely be determined insane; he's clearly got psychological and anger problems. Of course the police will need his side of the story. There will be a long investigation and he'll likely get acquitted due to insanity or some other psychological bullshit. Juanita will definitely get some time for being an accessory to something short of manslaughter, but given she didn't participate, and is a minor at 17 years old, she might get some sort of leniency."

Higgs summarized, "In a nutshell, it's a huge clusterfuck. This is going to cost big bucks before it's all sorted out. I just hope J get his just deserts because I don't think we're going to be able to locate him without more information"

"That's for sure," added Peters. "It's people like John I worry about, I hope he never picks up one of those serial killer novels, he's the type that'd try to re-create Dante's Hell, except on earth when he's older."

"What about the baby?" I asked.

Peters answered, "I think its best we don't come up with a name for her. I'd wager she'll make it out of surgery but likely won't survive more than a couple weeks given the extent of her injuries."

Higgs and Peters split up, Higgs to talk to his partner and Peters to see what she'd missed in the rest of the ER while she was dealing with this fiasco.

Higgs and his partner decided that they'd be taking both John and Juanita to the station for further questioning and procedures. Peters was quickly busy with another emergent case, an acute MI from what I could tell.

Again, I was left standing alone and confused. There was nobody to whom I had to report or check out with, and my shift had ended over an hour ago. With nothing else to do, I started on the walk home. Not exactly what I'd expected to experience my first day of entering into clinical medicine. But as the year would prove, this was far from the most interesting or tragic case to which I'd be exposed.

Chapter Two:
Two Enter, One Leaves

"THE WORST THING isn't that you saw your mom in the shower, or even that you took a photo of her, but that you're stupid enough to tell us about it!!"

"You make me sound like a pervert; it wasn't like that at all. Dude, digital cameras had just come out and all my friends thought my mom was hot," explained Adam.

"You mean a MILF."

"I didn't know what a fucking MILF was when I was 14. My biggest stressor was the SAT ... something I doubt stressed you out, or else you wouldn't have been stuck going to Brown."

"Yeah yeah, not all of us can be *Harvard* alums like you. But we still ended up at the same med school either way."

"Anyway ... I only took the photo 'cause my friends kept saying my mom was super hot. That, and they double dared me to do it, plus offered me a hundred bucks. And don't forget, that was like a zillion dollars back then."

Another med student joined in the conversation, this one clearly a jock type with a fit physique. He was what one of my former residents dubbed an 'orthomorph'; a med student with the trim and athletic body of someone who was likely to enter into orthopedic surgery. An orthomorph was the dumb jock of medical school. "It's ok as long as *you didn't* think your Mom was hot. If you know what I mean," he winked.

"Yeah!" piped in another student. Now everybody was engrossed in the conversation; with four guys and two girls, only I stood in the corner observing—clearly the outcast. Though I must admit I was mildly amused; this is not what I envisioned future physicians to be discussing in the 10 minutes before morning rounds began.

"Wasn't your mom a Yoga instructor or something?"

"Yeah, but she mostly just managed a few studios that she owned. It kept her busy 'cause my dad was always working long hours and pretty busy with trauma surgery call when I was younger."

The jock spoke up again, "Dude, if she was a Yoga instructor, I bet she was a MILF. Hey, you still got that photo? Maybe on your phone or something?"

On cue, both girls gasped and shouted, "GROSS!!! How could you ask that?"

"Actually, it's not that big of a deal … the other reason my friends wanted me to take that picture was because my mom was in *Playboy* two years before I was born and they wanted to compare her photos from then to after my being born."

The three other guys all high-fived each other; I'm sure Adam would have too. Why, I still to this day don't know, but I guess it's why I never really fit into medical school. I didn't come from the world of Playboy mothers and private schools, which was the norm for a significant portion of our class. Particularly on this rotation in internal medicine, I found myself surrounded by students from a pedigree of successful high income households and top tiered educational institutions.

"What I wanna know is how'd your dad hook up with a Playmate?"

The girls attempted to act repulsed, but you could see they were just as intrigued with the question. While their arms were crossed trying to seem disinterested, they were leaning into the circle and eagerly waiting for Adam to answer.

"My dad was into the Hollywood scene. He was somewhat of a celebrity after CNN did a few interviews with him describing some new surgical techniques he innovated. From that interview, he became the go to surgeon for the VIP crowd around here. He met my Mom at some party a couple months after her centerfold issue came out."

"How is it you have a MILF mom and a rock-star dad, yet you look like 'Where's Waldo'?" contributed Jocko the Orthomorph to the conversation, and then playfully hit Adam's shoulder. They all shared in the amusement as though this were a perfectly normal conversation.

I'd heard enough and bee-lined to the door in an attempt to exit the small conference room. Just as I grabbed the doorknob, Jocko hollered in my direction, "Hey Rajeen, how come you don't sit with us before rounds?" Nobody ever gets my name right; I think it's on purpose, but I'm not sure.

Fuck, I almost escaped, and now I was dragged into the morning summit of meaningless pretentious drivel.

The summit leaders are Jocko the former Princeton lacrosse player who's name I've never bothered to commit to memory, Adam the playmate offspring, and his other Harvard colleague Chris. All three come from families that are highly successful and rooted in social circles frequented by such captivating sources as the illustrious *Enquirer*.

Then there's Donovan from Yale; he's the mousey one who never quite fits in, but is always included because his net worth alone is a sum so high I cannot even fathom. Let's just say when visiting home he travels via private jet, his *own* private jet.

The group is rounded out by Crystal and Paige, BFFs from Columbia who both managed to get into the same top medical school almost immediately after applying. How exactly they pulled that off is anyone's guess. But it clearly wasn't due to the fact that all of their parents and step-parents are successful physicians with a great deal of pull in the medical community. Nor did the Bel Air addresses, fund raising events, and deep donations made to the campus have anything to do with their acceptance letters. I'm sure it was a complete meritocracy.

Don't get me wrong, all six here are brilliant individuals, always in the top 1% of whatever they do despite external factors. But they are so detached from reality it's amusing. They come from a world of nannies, au pairs, chauffeurs, gated mansions, private schools, privilege, power, and, well, you get the idea.

Fortunately not the entire medical school is filled with such creatures. I'd say only about 50% of our 150 person class is of their ilk; the rest actually worked hard to get here. Unfortunately I happen to be on a seven student rotation in which I'm the sole outcast.

I eventually responded, "No reason other than in my culture, discussing the nudity of one's mother is considered disrespectful." My condescension was lost on them.

"You just don't want to sit with us 'cause you think you're so much smarter than us."

And on the first day of the rotation … it starts.

I hate conversations like this; unfortunately they occur far too often. In medical school there aren't so many physical fights, mostly due to the zero tolerance for violence and instantaneous suspension bestowed upon all involved should it occur. Thus, everybody is judged by their academic performance; it serves to stratify the entire class. And in this morass of high achievers, where egos are more delicate than a Fabergé egg, academic prowess and achievements become all encompassing and essentially the entire world view of a medical student, far more so than other frivolous traits such as kindness, humor, empathy, interpersonal and other social skills the rest of the world perceives as important.

Medical students want nothing else than to ace every test, make it known to everybody else that they aced the test, impress all their superiors, publish a few scientific articles, get great letters of recommendation, and then move on to a prestigious residency in which the cycle repeats in an effort to obtain a top notch fellowship after which the cycle *again* repeats in an effort to obtain one of a handful of sought after jobs in desirable locations. Those of us that don't fit into this paradigm are often the butt of most med student ridicule.

"That has nothing to do with it," I try to reply, but before I can finish the door bursts open and a dozen residents pour in.

Instantly the summit ends and all six toadies are standing raptly at attention, ready to please their teams in an effort to do well on this critical inpatient internal medicine rotation. This is one of the core rotations in which a stellar letter of recommendation is crucial to secure, regardless of which field a student ultimately decides to apply.

And thus, begins day one of a six week audition, the goal of which is to obtain the best letter of recommendation possible.

There will certainly be lying, cheating, and stealing involved. The only caveat is you can't get caught, or else you can forget the letter and likely face suspension. And I'm stuck with six of the most cunning sycophants in our class. They'll stop at nothing to prove they are the best—this rotation's going to suck.

I was right about the sucking, just wrong about the why.

The room instantly began to reek of shit, and not from somebody's flatulence or bowel dysfunction, but from all the brown nosing that'd already started. The six immediately had their noses so far up the chief resident's ass that they might as well have biopsied any polyps they found.

Instead of mingling I occupied a now vacant seat and dedicated my undivided attention to devouring my bagel. It may well be my only caloric intake until dinner if I got stuck being on call tonight.

"Attention everyone," the chief resident announces, instantly commanding attention and complete silence from the 20 or so bodies in the cramped lounge.

"I'd like to welcome our new third year medical students to their inpatient internal medicine rotation. This will be a very rigorous six weeks, and I'd like to set some ground rules. First, there are four teams and seven students. One team will have only one student, that's team Red. The medical students will be on overnight call with their respective teams and be expected to be fully involved in all patient care activities. I will personally meet all students from 7 to 8 a.m. every morning for lecture; thus, all pre-rounding patient care should be taken care of before then ..."

I'm sure he droned on further, but I lost interest after the 7 a.m. lecture notice. A quick mental calculation taught me all I needed to know, namely, that I'd have to show up at 5:30 a.m. to be able to see my patients before being rewarded by a lecture, which was to be immediately followed by more work. Doable? Sure. Great learning opportunity? Check. Fun? Negative.

"And finally Rajen will be assigned to team Blue." I startled to attention only to notice everybody was exiting the room. Shit, I already started off on a bad foot. Luckily I saw Adam being handed some blue cards, so I figured I was on his team and joined the group of five in the hallway.

"Hi, Raj, is it? I'm Duke, the senior resident; this is Kelly the second year resident, and Amy and Jason, the interns of the team. I'm guessing you already know Adam, your co-med student. I think we have a couple pharmacy students, but they'll join us later and only sporadically."

"Pleasure to meet you all?" I wasn't sure myself if I was asking or stating. It's intimidating when the whole team is sizing you up on the first day of a critical rotation.

"Hey, are you the one everybody talks about who crushed the board examination this year?" Amy instantly asks me. Clearly, she's the overachiever of the group, and judging by her Fendi pumps and Versace bag, also comes from a life of privilege and status. I'm hoping she works with Adam.

I notice Adam frown. While a genius and accustomed to being the smartest kid around, he full well knows that I hold the title of virtuoso test taker in our class. This was a title that I did my best to conceal, but rumors in med school are like fleas in a kennel, ubiquitous, annoying, and unrelenting.

There was always one outlier in most of our tests, a single individual known to mess up most of our grading curves and who reportedly got one of the highest scores on our board exams in the history of the school. While many people took credit for all the high scores, I was the only one who knew the true answer, but I had no desire to claim credit. Eventually rumors spread that I was this individual. To this day I vehemently deny it, but most are certain it's me.

"Rumors will be rumors." I reply and leave it at that.

Amy winks in that all knowing style girls have, indicating that this wouldn't be the end of the topic.

"So Raj, hopefully we can make good use of your brain power to take excellent care of our patients. You'll be working mostly with Jason," instructed Duke.

I looked over to Jason; he was in scrubs, bad sign. He nodded, knowing I wouldn't like what came next.

"Thus, you'll be on call overnight today. Hopefully you brought some scrubs to change into."

Damn it, I knew this was going to happen. That meant that Adam would be on call as well, and everybody knows that misery loves company. His company would lead to my misery.

Duke pulled us all in close for a team huddle and continued, "Our attending is Dr. Miley. She's brilliant, and more importantly she's no nonsense and incredibly fast. Her goal is to get out of here as soon as she can. The best part though is that her husband is Dr. Manis, the CEO of the hospital. Thus, anything we want, we get, and fast, so our lives should be quite good in regards to minimizing red tape."

Just then the infamous chirp of a pager went off. All six of us instantly checked the beepers on our waists. Like gunslingers in a duel, Duke is the first to remove his from the little plastic holder and quickly reads the message, announcing, "It's the ER—looks like we got our first hit (a resident's way of describing a patient admission, or basically work to do). Jason, you wanna take this with Raj?"

Jason nods and pats me on the back indicating I should follow. Great, just minutes into the first day of the rotation and I've already been antagonized by my classmates, told I'm on call, and received the first patient. Could be worse, at least I didn't have a kidney stone.

As we're halfway down the massive hallway Jason put out his hand, "Hi Raj, I'm Jason Bates, nice to meet you." We shake and he continues, "don't mind Amy, she's constantly going to harass you about your scores, she can't stand it when somebody does better than her and she can't rest until she knows your numbers. We both went to Hopkins together; she was lazy then, and she continues the trend here. Seriously, she'll do anything she can to avoid work. Kelly is cool, married with a young kid. Duke is a nice guy, very decent and ethical, but not the sharpest tool in the shed."

I'm not sure how to respond, so I just nod. The hospital is full of gossip. Jason doesn't seem as though he's very interested in it other than to give me a quick background on the team.

"I know you're a bright guy, so just let me know what I can do to help make this an educational experience for you, okay?"

I already liked Jason; he seemed bright and professional but unconventional, though my ability to read people is akin to my literacy in Mandarin, namely, non-existent.

We enter the ER and Jason rushes off towards the phone, "Raj, I'll meet you at the control desk; I forgot to get the name of the patient we're supposed to evaluate."

I'm well acquainted with the layout of the ER and before I even make it to the nursing station I run into Dr. Peters.

"Rajen, don't you ever go home?"

"Same can be said about you Dr. Peters."

"I'm guessing you're here for the admission; I think I just paged Duke about him?"

"Yes, ma'am."

"Well, I have to go to radiology right now. Some little girl put a bean in her ear a few days ago and now it's started to sprout! The radiologist said he can see a stem emerging on her scan; I want to check it out personally. But your patient is a healthy 45-year old male with no past medical history who comes in because of a 72 hour history of right flank pain, fevers, and hematuria. See you in a bit." With that she rushed off.

The ER is bustling. I catch Jason entering from the other end. "Duane Little, Bed 8."

"Let me guess, 45-year old male with fevers and kidney pain."

"Damn, I heard you were good, but nobody told me you were psychic."

"I wish. I ran into Peters on the way over and she gave me the lowdown."

"Cool, tell you what, I'll let you run the show and I'll just be your shadow. I'll try not to interrupt if I don't have to, and if you're stuck just nod towards me and I'll take over. Cool?"

"Sounds good."

I enter Bed 8 and find Duane pacing around the little space with his hand on his right lower back nearly in tears. He's a typical guy you'd see in a department store clothing catalog, about six feet tall, 170 pounds, fit, dressed in khakis and a polo with a clean shave. In other words, he doesn't belong in an ER.

"Hi, Duane."

"Oh thank goodness Doc, I'm so happy you got here so fast." He tries to sit on the gurney but the pain prevents him and forces him to stand and resume his pacing.

"Name's Rajen, and this is Dr. Bates."

"Pleasure." He cringes as he reaches out to shake our hands.

Sure I'm used to seeing people in distress, but never have I encountered a patient that is respectful or thankful. Usually they're aggravated and insolent, so this was unexpected.

Sizing up the situation Jason announces, "Raj I'm going to get an IV kit and some morphine so we can get Duane here comfortable immediately. Go ahead and get a history until I return."

Duane and I nod.

As if Duane knows exactly what I need, he starts talking as he limps about the room clutching his right flank. "Thanks again for your time. I usually only see a doc once or twice a year for a physical, and all's been well. I have no medical history to report, no medications, only some occasional alcohol, no drugs or tobacco. Family's healthy too, just a grandfather who died of a heart attack. I'm married with a seven year old daughter. She's in school now, but my wife took off work and will be here soon. I drove here myself."

He groans in pain and then moves to the sink where he dry heaves. Amazing, he told me in 15 seconds what most patients require 15 minutes of coaxing and interrogation, only to report details that are mostly incorrect.

The severe pain subsides in another 15 seconds and I decide to resume our interview, "Dr. Bates will be here shortly and we'll be able to get rid of that pain for you. In the mean time is it ok if I get some vital signs and ask you a few questions?"

He nods. I sit him down and we chat while I gather my data.

"Tell me what's been going on."

"Basically Doc, I noticed this pain on my right side, I'm guessing where my kidney is, about 3 days ago. At first it was tolerable with some ibuprofen, but it's just gotten worse and worse. Yesterday I started getting a fever to about 101°F, but thought I could ride it out despite my wife telling me to go to the hospital. This morning right before leaving for work the pain increased and I noticed my urine looked like V-8. So here I am."

"Any trauma, recent travel, sick contacts, drugs or medications?"

"No to all of the above. I did have seafood a couple nights ago. Do you think this could be food poisoning?"

"No, that doesn't explain it. What do you do for a living?"

"I'm a software programmer and soccer coach. My wife's a high school teacher. Daughter doesn't work yet, being in second grade and all."

We both manage a smile despite his distress.

"Duane, your BP is a little elevated. That's likely due to your pain, but you also have a fever of 103.8°F. I suspect you have an infection."

Jason rushes back and immediately gets to work on placing an IV in Duane's arm. He gets it on his first try. Duane was a model patient despite another bout of colic. Jason quickly injects an entire ampoule of morphine through the IV.

"How do you feel now?"

"No different Doc … oh, wow … ok, you gave me some serious stuff, huuuuugh?"

Duane's words slur and his eyes take on a glazed appearance as the Bell's reflex causes them to roll upwards. Soon he's snoozing and barely breathing.

I quickly affix an oxygen mask and crank it up to 12L/min. His oxygen saturation and other vital signs normalize almost immediately.

Satisfied with our work, Jason says, "Well, we know he's not a drug user, seeing as how I only gave him 10 mg, a very moderate dose of morphine for a guy his size. He's already down for the count. So you discover anything Raj? What's your diagnosis?"

I recap what Duane told me. "Basically, I think he has a kidney stone which is stuck in the ureter somewhere and it's been causing intermittent obstructions and hydronephrosis. Now he's gotten infected."

"Is that your final answer Dr. Raj? Renal calculi with secondary urosepsis?"

"It is."

"Ding ding, I think we have a winner here folks."

"You mean, that's all?"

"Well, the fun part's over, now we get to do all the paperwork, admit him, get some blood and urine cultures, along with some basic labs. We should get a CT to confirm our diagnosis. I think we should admit him for a couple days until we know what bug is causing this and get his fever under control. Then he can go back to his happy life at home."

"So you think he'll be alright?"

"Oh yeah, you kidding, this is what ER's and hospitals were created for, diagnosing and treating acute illness. Not the homeless shelters, hospice facilities, and drug dispensaries they've become."

"Good. He's a super nice guy, his wife's on her way over, and his daughter …"

"Wait, did you just say he's a 'super nice guy'?"

"Yeah, why?"

"Nothing. Just silly superstition that bodes poorly for him. Always remember this dictum in medicine: bad things happen to nice people. *Especially* in a hospital.

"Haven't you ever noticed most patients are annoying, and some are complete assholes? And that it's always the assholes who beat the odds and survive the fatal heart attack or somehow live ten years with metastatic cancer? It's the nice guys that finish last in hospitals, probably why we don't see many of them; they're smart enough to stay the hell away from us."

In medicine, the joke is that prognosis is inversely related to niceness. The nicer a patient, the worse their disease, and poorer their outcome. I certainly hoped this wasn't the case in Duane's situation. In fact, I was looking forward to meeting his family and informing them that he'd be good as new in a couple days.

Boy, was I wrong.

~~~~

The rest of the day was not nearly as interesting as the morning, but at least there was no further discussion about MILFs or board scores. We were back in the lounge just finishing up the paperwork from the day. We'd received three other patients after Duane; a steady but very manageable amount of work.

Adam and Amy seemed to get along fabulously, judging by their constant giggling and newfound BFF behavior—not to mention their mutual penchant for avoiding any type of work.

It was a pleasure to work with Jason; he was diligent, thoughtful, caring, and never said no to more work. Right on time, just as I thought about more work, Amy sauntered over to Jason with puppy dog eyes. A request for a favor was sure to follow, which likely involved more work for us.

She just stood next to Jason. He was first to break the silence. "Can I help you with something Amy?"

"Well, since you asked … I just got this admission from the ER, and I was wondering if you wouldn't mind taking the hit, given you're all done with your work and we're still working on our last patient."

"Not sure how that makes it my responsibility."

Way to go Jason! Perhaps his reputation for being a "black cloud," someone who always has bad luck and more work than anybody else on the team, was incorrect.

Nope, I was wrong.

"Yeah, you're right technically, but remember the time I signed you in for lecture and you didn't attend?"

"Sure do, I had a dislocated shoulder and was getting it repositioned."

"Fact is that you weren't there and I still signed you in, so this would make it even." She even batted her lashes to emphasize the point. "And I really need to get done early tomorrow. I got a date with this venture capitalist who's taking me to Urasawa and I don't want bags under my eyes."

Nooooo! I could sense Jason wavering, and he was doing so well, too. I knew he was going to cave in to Amy's assault to pawn off her work.

"Fine, what you got?"

She yelped for joy and handed him a card and rushed out of the lounge with Adam in tow before Jason had a chance to renege on his offer.

"So this is how you got your black cloud, huh? By doing others' work?" I asked Jason.

"You ever heard of the mantra of old school surgeons?"

"Nope."

"What's the problem with being on call every other day?"

"I don't know."

"You miss half of the cases."

"Nobody thinks that way nowadays."

"Agreed. But there is some truth to the saying; the more we work, see, and do now, the better we'll be in the future when it really counts. Thus, while it's more work for us today, I think it's an investment in the future and an opportunity to learn now. Besides, right now, we have operational immunity, we're covered for over $10 million in malpractice, and everybody who comes through the door signs a waiver that they are *willingly* entering a teaching institution. Unless we perform 'egregious negligence' we won't be fired or lose our license. In the real world, if you so much as make a bad joke, you can get a formal complaint against your personal medical license. Two of those infarctions and you might lose your hospital privileges if you're in a desirable location or top hospital."

He had a point. "You're the boss." Pay now, earn dividends later.

"Let's see what she dumped on us." He read off of the blue card she had handed him. "Appears to be a 96 year old female with altered mental status in ER Bed 9."

We both looked at each other, "GOMER."

The infamous 'Get Out of My ER' acronym is used to describe patients that the ER wants nothing more than to get rid of ASAP; typically your homeless, psychotic, nonagenarian, or liver bomb.

"Raj, why don't you get started on," he squinted to make out our patient's name, "Matilda Margaret Maude, while I go check up on Duane? I'll make sure he's doing well and meet you in the ER, with any luck we can hit the sac by midnight."

"Sounds great," I lied. Dinner sounded great, not interviewing a patient who was bound to smell like urine and have advanced dementia.

As I made my way to the ER I recalled an interesting factoid I'd read recently. Something like greater than 40% of annual Medicare spending is utilized during the final six months of peoples' lives. Even worse, the quality of these final days are usually terrible, given they're spent mainly inside hospitals fighting off one infection or another. Just as I started daydreaming of what other uses this $180 billion could be put towards, I entered the ER.

I was secretly hoping it'd be jam packed so that Amy and Adam would be up all night. To my chagrin it was a ghost town with about four patients and nobody in the waiting room. Perhaps the calm before the storm I hoped.

Before entering the room to meet Ms. Matilda Margaret Maude, I had to do a double take at what I was looking at. Ms. Maude was essentially rice paper thin skin draped over a skeleton covered with liver spots and missing dentures, making her mouth look like a black sinkhole with her lips pointed inward. She lay supine in bed but was so kyphotic that the roll in her back prevented her head from touching the two pillows under her. Her fingers were so thin and frail I was afraid that if I shook her hand they might just turn to dust.

"Ms. Maude." No response. I tried again louder, nothing. "MS. MAUDE," I shouted.

She opened her eyes, and whispered, "Abigail?" This was followed immediately with a return to her somnolent state, with mouth gaping open and spittle dripping down the corner of her sinkhole, er mouth.

I tried gently rubbing her sternum, but she didn't seem to notice. I tried again harder and felt a soft crack. I recoiled in fear of having possibly just fractured one of her ribs. Thankfully she still didn't seem to take notice. An incidental finding on a later x-ray would tell all.

She started smacking her lips and again asked for Abigail.

Nobody had bothered to check her BP, likely for fear that placing and insufflating a cuff on her arm might destroy her humerus. No wonder the ER wanted her out of here. I didn't even know how I'd start an IV line on her; she was so covered with age and liver spots and redundant skin that I couldn't see any veins on her arms.

She clearly wasn't going to be of much use in giving me a history. Thus, I'd do the next best thing, research her old medical records, known as a chart biopsy.

Of course I came up with nothing; apparently she'd never been here before. So far all I knew was her name, that she was breathing, and might have a broken rib.

"Who's in charge here?!"

I looked up from the work station to see a well-dressed forty-something gentleman yelling in my general direction from Ms. Maude's room.

"Uh, hi. I'm Rajen, who might you be?"

"Are you her doctor? I want to know why nobody is taking care of my Grandmother."

"I'm the medical student on the team who is going to be admitting Ms. Maude."

He cut me off and berated me, "MEDICAL STUDENT?! What kind of nonsense is this? When I called I told them I wanted the Chief of Medicine to see her, she's critically ill. This is nonsense. I'll report this to the Board of Directors!"

Just what I needed, an irate family member who had no idea what he was even upset over.

"And you are?"

No response. So I went on, "this is a teaching hospital and the admitting doctor is on his way over. He just had to check in on another patient. Can I ask you some questions so we can take the best care of your grandmother?"

"Fuck. Is this where healthcare dollars are going these days, to have medical students see patients while the real doctors can go golfing?"

"I assure you that no doctors are golfing at this hour." It being 10:20 p.m. and all.

"I don't approve of your insolent tone MISTER."

"My tone? You were the one that was using profanity and raising your voice."

"Fine, I'll answer your questions, but make it quick, I need to get home."

"Great, thanks. And you are?"

"Richard, her grandson. Most of the family will be in later tonight. We all live around here."

He again ignored me to answer his cell phone, right next to the sign stating 'NO CELLULAR PHONE USE IN THE EMERGENCY ROOM.' "Yeah, just wait by the ER entrance, next to the ambulances; I'll be out there as soon as I talk to a real doctor."

I assume he was talking to his driver, but I had no way of knowing and didn't want to indulge him.

"What brings your grandmother to the ER today?"

"You're the *doctor*, isn't that what you should be telling me?"

"Look Richard, you can be a smart ass or you can help me out here. I'm not an oracle who knows her entire medical history. If you could provide that, in addition to all her current medications, doses, and allergies it would be a good start."

"Bernard knows that information, not me. He should be in shortly, I sent the other driver to pick him up immediately. They said there wasn't enough room in the ambulance for him to ride along because two paramedics were in the back with her."

"Who's Bernard?"

"He's the live-in butler and caretaker. Grandmother lives alone next door, and he looks after her. She also has a nurse during the day; she'll be here tomorrow; I'm sure they can answer all your questions."

"Are you two close?"

"Look, I don't know what you are insinuating, but we love our Grandmother. She has one other grandson and a granddaughter. If they don't come by tonight, they'll be in tomorrow before work. Her husband passed away about ten years ago and she didn't want to live in a nursing home, so I bought her the mansion next door so that I'd be close by in case something happened."

Just then two other well dressed people stormed into the ER and darted straight towards Ms. Maude.

"Grandma, are you ok? They aren't hurting you are they?" The female asked as she glared accusingly in my direction before attending again to Ms. Maude.

"Abigail?"

I had to take control, or else this family would drive me nuts. "And who are you two? The ER is closed to visitors, only one family member is allowed by the ..."

"EXCUSE ME? Another outburst like that from you and I'll call the Board of Directors and have you fired," she announced loud enough for everybody nearby to hear. Nobody cared. ER personnel are accustomed to people under duress trying to flex their power and position. It's meaningless and doesn't change a thing. In fact the more power one overtly flexes actually demonstrates how little power they actually have.

I sighed, since it was all I could really do at this point. It seems like people always feel more entitled at the hospital. I've already noticed those that drop names are frequently the most impotent, without any real power or influence.

Just then Jason arrived, allowing me to escape the family from hell. Intercepting him before he came too close, I gave him a quick update at the workstation. Luckily while we were conversing, the grandchildren were trying to arouse their comatose corpse of a grandmother.

"Fuck-an-A man, this is the classic situation in which a family that clearly knows diddly about the last remaining grandparent suddenly feels guilt that she's in the hospital. They'll want everything done for her while being able to provide no useful information other than to give us heartburn. Remind me to thank Amy!" Jason sighed, clearly having seen this scenario before. "Raj, watch me handle this, and try to take notes."

He entered the small room and instantly got everybody's attention, "Greetings, I'm Dr. Bates and I'm in charge here."

"Finally, a real doctor." Richard introduced his siblings and demanded an update be given on their grandmother.

"Well, it appears as though she has come to the ER due to altered mental status. This is something we take very seriously and are going to get started on immediately with the appropriate CT scans and blood tests. I will have more information for you in the morning when we start to get some results back."

The granddaughter spoke, trying to appear smart and knowledgeable, "won't the radiation put her at risk for cancer?" With that question she failed, her ignorance obvious.

I wanted to slap her silly. She'd be lucky if her grandmother made it through the week as cachectic as she appeared. Hell, a CT scan of the head is only about the same amount of radiation as a trans-Atlantic flight.

Ignoring her question, Jason turned to me and said, "Dr. Raj, can you kindly go to radiology and personally notify them we need an immediate scan for Ms. Maude here? Tell them she's a VIP and they better make her comfortable and be quick. Also ask for the special 'low radiation' protocol." His wink was almost imperceptible.

Taking the hint, I rushed off to the radiology department where they looked at me like I was some confused medical student and told me to be on my way. Later I learned that I was just supposed to disappear, not actually do what he said.

Returning to the ER five minutes later, I found Jason putting his medical knowledge and training to good use: surfing the web.

"After you left I was able to kiss up to the family. They decided she was under good care and went home. They especially liked the VIP part," he winked, obvious this time. "They are all successful attorneys at some law firm their grandfather started ages ago. They have no clue what's going on with their grandmother. Fortunately the butler should be here soon and will fill us in on everything."

"What do we do in the mean time?"

"What we do for all GOMERs … pan-scan her."

In patients who are poor historians the physical exam cannot be focused appropriately (these are the same patients who don't know why there are in the ER in the first place) and is of limited or no benefit. So instead of wasting a long time on an exam which is likely to be useless, a CT scan from head to toe is performed to look for any abnormalities. The physical exam can take a solid 45 minutes while the CT scanning can be performed in less than 8 minutes with modern scanners. Sounds great in principle; the only problem is cost. A pan-scan from the ER starts at around $15K and quickly rises from there if special dyes/contrast agents are needed or if MRI scanning is required.

We ordered the pan-scan and waited for Bernard.

~~~~

Bernard was a class act, the epitome of classic hired help. He arrived in a British butler's uniform, nicer than most tuxedos I'd seen. And more importantly, he had Ms. Maude's entire medical file for the past 35 years that he'd been working for the family. He reminded me of Alfred, the butler from Batman.

Thanking Bernard, we let him settle into Ms. Maude's room while we started to go over the records. Apparently he and Josefine,

Maude's personal nurse, were going to take turns so that somebody was by her bedside at all times.

"Dude, don't you think he resembles Alfred?" asked Jason as soon as we were out of earshot. Guess I wasn't the only one thinking about the caped crusader.

"That's what I was going to say! He's just as organized too; look at these meticulous records."

We began to familiarize ourselves with Matilda Margaret Maude. The records were so well organized that their review was only a one man job, thus; Jason decided his time would be better spent speaking with Bernard to get his perspective on what was happening. More medical information was soon to arrive once Josefine brought her even more comprehensive medical records about Maude's history. While both records were very complete, I later noticed that some minor details were missing from both accounts; while nothing crucial, when taken together they were incredibly comprehensive.

It was quite amazing she made it to 96 years of age. She'd smoked since she was 17 until just a couple years ago, quitting only because her dementia had advanced to the point that she'd forget how to operate a lighter. She was on medications for dementia and high blood pressure. She'd survived breast cancer, typhoid, malaria, 2 MIs, and was on about four anti-depression and anti-anxiety drugs. She also had a history of heavy alcoholism.

Matilda used to be quite the socialite, always surrounded by people, until about five years ago when she began to withdraw from just about everything. The decline the past couple years had been dramatic; leaving her essentially non-verbal, incontinent, and visited by her grandchildren about once a month, and that too, begrudgingly. Apparently the commute from next door is pretty difficult.

"Why do you think Bernard and Josefine are so protective of her?" I asked Jason when he returned.

"Apparently her husband was a standup guy. He was an excellent lawyer with a reputation of treating everybody with the utmost respect. The combination made him very prominent in the community. I'm sure the fact he was uber rich helped too. Anyhow, Josefine and Bernard loved him like a son, and in his will he requested they honor his memory by taking care of Matilda. So part of why they act the way they do might be out of deference to him. I wonder if the inheritance goes to the two of them or the money hungry grandkids?"

"How was Matilda, before she went all comatose?"

"Reading in between the lines, I think she was the quintessential trophy wife and bitch. She came from a background of privilege and never worked a day in her life, just looked pretty on her late husband's arm. He was happy with that setup because she'd entertain herself, allowing him to work and build his empire. She was also adept at arranging the appropriate social gatherings for a family of their stature."

"I bet her family is just here to show *their* attorneys that they care. I'm guessing if there is any inheritance dispute in the future, their names appearing in the medical record as proof they were here when grandma was ill will only be to their benefit."

"Raj, there's hope for you yet. Trust me, she'll be a royal pain in our ass for as long as she's here." Again Jason's pager went off, this time with a text page. "Well, the radiologist reports that all her scans are essentially normal. Just the expected osteoporosis and cerebral atrophy, all consistent with her age."

"Remind me again why she's here?"

"Her grandson called emergency when he was visiting her claiming she didn't recognize him and kept moaning something he'd never heard before. But he's a lawyer, so he used the altered mental status buzzword, and voilà, here she is."

After finishing up all her admission orders I ask, "How do we get her out of here?"

"Good question. Smart to think about disposition/discharge early on. I figure we have two options: number one, we keep her here long enough until she gets a nasty nosocomial infection and ends up in the morgue; number two, through frivolous testing we arrive at some bullshit diagnosis, treat it, cure her, and get the family to agree to allow her back home all fixed up. If it's the latter, I'm sure the hospital will hit her up for a huge donation and name some stupid hallway after her."

"Great."

"Yeah, tell me about it. On the plus side, Duane is next door, so at least we don't have to walk far to check up on him."

We entered Duane's room to find him sleeping peacefully. All was stable. His heart rate had increased by 10 BPM, but thinking nothing of it for now, we headed to the call room for some long awaited shut eye.

~~~~

Sleep came quickly and the four hours it lasted was far from enough. Getting out of bed I made it to the locker room to brush my teeth and wash my face. The nice thing about being on call is you can go from being sound asleep to starting work in about three minutes; the bad part is you wear the same clothes as the day before and sleep on a communal mattress. Showering and breakfast are usually forsaken because the extra ten minutes of sleep are too valuable to squander on such activities.

The first thing I did was check up on Duane. Still sleeping, I gently nudged his shoulder to wake him up.

"Oh, hey Doc. Good morning." He sat up in bed rubbing his eyes. "Wow, you weren't kidding when you said you'd be by early. Is it even morning yet?"

Pre-rounding, the process of seeing patients and gathering data before actually rounding with the attending physician frequently started well before 6 a.m., and even earlier on surgical services when one had to be in the OR by 7 a.m.

Cutting to the chase, I ask, "How was your night? How are you feeling?"

"I slept like a baby." He straightened his back and stretched his muscles as if wondering himself how he was doing. Pleased with the results he nodded in approval. "I think I'm a lot better, the pain is about 80% less, and I'm not feeling sick like before. Do you think the infection is gone?"

"Well, you're on some very broad spectrum antibiotics, so they'll likely kill most anything that could be causing your infection. We'll tailor the therapy further when the culture results are back and we know exactly what we're up against."

"Thanks Doc. My wife and girl are coming in later this morning. Do you think you can meet them? I want to introduce them to the Doc that saved my life."

I was flattered by his kindness. "We're not out of the woods just yet, but I'd be happy to give them an update on your status. Hopefully the cultures will be back by then, and if we're lucky we'll know exactly what is causing all this."

I shook his hand and went next door to check in on Ms. Maude.

She appeared frail as ever, nearly every bone visible beneath her tissue paper thin skin. Nobody had dared start an IV on her, thus, interventional radiology placed a subclavian line under fluoroscopy guidance sometime in the middle of the night. It was through that that she received her fluids and had blood drawn for testing. She was so decrepit in appearance I was surprised the IV afforded actual blood and not dust.

I was about to wake Ms. Maude up when I noticed some movement in my peripheral vision. A petite figure hidden in shadows stood up and headed in my direction, picking up a file from the adjacent table on her way over. "Hi, are you the medical student looking after Matilda?"

"Yes, you must be Josephine? Bernard mentioned the two of you would be taking turns being with Ms. Maude."

"The one and only. I brought a summary of Matilda's medical history for your review. Her grandchildren aren't exactly savvy to all that Matilda's been through. And with her dementia, you can't really trust what comes out of her mouth."

Josephine didn't look within a decade of her sixty plus years of age. She was extremely well put together, fit, and organized. Even though she had spent the last 30 years being a nurse for only one family, she was more competent than just about any nurse on the floor here. That's what private practice is like; you get what you pay for.

I scanned through the records. They were similar to Bernard's, but more complete.

Ms. Maude had quite the medical history, over sixty years of heavy smoking, half of that was accompanied with alcoholism, depression, anxiety, bilateral hip and knee replacements, a spinal fusion, breast cancer complete with bilateral mastectomies and reconstructions, half a dozen cosmetic surgeries, malaria, and numerous bouts of pneumonia. A total of five vessels in her heart had been bypassed with three of those receiving secondary stents courtesy of her two MIs. Oh I forgot to mention the two strokes she'd survived and completely recovered from. By all accounts Ms. Maude should have been dead many times over two decades ago.

"How does Ms. Maude look to you today?" I asked.

"Well, she seems a bit weak. Usually she can sit up in a chair. She loves playing with her pets, not that she remembers their names. Watching television and petting her dog and cat are her main activities. Bernard and I take her through the gardens at least twice a day. She's a big fan of the roses when they're in bloom."

"Is she verbal at home?"

"Oh no, she barely says anything as it is, and almost none of what she does utter makes any coherent sense. I've been feeding her for the past four years and changing her diapers for about three years now." Nodding Josefine added, "Sadly, some consider her current status a significant improvement over how she used to be." As soon as the words were uttered Josefine went rigid and turned around, clearly regretting having divulged too much information. "I apologize, that was rude of me. She was loved by her husband, and that's what counts."

I figured I'd gotten all the information Josefine would provide me for the time being. I needed to build some rapport before I learned more about Ms. Maude.

A quick physical exam, which consisted of me looking at the monitors to ensure they were rhythmically beeping, confirmed that she was indeed still alive. The days of performing an actual physical examination are long gone. Nowadays it's all about interpreting numbers and letting the automated readings tell you what's going on. And Maude had numbers on the screen, they weren't zero, thus, my initial interpretation was confirmed; she was alive.

I ran into Jason in the lounge. He asked, "Hey Raj, how are our peeps doing?"

"Well, Maude is alive, and Duane says he's feeling 80% better."

"Good."

"I met Maude's live-in nurse, she seems quite competent, says Maude's energy level is down from baseline but otherwise she's demented and incontinent as ever."

"While you were checking up on them I made some phone calls and did a little bit of sleuthing myself. Got some interesting news for you; we've got diagnoses for them both."

"Sweet, what's Duane's bug?"

"Well, I talked to his wife this morning. Seems like they have a healthy sexual life and she recently had an *E. coli* urinary tract infection that was sensitive to penicillin. A quick call to the lab confirmed that Duane likely has the same bug. It always comes back to sex or drugs."

"I bet his wife's hot."

"I'm not willing to disagree with you on that point."

"So we just treat him for a couple more days on IV Zosyn and send him out on something oral?"

"Yep. Ms. Maude is a little more interesting. Her last hospitalization was due to pneumonia from MRSA. She was in the ICU for almost three weeks followed by another couple weeks on the floor before being sent home only two weeks ago. But when I checked her labs this morning her troponin was elevated. She's having a silent heart attack."

"Damn! I wouldn't have guessed. How'd you think to get those labs?"

"After we went to our call rooms I remember thinking that in her age group silent MI's are common. I reviewed the CT scan in my head and all those stents she had bothered me. So I figured what the hell, and called the lab to add a troponin to the tests we already ordered. Best part is, on rounds, I want you to mention that you did it. You'll look like a superstar."

"I can't do that, it was all you."

"Dude, I don't give a rusty fuck what people think of me here. This is only my internship, and then I'm off to Dermatology residency and the easy life. You still need your letters of recommendation, and this will help cinch you a good one from Miley."

"Thanks man, I owe you. Shouldn't we get her seen by cardiology?"

"Already on it, I called them like five minutes ago. They're going to take her for a cardiac catheterization in about an hour. I heard in some European countries they don't even allow people to get a cardiac cath after the age of 65 for unhealthy individuals and over 75 you're out of luck no matter who you are. But here they're more than happy to spend another 100k to add a few days to Maude's life so she can go home and do whatever the fuck she does."

"She pets her dog."

"Awesome, we'll spend a quarter million on this hospitalization so she can go pet her dog. I bet she can't even remember the damn thing's name. Gotta love medical care in the US. Let's grab a bite before rounds."

~~~~

We met the team for rounds, but Adam, Amy, and Kelly were nowhere to be found. Jason and I quizzically looked at each other as Duke rounded the corner and fast approached.

"Jason, I gave the rest of the team the day off. They only got one admission overnight, so I figured you and Raj could handle that."

We were both cursing up a storm, in our heads, but on the outside we welcomed the opportunity for more work with no reward as Duke gave us the lowdown on our newest patient.

Rounds flew by.

"Strong work Raj, most residents wouldn't even have thought that Ms. Maude was having a heart attack. You keep this up and I'll make sure you make honors on this rotation."

Before I could thank her, Dr. Miley was off to attend to whatever it is that attending doctors do all day. My guess was surf the web.

"Well, looks like you guys have it under control. I'll be around if you need me," said Duke.

Ah, the code words that Duke was leaving for the day and all the work for the team was bestowed upon our shoulders. In medicine it's never appropriate to say one's leaving, instead one makes a false offer to be available, when in fact they are likely to be unavailable and definitely do not want to be called or bothered. It's a strange culture.

"Guess it's just the two of us Raj. Ohhh … check that out."

Both our heads turned toward the "click click click" of stiletto heels hitting hospital tile. Growing out of those heels were gorgeous legs with a miniskirt that left less to the imagination than a hospital gown, and a body which deserved even less clothing. She walked straight into Duane's room.

"You were right Raj, she's definitely hot, now we know where he got his *E. coli* from. Can't say I blame him either. Shall we introduce ourselves?" Jason winked while he said it.

I followed Jason into the room where the sultry Mrs. was seated on the side of Duane's bed gently stroking his head.

"Hi Duane, just came in to check in on you. Is this your wife?"

"Hi Doc. I'm the better half. How's my darling doing?" She replied.

"Pleasure to meet you, I'm Dr. Bates and this is Raj, our medical student. He's been working hard on your husband's case. The good news is that the blood cultures came back positive for *E. coli*, likely from the urinary tract infection which you were treated for last month per our discussion on the phone. The other piece of good news is that it's sensitive to the antibiotic we already have Duane on, which explains why he's doing so much better."

"Oh, that's great news. Do you think he'll go home soon?"

"I think that's a reasonable possibility in the next day or two. We'll keep him over night on the IV antibiotics and then transition him to something he can take orally tomorrow. If he does well, he's all yours."

"Wonderful!" She kissed him on the cheek.

"Hey Doc, not to rain on the parade, but my arm here kinda hurts. Can you take a look at it?"

I rushed over to Duane's right arm and it was almost double in size compared to his left arm, and very tender to palpation. I immediately looked up at Jason whose nod conveyed that agreed with the diagnosis without saying a word. His prolonged silence was my cue to speak up.

"Well Duane, it looks like your IV line has infiltrated; instead of pouring the fluid into your vein, it's basically leaked it into the soft tissues of your arm. Thankfully it's not a big deal; we'll just remove this line and start one on your other arm. I'll let the nurse know on our way out and get his taken care of this right away. The swelling in your arm should subside and normalize in a couple hours."

"Phew, thanks guys. I thought it was another infection."

"I'll turn this IV off for now. The nurse is next door and she'll be in as soon as she's done there. I figure that gives the two of you about 15 minutes of alone time before the next interruption."

Both Duane and his wife were smiling ear to ear with sheepish grins. I have little doubt they thoroughly enjoyed the next 15 minutes. In fact I think I heard a zipper open before I even shut the door to leave. I doubt it was the one to her purse.

"Raj, why don't you tell his nurse to swap out his IV and place a new one in his other arm, I'll take care of his orders and morning labs. He's got the same nurse as Maude; I think I saw her in Maude's room preparing her for transport to the cath lab."

"Sure thing."

The nurse was indeed helping the transport team move Maude into a gurney for transport. She seemed quite frazzled and anxious …

the nurse, that is. Maude was still moaning 'Abigail' to whoever was listening. I made a mental note to figure out what that meant.

I relayed our orders to the nurse and she agreed. On my way out she hollered after me.

"Hey, on second thought, I'm busy here; can you just start his new IV?" The nurse had the audacity to ask me this even after she'd already agreed to take care of it, not to mention it was her job, for which she got paid over $50 an hour to do.

"Sorry, I was on call last night, and we only start IV's in emergent situations. I'm sure you can handle it, but if you are unable to start a simple line, please feel free to give me a page after you've failed," I replied with some spice in my voice.

She didn't respond audibly, but I could swear she mouthed something inappropriate. Nurses were always trying to get out of procedures, and medical students were prime targets to dump the menial tasks onto. But I wasn't in the mood to deal with any attitude, perhaps it'd have been different if she'd asked me nicely. The last thing I noticed when I left the room was that she was only wearing one glove. Odd.

Fortunately the morning and afternoon went by smoothly, though the nurse did complain to Jason about my lack of enthusiasm for patient care. Jason was very PC in how he dealt with it, telling her he'd talk to me about it. Our talk consisted of us making fun of her cartoon-themed scrubs and how grateful we were we didn't have to collect urine and stool samples all day.

Sign out rounds, in which the team that was on call quickly presents their patients to the team that is on call for the night, took all of six minutes. Before I knew it, we were exiting the hospital 35 hours after we last entered, only to return in 12 hours.

~~~~

The morning started before I even parked my car. I received a page from Maude's nurse asking if I wanted to change her heparin, a potent blood thinner, drip. She wasn't on heparin when I'd left the hospital; something had clearly changed for the worse overnight.

I rushed to the intern to whom I'd signed out the night before to get an update. Apparently Ms. Maude had quite the eventful night. She did not get the cardiac catheterization during the day as planned due to two emergent cases that bumped hers to later in the day. By that time her labs were rechecked her troponin levels had risen. The cardiologists concluded she was having an acute heart attack. While she was undergoing her procedure they found that three of her bypasses had nearly closed off and required stenting. Remarkably, she underwent the procedure without complication.

All five of her major cardiac arteries had already been bypassed surgically, and now all five bypasses had been stented, with one being stented twice. I didn't even know such a thing was possible.

I later learned that the cardiologists didn't think it was possible either, but the risk of putting her through open heart surgery was too great so they tried to dodge that bullet with the stents. If the procedure worked it might be a reportable case; that seemed to excite the cardiologists. I can imagine the title of the article, "Living Corpse Undergoes Repeat Stenting and Survives."

That explained why I was paged about her heparin. She needed it to prevent the new hardware in her heart from acutely thrombosing, in which a blood clot forms and completely obstructs the now artificially opened arteries.

I swung by her room, the incessant beeps informing me she was still alive. She looked no different from before except now a sandbag was applying pressure on her right groin, the entry site from where they performed her stenting procedure.

"Good morning Doctor," said Bernard.

I turned to see him in full regalia reading *BQ: Butler's Quarterly*. He definitely took his job seriously.

"Morning Alf … uh, Bernard. How has she been?"

"Amazing, actually. Just a few hours after the procedure her energy seemed to have come back and she was asking to eat again. You folks are really magicians in what you can do here."

"I can't take credit for it. I'm glad she's recovering so rapidly." The only problem was that I failed to see any recovery; in fact if it wasn't for the monitors informing me she wasn't dead, I'd have thought her ready for transfer to the morgue.

As I turned to leave I heard her whisper what sounded like, "Abigail."

I was going to ask Bernard about it, but got distracted when my pager went off. It was the nursing station. Instead of calling, I just walked up and asked for who paged me.

It was a very young nurse, who I wondered if was even old enough to vote. She still had that look of excitement and caring that had not yet been eroded away and transformed into jaded cynicism.

"Hi." She looked at my nametag, "Rajen, I'm Breanne, I just took over for Duane. Great guy he is, but I wanted to ask you, is it ok to give him something more for his pain?"

"More? He was doing so much better when I left yesterday that we stopped his pain medications. Did anything happen overnight?"

She consulted her little notepad, "Not really. Cynthia changed his IV last afternoon after transferring Ms. Maude to the cath lab for the second time. Duane received all his antibiotics on schedule. He even took a short walk with his wife and daughter."

"So his kidney pain is back?"

"Oh no, I forgot to tell you. He passed his stone last night; we collected it and sent to the lab for evaluation. The pain is in his arm."

"Yea, the IV in his right arm infiltrated yesterday, that's why it was switched over to his other arm. But the pain should have resolved within a couple hours. In fact, he was back to normal when I eyeballed him before leaving."

"I'm sorry, he's complaining of pain in his left arm."

"Fuck. Oh … sorry, you didn't hear that." I took off power walking to his room.

Duane was sitting up in bed. A quick glance at his monitors showed that his heart rate was almost 100. Not what I'd expect in a healthy guy like him on the road to recovery. His BP was normal, but his temperature was 99.4°F, a full degree higher than when I'd left yesterday. His respirations were also increased from 12 to 15. I didn't like what I saw. Something was awry. He was behaving as though his infection was coming back.

"Hi, Duane."

"Hey, Doc. How you doing?"

"Forget me, what's going on with you? I heard your arm has been causing you some discomfort?"

"Yeah, it's not a lot, but it woke me up a couple hours ago and it's been getting worse since, so I thought I'd ask for some of that pain medication you gave me before, worked really good last time."

"Is there any pain in your back or elsewhere?"

"No sir, if it wasn't for this arm thing, I'd say I was back to 90% of normal."

"Can I take a look at your arm? Where is it bothering you?"

My stomach knotted up, turned cold, and sank before I could even grab some gloves to examine Duane's arm. I immediately noticed as he raised his left arm that it was swollen, red, and likely warm. There was some erythema and a small amount of discharge around the IV where it penetrated his skin on the dorsal side of his right hand.

His forearm was swollen by about 25%, extending nearly up to his elbow. But the most ominous sign was that I could see tendrils of redness emanating from his IV site and extending about midway up his forearm, like long spider legs, corresponding to his superficial veins.

I gently squeezed his forearm. He cringed in pain. His eyes watered and his arm involuntarily retracted, all from a squeeze so gentle it'd be considered a weak handshake. I bit my tongue to keep from saying anything to scare Duane. It was all I could do to keep my composure and exude confidence.

"Well. Duane, I'll definitely make sure you get some pain medications ASAP. I'll also need to culture that discharge and remove your IV. We'll have to replace it with another one, likely a PICC line. That's a catheter line that will be located on your other side. Just think of it as a super IV."

"Sure, Doc. Do you think I'll be going home soon? You heard the stone came out last night?"

"I think we should wait until the laboratory evaluation of your stone is complete and we know what this discharge on your IV is from."

"Well, you know where to find me." He still managed a smile. I'm sure he wouldn't have smiled if he knew he was about 24 hours from death had this gone unnoticed.

A lot had to be done in the 30 minutes remaining before rounds. I called Jason and gave him a recap on what had transpired. He cut me off and said he'd be right there as he slammed down the phone. I called the pharmacy to get them working on preparing a Vancomycin solution STAT. Meanwhile, I got the culture supplies ready and notified the procedure team of our STAT request for PICC line placement. I took care of all this in 90 seconds flat.

Flesh eating bacteria wasn't something that allowed for lollygagging.

We entered in Duane's room together, armed with culture supplies and pain medications. He looked worried when he saw we were garbed in gowns, gloves, and masks.

"Duane, Dr. Bates here behind this mask. Sorry to barge in on you like this, but you have a serious infection in your left arm that is contagious. We're going to take the cultures that Dr. Raj mentioned and then we're going to give you some different antibiotics that will make you all better." Jason attached a syringe to Duane's IV port and quickly injected the clear liquid. "Here's some medication for your pain."

The Toradol afforded Duane some immediate relief.

We set to work culturing the discharge around the IV, the amount of pus had almost doubled since I was last in his room just a few minutes ago.

"You're starting to worry me guys. Is everything thing ok?"

"It appears you've developed a Staph infection in your left arm. The bad news is it's started to get into your bloodstream. Once we get these cultures we can tailor the therapy to kick this bug's ass and get you home to your family."

Twenty minutes later the Vancomycin solution was ready. In that time, Duane's temperature had escalated to 100.5°F and his arm became even more painful, requiring morphine to alleviate the discomfort.

The PICC team was busy and wouldn't be able to insert his line for almost 2 hours; thus, we decided to administer the Vancomycin through his infected IV. We didn't have time to wait. Being aggressive, we set the infusion for 20 minutes instead of the usual 1 hour.

Leaving Duane in a state of morphine induced haze as we rushed off for rounds, both of us worried about his outcome.

"Raj, you realize he's probably got a fucking MRSA infection? This is not good!"

"Hey, remember yesterday when I asked the nurse to change his IV? I didn't think anything of it at the time, but when she was transferring Maude, she was only wearing one glove, and no gown. And we know that Maude is colonized with MRSA."

"SHIT. FUCK. God damn it … that's where he got it from. He should have been going home today; instead he got one of the worst nosocomial infections out there. And it was introduced right into his blood stream where it's been reproducing like mad for the past 18 hours. Normally people get this in their lungs or through a skin abscess in which there are some barriers before it hits the circulatory system. Those barriers were bypassed in Duane's case. If you're religious, pray for him, man." Jason was getting visibly upset.

"It's that bad?"

"Well, if he responds to the Vanco over the next 12 hours or so, we might dodge this bullet, but a direct inoculation with MRSA straight into the blood stream can kill a healthy person in less than 36 hours, dude. That's why we have all these precautions throughout the hospital. That nurse should never have been without a gown or gloves in Maude's room. All those signs you see for various precautionary measures on patient doors are to prevent this exact scenario."

"Damn."

"You go off to rounds, I'm going to be a little late. I've got to get him on isolation precautions; luckily he's already in a negative pressure room. I'll call the lab to get the Gram stain results before I come over."

Dr. Miley was very impressed at Maude's recovery. But she gave us her soapbox about how medical advances are keeping people alive longer and longer, however, quality of life is usually severely diminished, and the costs go through the roof. From a business perspective Dr. Miley said it was atrocious, to keep people alive with such 'piss poor quality of life.' She went so far as to claim, in certain instances, prolonging life might even be unethical, just because we have the knowledge, technology, and means does not mandate that we utilize them all on every case. But we must uphold the wishes of the patients and family.

Speaking of family, none of Maude's grandchildren had bothered to make an appearance since that night in the ER. However, through Josefine and Bernard, they made it clear that *everything* was to be done for their Grandmother's survival.

Just as we began to round on Duane, Jason appeared. Miley said we did all the right things. She'd personally notify the infectious diseases committee about this infection since such a definite link was apparent, clearly implying that heads were sure to roll. She didn't go in to see Duane in an effort to minimize the risk of contaminating others given his active infection.

Maude was on autopilot and the cardiologist said she could go home in 2–3 days if all went well. Given her advanced age, he wanted to keep her for observation a little longer than normal.

Fortunately, Duane was also doing well. That same evening, after his second dose of Vanco, Duane reported his pain had significantly subsided and he was starting to feel better. Hopefully by tomorrow we'd have his infection's sensitivities and might even be able to transition him to oral—or PO as we say—antibiotics in a couple days.

I went home that night thinking I'd made a difference in someone's life and that tomorrow would be a good day.

~~~~

Tomorrow arrived and began as ordinary as a day in medicine can. Both Duane and Ms. Maude were doing well.

In fact Duane's culture results arrived just before rounds. The causative bug was in fact MRSA; fortunately the strain responsible for his infection was sensitive to Bactrim, a very common and generally well tolerated antibiotic that was available in both IV and PO formulations.

"Thus, given the bacteria's sensitivity to Bactrim and Duane's positive response to IV Vanco treatment, I think we can transition him to IV Bactrim for a day, and if he responds favorably, send him home in two days on PO Bactrim." That concluded my presentation on Duane for morning rounds.

"Raj, that is an excellent plan; make it happen. Switch him over so that his a.m. dose is Bactrim instead of Vanco today. How is Matilda doing?" asked Dr. Miley.

"Status quo." Jason and I both remarked simultaneously.

"Well, I guess we're still babysitting her until cardiology allows her to go home, so just keep everything the same and hopefully she'll be off our service by the week's end. Ok team, good job, get your work done and get out of here. We're on call tomorrow, so get some rest tonight."

While Jason wrote the orders for Ms. Maude, I decided to check in on Duane.

"Good news, Duane. The culture results came back and it looks like the bacteria causing your infection are sensitive to a very common antibiotic we use all the time. We're going to switch you over to the new medication via IV for a day. If you do well we'll give you the pill version for another day, and if you tolerate that ok you'll be out of here on the pill version of Bactrim for a couple weeks or so at home."

"Hey, thanks, Doc, no offense, but I'd be happy if I don't ever have to see you again."

"That's the same thing the girls say. Guess I should hit the gym a little harder," I deadpanned.

"Oh, no, no, I didn't mean ..."

My smile gave me away.

"Good one, you had me there for a second. You don't have a girlfriend? I thought Docs had chicks chasing after them like no tomorrow."

"Ah, my friend, you speak of the old school. Today's girls know that the title 'intern' or 'resident' or 'fellow' is synonymous with poverty and sleep deprivation. They don't waste their time on us lowly trainees. Girls only want the fully board certified physicians or 'attending' doctors. That's where the money is, and the girls know it … unfortunately."

"For real?"

"Yeah, no joke. Used to be that you go to a bar and once word got out you're a Doc, girls would find you. Nowadays that strategy is a bust; girls not only ask if you're done with your training, but in which field you specialize."

"Why would they care about that? A Doc's a Doc, right?"

"You kidding me? Girls don't want to date a general or primary care Doc these days; they want a specialist; that's where the money still exists. My friend's a fully-fledged single neurosurgeon and he's got no trouble getting a girl now. BUT, in med school it was a whole different ballgame. He had to beg for a date. However, now that he makes north of $800k a year, he's a very sought after quantity, despite an extra 20 pounds and some male pattern balding."

"Geez, man, and I always thought Docs and jocks get the chicks, in that order."

"Maybe jocks, you're the soccer coach and you have a gorgeous wife."

"See, that's the funny thing, I met her in college at Cornell, and the pickup line I used was that I was studying to get into medical school. She thought I was smart and going to be a doctor one day. After not getting accepted anywhere, I got my master's in software design, but I already had her by then."

I patted him on the back as I prepared to leave. "Well, I'm glad that line worked for you, I've had no such luck."

"You're a nice guy, I bet you'll meet someone great; and if not, you can just stick to saving lives. You seem to be pretty good at it."

"Thanks Duane. I've gotta get going, I'll make sure you get your new medication now, and I'll be back later to check up on you."

"Thanks, Doc. Once I get home I'm going to put the word out that I know a great eligible bachelor who saves lives in his free time."

I bet Duane never suspected that within a week he'd be asking me to take his life, not save it.

~~~~

I entered medical school thinking that by becoming a physician my goal would be to save lives and end suffering. What I didn't know was that the two didn't necessarily go hand in hand. Duane was about to teach me that sometimes they are mutually exclusive. And that distinction is precisely why my life just got a whole lot more complicated beginning this very morning.

Before I got to Duane's room I ran into the covering intern for the night. He was shaking his head as he approached.

"Dude, your guy didn't do so well. Luckily he's still alive, and the good news is that he's off your service."

"Off our service? We were thinking of discharging him home tomorrow."

"Cancel that plan. He developed TEN early in the evening and it progressed rapidly. At first he just said his eyes were itching badly, but that got worse and worse, so I got an emergent ophthalmology consult. They said he had severe abrasions in both corneas. But it gets worse. As the eye doc was leaving the room your patient coughs up blood all over the place and freaks the eye doc out. Guess they aren't used to seeing much blood. Anyway, he called a code. Smart thing he did that 'cause that's what saved his life."

I was in shock trying to take it all in. Just yesterday Duane was laughing and talking about setting me up.

"So by the time the code blue team arrives he's in a full blown seizure, his skin is so excoriated and pustular it looks like he's got third degrees all over his body. The seizure was so violent that he fell out of bed onto the floor with chunks of skin just sloughing off.

When he fell off the bed his PICC line got caught up on something and came out, so we lost IV access. He was seizing, coughing up blood, and vomiting simultaneously, all while his flesh was flying off with each new wave of seizures. Since we didn't have any IV access we had to give him some serious IM sedation. But that stuff doesn't act right away and he was literally choking on his vomit. So we had to do an emergent intubation, which was impossible during his grand mal, so we did an emergent tracheostomy. Once things finally calmed down we transfused him with six units of blood. But due to all the areas of missing skin—I'm talking about 50% of his body. He's needed steady blood and platelet transfusions all night long. The dermatologists actually came in during the middle of the night to help cover all his skin wounds; I've never seen them around after 4 p.m. so *that's* saying something. Then we transferred him to the ICU once he was a bit more stabilized. Worst thing is that his daughter and wife were in the room when it all happened. Daughter freaked out and was admitted to pediatric psychiatry for monitoring. The wife's a mess; cute though, I must add. She was asking for you, something about you saying all was going great."

"Where is he now?"

"Shit, I'm late, here's his sign out card. He's in the medical ICU." The intern ran off already thinking about his next task at hand.

Fuck, FUCK, *FUCK* … this was *not* good. I just stood there in a state of semi-shock. Sure I'd read about toxic epidermal necrolysis, or TEN, and how catastrophic it can be. Most people with a severe case don't survive, but it's so rare, only a 100 or so severe cases in the U.S. per year.

Then I realized what caused it. It was the IV Bactrim he received. Sulfa medications are associated with TEN and that's the only thing that changed in his care yesterday.

My heart turned into a chunk of ice and I felt it sink to my stomach. It was my idea to start him on this new medication! If he'd just stayed on the Vanco for another week he'd have been fine. Or if I'd inserted his IV instead of that wretched contaminated nurse, he'd never have gotten the MRSA infection in the first place.

Just a day ago he was thanking me for saving his life, not realizing I was the one responsible for almost taking it away.

My legs started moving, but my mind was a cloud of confused thoughts, none of which was completely formed. I was still grappling with how this could have happened; he was doing just fine yesterday.

Before I knew it, I exited on the fifth floor and was entering the ICU. There was much commotion two rooms in front of me. The cramped space was filled with five people, four in long coats and a nurse in scrubs. A ventilator with some long tubing and two full bags of RBCs were being rapidly infused.

I couldn't see who the patient was because he was covered from head to toe in a thick salve with white dressings covering most parts of his body. His eyes were open but doused in thick lubricating ointment. I couldn't recognize Duane, but the fact that the ventilator tubing was entering in the middle of his neck and his skin was missing clued me in pretty well that it was him.

I was close enough to hear the attending physicians discuss the case and I made out bits of conversation.

"It's amazing he's alive, but his clotting factors are quite low. We're going to have to give him some more platelets. I think after these transfusions are complete, we can dedicate one of the central lines for blood products and the others for medications and fluids."

"Agreed. The ophthalmologist was here earlier this morning. He said that his corneal abrasions were severe and worse than yesterday. He might lose one or both eyes if we don't make sure they're always lubricated."

"We should start the IVIG sometime today if the steroids don't make a significant difference by about noon. If he keeps losing skin like he is now he'll die of dehydration, blood loss, or both, in the next day or two."

"Not to mention infection. He had MRSA septicemia; if he gets that in these open lesions the game's over."

I'd heard enough, and turned to leave. The chipper and improving Duane was now reduced to being mechanically ventilated and nearly blind. Not to mention that he was losing both skin and blood at an alarming rate. IVIG was a treatment of last resort with only a slim chance of success. But if the steroids didn't do the trick, this was the last option in the armamentarium for treatment of TEN, aside from supportive skin care measures and blood transfusions.

Just when I thought things couldn't get any worse, they did. I ran into his wife as I exited the ICU and she came running up to me.

She wasn't doing well, and who could blame her? In the past day her husband went from recovering nicely to knocking on the pearly gates, her daughter was admitted to the hospital for a psychiatric meltdown from witnessing her father losing half his skin and blood during a seizure immediately after having an eye exam indicating he was rapidly going blind, and she was left alone to deal with the fall-out. She looked as one would expect: disheveled, confused, eyes and nose raw from crying and sniffling. But she still managed to dress well, likely the only bit of armor she had left against the cruel world suffocating her.

I braced myself for the onslaught I thought was to follow. I just knew she was going to blame me for everything and yell and curse me out. She might even attack me and report me to the medical board and perhaps sue me. My career would end years before it was even to begin.

I took one last deep breath and prepared myself. As she approached me she slowed down and patted down her dress and coat, in an effort to compose herself for the upcoming *battle royale*.

What happened next caught me off guard.

"Are you ok Dr. Raj?" she managed to ask between sniffles.

My body managed to seize briefly at the question. I took a moment to take myself in. I didn't look so hot either. I'd managed to splatter hand sanitizer all over myself as I rushed out of the ICU, my hair was a mess due to my fidgeting once I learned about Duane, and I must have given off the vibe that I was somewhere in between constipated and about to vomit as I prepared for her arrival. What happened next came naturally without thinking.

"Me? You poor dear," I patted her shoulder, "I can't imagine what you are going through, and I won't pretend to." She embraced me and sobbed on my shoulder.

"I think Duane developed a severe reaction to the sulfa antibiotic we placed him on to try and treat his infection. His body is now registering his skin as being a foreign invader and doing all it can to protect itself by firing his whole immune system's arsenal at his skin. That's why it was falling off and bleeding. Same with his eyes. The worst seems to have passed. The seizure was because his brain overloaded and needed to reboot itself. The ventilator is breathing for him at present because he is so heavily sedated from the pain medications, but they are keeping him comfortable."

"Thank you." I was perplexed at why I was being thanked. Unable to figure out the reason I continued with my report of his condition and treatment plan.

"They are giving him steroids to try and turn off his immune attack. If that doesn't work the next step is IVIG, which attempts to scavenge molecules and various cellular and protein fragments that are also playing a role in this havoc being wreaked on his body. This couldn't have happened to a nicer person. He didn't deserve this and we're going to do our best to help him recover."

"Thank you."

Again I couldn't for the life of me fathom what she was thanking me for. I was just blabbering on about what was happening in an effort for her to understand. I was almost about to ask what she was thanking me for. She should have been using me for a punching bag if anything. Instead I just remained silent until she broke the ice and answered my unspoken question.

"You're the first one out of the dozens that have been running around Duane to tell me what's happened. The scariest part wasn't thinking he was doing to die, but not knowing why. You've given me answers, and now I can start to come to terms with what is happening."

I hadn't realized until that moment what power we carry in something so little as an explanation. After all, what people fear most is the unknown. If you can tell someone what to expect he or she can mentally prepare for it; but if you pull the rug out from someone it's just a huge mess.

"Can I see him?"

"I don't think this would be a good time. There are a lot of people around him right now. Tell you what, I'll call you once he's more situated and walk you into the ICU myself."

She agreed and gave me her cell number while walking towards the waiting area with a head hung so low that I feared she might topple over. I had no idea what to do next, so I just stood against the wall until gravity pulled me down and I sat catatonic in the hallway. I don't know how much time passed but Jason eventually came over and helped me up. We discussed the events that had transpired.

"Raj, you can't blame yourself. It's not your fault because of your *intent*, nay our intent. Ultimately it was a team decision that changing medications was in his best interest. Not to mention the actual name behind the order is mine, not yours. The goal was to get him home as soon and as safely as possible. The intention was not to hurt or cause him harm; if we knew this would happen no way in hell would we have given him that medication."

"Yea, but it was my idea."

"And a damn good one at that! You assessed all the options and picked the best one. What occurred was an unintended consequence, a grave unforeseeable disability in his treatment plan. Man up, Raj, this is the real world, and shit happens. We're not here to be friends with our patients, we're here to help them. Unfortunately, nothing in medicine is 100%. The sad truth is that we're going to have some complications and tragedies such as Duane. The measure of a true doctor is how he handles the situation when things go to shit. It's easy to give good news; bad news is what this job is all about."

I listened and knew what he said was true; I just couldn't detach myself from the events that had occurred.

"Come on, we'll grab a bite to eat and talk to his wife again after rounds."

Rounds went well. Ms. Maude was continuing her nonsensical yearning for Abigail, while her grandchildren still remained MIA. Dr. Miley shook her head about Duane and said let that be a lesson to us all that what we do is very real and not a game. We can't ever take our jobs lightly when human lives are at stake every minute of every day. With that, she wished us a good call night and headed off.

A half hour later, Jason and I headed to Duane's wife and escorted her into the ICU. I could immediately tell that Duane's condition had deteriorated; he was on pressors, meds used to maintain one's BP because it's too low due to extreme illness, blood loss, or sepsis. Duane had all three. I let Jason lead the conversation. I wasn't up for anything besides being a passive observer.

"Mrs. Little, looking at his labs I have …"

His voice fell on deaf ears, Mrs. Little was immediately by her husband's side holding one of his bandaged upper extremities and sobbing by his side.

"I love you, dear, we're going to get through this and take you home." Her body was trembling as she spoke; leaving her gasping for air in between fits of sobs as she tried to communicate to her husband. "Jenny is also in the hospital. She went into shock when she saw your seizure last night, but she's going to be ok by the end of the week. I'm falling apart here honey … I really need you by my side. The last nine years have been the best of my life … I can't imagine the next 90 without you. You've *got* to pull through. If not for yourself, for me, babe." She put her forehead against his bandaged arm and just remained in that position.

Hearing her heartfelt conversation brought moisture even to Jason's eyes, but he would never admit it. We slipped out of the room and brought down the curtains to give them some privacy. We planted ourselves at the workstation and waited.

"The fact he's on pressors isn't a good sign?" I asked, but noticed Jason was in deep conversation with the ICU attending who was doing a lot of gesticulating and brushing his hand through his thinning head of hair. At the end of their conversation the attending wrote some orders and spoke to the nurse.

"What was that all about?"

"I was just getting an update from Dr. Benson. Bad news. In addition to the TEN and MRSA, Duane's going into SIRS, a precursor to DIC. Basically, his clotting factors are all out of whack and he's getting a unit of blood every hour and a ten pack of platelets every four to six hours. He said the steroids aren't working despite the mega doses he's getting."

"IVIG time?"

"Yep, that was what he was telling the nurse to get prepped. The infusion should start in the next couple hours."

"Isn't that like $10k per treatment cycle?"

"Dude, it's like $10k per *dose*, and he's slated for 2 before nightfall. It's a last ditch effort. This isn't looking favorable." Something caught his attention, it was Mrs. Little exiting from Duane's room. "Oh, she's coming out; follow my lead."

We walked up to Mrs. Little and gave her some fresh tissues to dab the rivulets of tears streaking down her face.

"Mrs. Little, unfortunately Duane is not responding to all our efforts, we're going to begin IVIG infusions within the hour to try and clear the offending molecules from his body. It's only a 50/50 chance that it'll help, but this is our only option. There's a 100% chance he'll continue to deteriorate without out it."

"I understand, thank you for your honesty. You and Dr. Raj were well liked by Duane, he spoke very highly of you both. I know you'll do your best to help him. Besides it can't get much worse, right?"

Wrong. But we didn't actually tell her that. The problem wasn't so much that he'd die; it was what would happen if he survived.

Duane did well after his first IVIG infusion and was off the pressors by dinnertime. There was even talk of taking him off the ventilator and lightening up his sedation. Everybody was optimistic.

During his second infusion is when all hell broke loose. He developed thrombosis, a rare complication from IVIG. But being Duane, he didn't just develop the local version, he developed the systemic variety and began to throw little emboli everywhere in his body. By the time it was recognized, he was not responding to pain and was unable to move the left side of his body.

The infusion was immediately stopped and he was sent for a STAT CT scan of his head which demonstrated a right-sided cerebral hemorrhage, or in other words, a stroke. The list of Duane's problems continued to grow.

"Shit, Raj, I wish he never came to the bloody ER."

"It's like what you said about nice guys. They don't do well in the hospital."

"Ha ha," Jason tried to laugh. It came out more like a cough. "You remember me saying that?"

"Yeah, I thought it was all BS."

"Here's living proof it's not. He came in with a simple kidney infection, and now he has sepsis, TEN, DIC, a stroke, and he's ventilator dependent with a tracheostomy. Not to mention he's legally blind. I just spoke to Dr. Sun, the ophthalmologist, a couple minutes ago. He said 50% of both of his corneas have eroded away and the likelihood of recovery without scarring is slim. If he ever hopes to see again he'll need bilateral corneal transplants."

"He must be going through hell."

"I'm sure he'd take hell over this. I spoke to his wife. I was completely honest. I told her he had about a 5% chance of making it through the night. So in an hour we're going to take him off all sedation and perhaps he might communicate a little bit. If he wakes up enough, maybe he can nod or blink his eyes to answer some questions."

I finished up my other work and entered the ICU just as Jason and the attending were reducing Duane's pain medications. He was starting to move the right side of his body and tried to blink his eyes.

"Duane darling, can you hear me?" His wife cried into his right ear. No response. She tried again. Then she switched to his left ear and he moved his right arm.

"Can you hear me, baby?"

A slight nod.

"Are you in pain?"

Affirmative.

"I love you ..."

And she hit the floor, sobs writhing through her body with convulsive force. Her screams of agony tore through the entire ICU. Everyone heard but tried to look away and ignore them. Jason and the attending picked her up and carried her to the conference room. I was alone with Duane.

"Hey, Duane, can you hear me?"

A nod. He tried to speak, but the breathing tube going into his neck thwarted any possibility of verbal communication on his part.

"Can you see?"

Negative.

"Can I do anything for you?"

An emphatic nodding and right hand shaking.

"What? You name it and it's done!"

More hand shaking, but I got the sense that neither of us knew sign language. Even if we did, his hand was so bandaged up his fingers couldn't move individually. He was wrapped up like a mitten.

This was going nowhere fast. Then I had an idea.

"Tell you what, I'll unwrap your hand a bit and put a pencil in it. Do you think you can write a little?"

Nodding and a forced grunt.

I ran off to get a big pencil and some paper. I unwrapped the mummy like dressing off his right hand and just stared. It was half raw pink flesh and half black eschar, as though it had been laid on a barbeque for too long. The black eschars didn't look much different from what a mummy's tissue looked like, as least the ones I'd seen in museums.

"I'm placing a pencil in your hand now. The notepad is just under it, ok?"

He tapped on the pad and tried to write, but his hand movements were clumsy at best, and he succeeded in only making some undecipherable streaks akin to an elephant painting

"I can't read that Duane, can you try again?"

He tried again.

Same result.

He started banging the pencil now, clearly agitated. But I couldn't tell if it was from frustration or pain. The pencil was slipping from his grasp, so I wrapped it in many layers of tape to increase its girth allowing for Duane to grip it easier.

"Still can't read it, are you in pain?"

Affirmative.

"Do you want some pain meds?"

Emphatic negative.

"Do you want to try and write something down again?"

Affirmative.

I again placed the pencil, now enhanced in circumference with surgical tape, in his hand, and he tried once more. Much more slowly and deliberately this time, he succeeded in writing a couple letters before the monitors started to beep and a nurse ran in notifying me his BP was dangerously low. She ran off to get the attending. I hit the silence button.

Duane kept at it with deliberate focus. His whole being was focused into what he was scribbling with his right hand. He finished the first word and started the second as the attending entered.

Chaos ensued. His BP crashed and every alarm in his room went off.

I dropped the pad when somebody bumped into me while hanging a new IV bag. Soon pain meds coursed through Duane's system and pressors were reinitiated. Within seconds he was again unresponsive.

I bent down to pick up the paper and stood in horror as I read his note, barely legible yet startlingly clear in what he was trying to convey. I saw two words I never believed would come from Duane. He wrote 'kill me' on this third attempt to answer what he wanted me to do for him.

Jason was headed over. I hid the paper in my pocket.

~~~~

Despite a quiet call night, I didn't do any sleeping. I was up all night thinking about Duane. I kept thinking about how I'd entered medicine to save lives, but now it seemed that the answer wasn't so clear cut. Could it be that to ease one's suffering our role might actually be to assist in their death? After all, if that's what Duane wanted, was it our right to refuse it?

Technically suicide is illegal. Something I always found amusing because if one succeeded, how were they to get prosecuted? I guess where it really comes into play is that if one commits suicide; their beneficiaries lose any benefits such as life insurance, pensions, and various other inheritances and such. That's why many people who end their lives make it look like an accident so their heirs can at least reap the rewards of what they had amassed when alive.

A very common way of doing this is death by cop—speeding and then pretending to draw a weapon of some sort when the officer is approaching the vehicle. The officer will discharge his firearm in defense and the investigation will find that the traffic offender only had his phone nearby. In this scenario the family gets all insurance and other benefits and the individual winds up dead in a rapid and painless fashion without actually committing suicide.

The problem with this scenario is that Duane will never be able to drive a car again.

I hadn't yet told Jason about the message Duane had written to me in his last seconds of consciousness. I was debating if it was even real. I mean can somebody in his state of duress be capable of making such a serious decision? And if so, should his wish be carried out?

After all, once he was intubated and could no longer communicate, his wife became his legal guardian. Thus, she is officially in control of any medical decisions concerning Duane. The problem being, when does she relinquish her power over her husband? Every time he is able to communicate or only once he is fully recovered? And what the hell is 'recovered' in his case anyway?

My head started to hurt. These were all very complex questions to which I had absolutely no answers. Medical school never touched on these topics. If they were covered, I must have skipped that lecture.

I lay in bed tossing and turning. When sleep finally arrived it was promptly interrupted by my pager. It was Jason, but he was calling from the ICU. That could only mean it was related to Duane. Any page during pre-dawn hours from another physician is never good news.

Instead of calling back, I hightailed it to the ICU. As expected, Jason was at Duane's bedside talking to the ICU resident on call for the night.

"Bad news Raj, I was paged about Ms. Maude. Her heart rhythm had a few irregular beats an hour ago, so I got a troponin level. It just came back elevated. Cardiology thinks she might be having another MI and is rushing her to the cath lab yet again. They're worried she might have had an acute thrombosis in one of her stents. Hopefully it's nothing. We should know in the next hour or so."

"Oh, I thought something was wrong with Duane."

"Since I was up here, I thought I'd check up on him. He's starting to respond to treatment, how I don't know, given he's only on supportive care and antibiotics. In either case, he's been waking up over the past few hours and I know you have a soft spot for him, so I thought I'd page you. Didn't mean for you to rush up here."

I was touched by Jason's thoughtfulness. Most people would be pissed at being woken up at 4 a.m. to deal with heart problems in a 90+ year old GOMER. But Jason managed to find the positive in the situation and share it with me, namely, Duane's progress.

I went over to Duane as Jason tried to salvage another hour of sleep before starting the day.

"Duane, can you hear me?"

Affirmative.

"You feeling better?"

Negative.

"Are you in pain?"

No response.

"Do you want me to get your wife?"

Negative.

His head movements were minimal, but definite and brisk. He was clearly hearing me and responding in a coherent manner.

"Is there something I can do for you?"

Affirmative.

"Do you want me to do what was on your note?"

Definitely affirmative.

"I want to do a bit of an examination on you if that's ok?"

Affirmative.

"I am going to open up both your eyes. I want you to tell me if you can see anything?"

Negative. I tried twice more, same response.

"Can you move the left side of your body?"

He moved his right arm and leg, but his left side remained unchanged, immobile. I assumed he had tried to move all his extremities, but only had luck on the right side.

With that I left and headed outside to clear my head. As I passed the waiting area I saw his wife cuddled up in a chair with a blanket trying to rest. Since she wasn't allowed in the ICU at night, she waited as close to her husband as possible. She hadn't even gone home. For as much as Duane was going through, she was going through quite an ordeal herself. The last few days had aged her ten years and completely changed the course of life, not only for her but her daughter as well.

I sat down next to her, I'm still not sure why I did it, but it just seemed like the right thing to do. I gently patted her shoulder and she startled awake.

"Oh no, Duane, he isn't ... is he?" She said in a voice laden with sleep and fatigue. But her face had that look of horror in which she was expecting the worst news.

"He's actually better." Her relief was palpable as she readjusted herself to face me.

"Oh, thank you, Dr. Raj. I could use some good news. It's been miserable, but I still hope he's going to make it. I can deal with a lot, but Duane's more valuable to me than my own life. His death would be worse than if I died. I'd gladly give my life for his. I'd take all his pain just to see him smile once again."

I was touched at her love for her husband and in that instant I knew I'd renege on my promise to do anything Duane asked of me. Killing him might be an act of compassion, but it would be worse than murder for his wife. I knew he'd hate me for that.

"Dr. Raj, do you think he'll make it? Nobody talks to me about him. It's like everybody's trying to avoid me to protect me, but even bad news is appreciated. It helps just to be informed."

"Well, you know he's sick. But I was just in there and he could hear me and nod. Definitely seems like he's turning the corner. If he keeps this up he might survive, though the recovery process is going to take months. And he's going to require multiple skin grafts in addition to possibly being paralyzed and even blind."

"But he'd eventually go home?" The look in her eyes was one of such pure hope. It was all she had. To say no would have been criminal. Now I realized why many docs avoided too much patient/family contact. It really was much more art than science, far more subjective and uncertain than the precise and predictable nature of numerical lab values.

"Yes."

She clutched my sleeves and buried her head on my shoulder, sighing in relief. Hugging me, she kept repeating, "Oh thankyouthankyouthankyou!"

I patted her back, and she eventually let go.

"You realize life will be hard once he returns home. And likely expensive with his care requirements and inability to work."

"That can all be worked out. I can take a second job. Our parents can move in and help. Jenny loves her grandparents. We might be an extended family under one roof, but at least we'll be a family."

Well, I had my answer. I wouldn't keep my promise and assist Duane in his request. I didn't like being stuck between upholding the wishes of my patient and those of his wife.

In the back of my mind I still had a nagging thought; I still wasn't sure who held the actual power of medical decision making. In either case, assisting suicide in the state of California was the same as committing murder. BUT, I knew that … I could easily make it look like an accident or due to natural causes, in which case his family would inherit at least a million or more tax free dollars from his life insurance. And I'm sure I wouldn't even be on the list of suspects. However, by allowing him to live, his wife would be much happier, or so she claimed.

"I applaud your attitude. Duane is one lucky man to have a wife so dedicated and caring."

"I'm the lucky one to have him."

I shrugged, uncertain of what else to do, "I'll be back later and make sure you can visit him before the chaos of morning rounds begins."

I left her with renewed hope, but deep down inside knowing that Duane did not want to continue his life as a mere shell of the vivacious person he was just a week ago. He would be going form breadwinner to bed wetter. From head of household to blind, incontinent, paralyzed parasite in need of constant assistance with everything from eating to bathing. He'd likely need both urinary catheters and rectal tubes to relieve him of his bodily wastes. Not to mention his appearance would be a haphazard quilt of numerous skin grafts, and that's with the best efforts of highly skilled plastic surgeons and numerous operations.

And that's the best case scenario.

~~~~

It turned out that Ms. Maude did in fact have an acute thrombosis, or blood clot, of one of her stents. But thanks to the efforts of the stalwart interventional cardiologist on call, he was able to perform a minimally invasive lysis of the clot. In a couple days Mr. Maude would be as new as a fossil again.

Duane also did well overnight and in another day he was extubated and breathing on his own with the assistance of some supplemental oxygen. However, his voice sounded like that lady from one of those 'dangers of smoking' television commercials in which her voice is raspy and guttural. That's because his voice is emanating from the hole in his neck instead of his mouth. At least he was making progress.

His daughter was discharged home, where she joined her mother and grandparents.

Two days later Duane was transferred to the burn unit where they would tend to his third degree burns as well as start his rehabilitation process now that he was off most medications except antibiotics, morphine, and his myriad eye drops and salves for his macerated corneas. The same day Duane was transferred from the ICU to the burn unit, Ms. Maude was picked up in her Bentley to be chauffeured home.

I saw her in the gurney on her way out of the hospital escorted by both Bernard and Josephine. No other members of her family were present despite it being Saturday.

I called out after them, "Hey, Bernard, we never did get to finish our discussion on who Abigail is?"

"Ha ha, you do have a good memory don't you? Even her family doesn't know who she is. She's the darling little girl next door who comes by every day and does her homework by Matilda's bedside."

"So she's not related?"

"Not by blood. Her parents are very high powered professionals and her siblings are grown up. She was a bit of an accident," he winked, "if you catch my drift. She used to always come by just to say hi and play with the pets. Over the years Josephine and I have adopted her as part of the family. We help her with her homework, and she usually has a snack with Matilda. She came by the hospital once, but I think you were busy attending to the gentleman next door. May I inquire about his status?"

"Let's just say nice guys finish last, shall we?"

"Dear, dear, he was quite handsome from what I recall before he was transferred away. I had figured he went home to his lovely wife."

"I can't divulge too much due to hospital security protocols, but I can say he's not going home for quite some time. Ms. Maude is the lucky one here."

"Well, you keep up the good work, and we thank you again for your kind care. I'll notify the board of directors, through an anonymous benefactor, about the wonderful care that you and the team have provided. Your name will be mentioned with high praise."

I watched as they loaded her into her chariot for the plush ride home where she would continue to drool and moan in the lap of luxury until she needed another part repaired or another infection fought off. We'd be ready and waiting.

The same was hardly true for Duane.

His stay in the burn unit was estimated to be at least two or three months, only to be followed by a two or more month stint in a skilled rehabilitation unit, after which he would likely require skilled nursing at home for at least a couple hours a day for potentially several years … and that was all if everything went according to plan. And we know how well things went according to plan for Duane Little.

For Duane's first three weeks in the burn unit all was well. He would have daily visits by his wife and daughter who were always encouraging him and taking great pride in the baby steps he was making towards recovery.

His burns and multiple skin grafts were healing nicely. He was able to slightly move the left side of his body, if you consider twitching real movement. The vision in his right eye was slightly improved; he could see fingers at about two feet in front of his face, though bilateral corneal transplants were definitely going to be required in the future.

The downward spiral for Duane started at about week four after discharge from the ICU. Daily visits from his wife had severely decreased to only a couple times per week. Thus, his progress stopped and the goal now became "maintenance" of what he had— which was not much, essentially a vegetable with a sharp mind, poor eyesight, a barely understandable voice, and very limited writing.

I had completed two months of other rotations and was meandering the hallways with nothing to do when I remembered Duane and looked him up in the computer database. He was still in the hospital, so I decided to pay him a visit.

I went to say hello and found his wife at the bedside. As I approached she turned and looked in my direction, there was a possible hint of recognition, but that was all. She didn't stop; instead she walked right past me. The lady who had opened her soul to me now no longer remembered who I was. Perhaps because I was dressed in formal shirt and tie instead of the scrubs I used to wear on that rotation. Easy come, easy go; wounds of the psyche, too, heal with time.

She no longer possessed that loving demeanor she once had. She was now cold and distant. I suppose such occurs as one realizes the person they once knew no longer exists. Even though the body is alive the person is forever changed.

I thought about saying hi to Duane, but I realized he might not want to hear me, and I doubt he saw me from the dozen feet away where I stood due to his limited vision. I slowly backed away, but his eye was locked onto me, unblinking.

Curiosity overtook me and I approached and introduced myself. He remembered and we communicated for a while both through nods and written words. His ability to write had significantly improved. Unfortunately this stroke had also progressed and his verbal ability was almost nil despite speech therapy.

He was quite mad at me for not upholding my promise. I sat at his bedside for almost three hours, and what I learned sent shivers down my spine.

His wife had met somebody else and just last week requested a divorce. She apparently didn't want to take care of a vegetable and thought that Jenny needed a real father figure in her life if she was to grow up normally. That would explain Duane's recent decline and unwillingness to participate in physical therapy. He had no motivation.

Against my better judgment I asked if his previous request of me still stood. He said it did and that he holds me to my promise. The only difference was now he had changed his will with his lawyer such that his estate would be going to his daughter on her 18th birthday. Apparently he didn't approve of his wife's moving on while he was still alive.

I'm sure she'd be quite surprised to learn of this. She was not savvy to this change as of yet.

I wasn't sure what I'd do as I left Duane's room. Months later I made my decision.

Chapter Three:
Pancreatic Scare

THE FIRST TIME in your life when an alarm clock rings at 3:40 a.m. to signal the beginning of your day is seldom met with delight; today was no different. It was the first day of my surgery rotation at the university hospital.

Coming off a recent rotation on the medical wards, I'd been exposed to a ton of sub-acute cases, not all with happy endings.

A surgical rotation promised to be much different. And this was not just a surgical rotation; this was the "Robor" service. Burt Robor wore many hats, including MD, FACS, Professor of Medicine, Chairman of Surgery, and Vice Chancellor of the university, to be exact.

The Robor service was the mother of surgery rotations. Dr. Robor is one of the most respected and sought after surgeons in the country. His clientele is comprised almost exclusively of VIPs. His outcomes are phenomenal. And the workload is inhuman. Well for us, not so much him. See, he gets all the glory, but his "team" (i.e.— us) does most of the work.

Promptly at 3:40 a.m. a good med student would immediately bolt out of bed fully awake and rush to the shower to get dressed in the appropriate medical student attire of shiny shoes, starched shirt, tie, slacks, and unforgettable short white coat with pockets full of everything from note cards to penlights to reflex hammers. I proceeded to immediately hit the snooze button ... repeatedly. Bad idea, though it seemed brilliant at the time.

Breakfast was a luxury that I couldn't afford in an effort to run to the hospital to be on time my first day. I never really thought of 4:10 a.m. as being morning; in my previous life as a normal human being it represented the end of a great night out.

Reaching the hospital eight minutes later and fully out of breath, I realized I didn't know where I was supposed to be or what exactly I was supposed to do. The hospital wasn't exactly welcoming either, with its 1950s brick and the longest hallways of any building in the U.S. except possibly the pentagon. Only every third light was on, most of which flickered, providing that welcoming environment found only in 1970s horror films.

It was surreal to be standing in one of the most famous and respected institutes of healing with hardly a soul stirring, but still knowing that miracles were being performed within these crusty old walls.

The lobby was so vacuous and deserted I could have fallen from a heart attack and nobody would have found me for ten minutes. Strange, since the bustling ER must have had a wait of over four hours. Snapping out of my reverie I promptly found the seventh floor which was where Robor admitted his patients and where pre-rounds were to begin.

Pre-rounding is the miserable process in which medical students and interns, the lowest rungs of the proverbial medical ladder (somewhere in between three day old non-refrigerated leftovers and unwanted fungus) collect all the vital signs, "ins and outs," and overnight events for all the patients on the service. Given that nobody had even provided me with the names of our patients, this task proved somewhat difficult.

I innocently walked up to the nearest nursing station and politely introduced myself.

"Hey gals, we got a new batch coming in. It's gonna be a looooong day!" barked the charge nurse to her colleagues without actually making eye contact or any other sort of gesture to indicate that my presence was acknowledged. I later learned this was the routine way of treating med students in the harsh world of general surgery.

"They just get younger every year," announced a voice from somewhere near the chart rack.

I coughed, but being in a hospital, that was a very ineffective strategy for getting noticed.

"So, does that mean my team is not here yet?" I innocently inquired of no one in particular.

That's exactly who responded to my question—no one.

Getting frustrated, I finally planted myself in front of the charge nurse and didn't move. "Oh, you're still here."

FINALLY the charge nurse looked up from her bench and saw me for the first time. "I think you're late. I saw one of the interns looking for their student. He was somewhere on the East wing, 703 or something." I barely caught the last part, as she had already returned to her charting while she was talking to me.

I hurriedly looked for East and darted down the hall searching for somebody in a long white coat that could perhaps guide me. Suddenly, I heard a shout from the West hallway. "HEY, are you RA-GERM?"

I quickly turned and replied, "Uhh, yeah, I'm Rajen."

I rushed over towards the tired looking intern in a long white coat. Scrap that, it wasn't white at all. The combination of over wear, hospital debris, and lack of washing had turned his coat into a very unappealing shade of light brown.

"Am I your medical student?"

"Yes, and you're late on your first day. Didn't anybody inform you that a medical student should be here before any real MD?" Apparently not. "Well, we can still teach you that students are the last to leave. Anyhow, I'll call you Ra, it's quicker. Here, take these four patients and get their notes written. We'll meet in 15 minutes at 5 a.m. in the conference room to come up with plans before rounds at 5:45 a.m."

Unfortunately I couldn't make out his name as his badge was backwards.

I took the well worn and coffee-stained index cards, or sign out cards as they were known, that were thrust towards me, as the intern quickly rushed into a patient room leaving me behind without another thought.

He looked slightly emaciated, a little too tall for his coat, and walked with a slightly forward stoop as though he was constantly about to trip. Not knowing his name, I quickly dubbed him Dr. Lanky.

Now to get started on my notes for the day.

I rushed back to the nursing station and was about to ask where my patients were located, but … I thought better of wasting my time only to receive some snide comment and ambiguous advice. Thus, I looked up on the board and saw that all four were on the West hall, conveniently in adjacent rooms. Apparently Robor's patients occupied most of this entire floor of 40 beds.

Locating the charts was next on the agenda, and with only 13 minutes left, I started to panic. Naturally, only one chart was on the actual rack where charts were *supposed* to be located. Another two were on the break room table; and the final one was conveniently located resting atop the giant paper recycle bin. Only nine minutes left to fully meet, examine, and document four patients who had all recently undergone major surgery.

Grabbing progress note papers from the charts I hurriedly scrib-
bled down the vital signs from overnight, including the "ins and
outs," a patient's total fluid intake compared to their total fluid output, inclusive of all orifices as well as a description of each fluid's
consistency. There are the chalky green nasogastric collections, the
coffee ground emesis, the bilious and turbid abdominal liquid, and
the ever popular colostomy output (lots more on this later).

I literally ran to my patients' rooms. Luckily two of them were
gone for CT scans. That left me with seven minutes and two patients
to examine.

The first was Bertha (if you think Big Bertha you're way off,
think HUMONGOUS Bertha). She's a morbidly obese female who
underwent bariatric surgery a few days ago, commonly advertised on
billboards as "stomach stapling" or "lap band." Her case went well
and she was scheduled to go home today. I lifted up her gown and
checked her wounds. They all looked good … at least good to me.
Her lungs were clear, and the fact that she was sleeping indicated to
me she was not in pain. She didn't even wake up from my exam. Perfect, no questions to slow me down.

Last up was Johnny, a homeless gentleman who had been in the
hospital for the past two months due to lack of 'placement.'

All hospitals have strict rules; namely, a patient can only be discharged from the hospital to a residence (read: not the street). Also, a
patient must be discharged *to* somebody. Of course Johnny had neither a residence nor a somebody.

Two problems all too common in medicine.

Sure, he could go to a homeless shelter, but he has an open
wound in his abdomen due to the exploratory laparotomy (ex lap).
Johnny had undergone surgery in which the entire abdomen is
opened up and the intestines 'explored' for injuries which are
repaired at the time of surgery. Most people who undergo ex laps get

staples to close the foot long incision. But Johnny's abdomen was infected and would not allow for staples or stiches—the tissues were too macerated and friable. The reason for that was because he waited three days before coming to the hospital after being stabbed in the abdomen with a shard of dirty glass.

The only reason he came in at that time was because he astutely noticed that his food wasn't getting digested. Instead it was dribbling out of his small intestine onto his shirt from his puncture wound. That realization only took him two days; another day was spent attempting to get drunk.

That's when the gravity of his problem hit home. Too much of the alcohol leaked out through his new fistula, preventing intoxication. This is what prompted him to seek medical attention.

The reason for his stabbing? He lost a bet and was dared to stab himself.

Johnny isn't the sharpest tool in the shed.

As a result of his lost bet he punctured his duodenum about three inches from where it connects to his stomach. The wound was repaired, but due to the infection, the tissues have to heal themselves from the inside out. Translation: Johnny has about another month left in the hospital before he is stable enough to be discharged to a homeless shelter without any medications. Since Johnny doesn't have any insurance, it's only costing tax payers about $2,000 a day.

Fortunately Johnny didn't bother to wake up for his examination this morning, either, leaving me a full minute to spare before I had to meet up with the team.

I power-walked to the conference room at the end of the hallway, if the converted closet could be called such. It was a small square room with a single round table surrounded by plastic chairs; to one side was a kitchenette and the other contained a row of three computers. The entire room was littered with used coffee cups and old newspapers.

I scanned the room and did a double take. The three long coats in the room were the most tired looking souls I'd ever seen. All had massive bags under their eyes. Two were yawning and the third dozing off in his chair while writing his notes.

"You made it," announced Lanky, and he went on to introduce me to the rest of the team, "this is Dr. Parker and Dr. Reed, they're the interns. I'm Dr. Cooper, the senior resident on the service. Team, meet Ra, our medical student for the next month." I'm not sure that they noticed me because they were too busy writing notes for the day.

I already didn't like surgery; it was too formal. Not only did I have to call the interns "Doctor" even though they were a whopping two years older than me, but I was expected to be in shirt and tie at 4:30 a.m.

"Ra, you can join me in the OR today and take call overnight tonight with Dr. Parker. You'll be in charge of all post-operative patients for which you scrub in on. We have three cases today, a couple Whipples and a splenectomy in OR number 18. Generally I expect you to see the patients the night before their surgery and complete the pre-operative H&P, but you're exempt from doing that today.

"We meet here at 5 a.m. on all weekdays and 6 a.m. on weekends to go over all the patients before formal rounds start at 45 minutes after the hour with the chief resident, Dr. Blake."

Shit, talk about information overload. I didn't even know where the OR was located. But given the lightning pace of the debriefing I felt it was the wrong time to ask.

Lanky continued, "Our attending is Dr. Robor; he's the chairman of the entire department of surgery and very well respected. I'm sure you've heard of him, as he's quite renowned. He expects formal attire at all times when not in the OR. Do not speak to him unless addressed if you want to pass this rotation."

I hazarded asking a question, "I thought Dr. Robor had a very VIP clientele, but the patients I saw this morning were ..."

Lanky cut me off, "Bertha is the daughter of a Congressman. Johnny, well, he's special; even Robor is on ER call and has to operate on whatever comes in on those days. Now let's get started before Blake gets here."

"Pre-rounds," as they are called is the time when we individually see our patients before "work rounds" when we go over the plan with the senior resident, finally ending in "formal rounds" when we present each patient to the chief resident. During "work rounds" we gather all the patient charts and place them in a rolling cart so they are ready and available when we round with the chief. During formal rounds all the notes are finalized and orders for the day are written by whomever is not presenting that particular patient, typically the med student or other intern.

As work rounds started, the morning went from bad to worse. I was reprimanded for not seeing the two patients who had been getting CT scans. Apparently I should have gone down to the CT scanner to examine them there. I was dismissed to do exactly that. Of course, by the time I returned, chief rounds had already started and nobody dared interrupt Blake to introduce me.

At the end of rounds the group immediately disbanded and I was left alone not knowing what to do. I thought better of asking a nurse for help given my earlier experience. Instead I just followed the signs towards the OR located in the basement.

I took the "restricted" stairs figuring I was qualified to take them based on the fact my badge unlocked the doors and no alarm sounded. Opening the basement door immersed me into a world of constant activity. It was like entering a beehive, only everyone was wearing scrubs.

I brilliantly spun slowly around in a circle taking everything in when I bumped into an EKG technician and almost knocked over her machine. Instead of being yelled at, she was sympathetic to my plight, "Let me guess, first day?"

"What gave it away?"

"Locker rooms are down that way, you can get some scrubs and change in there. Come back out and head in the opposite direction through the double doors and that'll take you to the ORs. Good luck. I'm Amy; I'll probably be seeing you around."

She was gone before I could thank her. Guess the ORs were a no-nonsense kind of environment.

Being a med student meant that I had no locker or any other place to put my bag or clothes. Thus, I had to dump them in the corner of the locker room and hope nobody stole anything.

By the time I found my way to the pre-operative area, our first patient had already been transported to the OR. So much for a pre-op examination and introduction.

I weaved in and out of scrubbed worker bees, all wearing masks and hats once I entered the OR clean area. After circling three times I finally found OR 18. The rooms are conveniently not numbered consecutively; instead even numbers are in one corridor and odd numbers in another.

As I entered, the door slammed into the anesthesiologist's cart, immediately garnering everybody's attention. I identified Dr. Lanky speaking to another scrub-clad individual whom I presumed was Dr. Robor; they were both going over some sort of MRI scan. Lanky shook his head at me; Robor didn't make any sign of acknowledgement.

The room was quite expansive with numerous bright lights. In the center was a patient hooked up to several monitors and IVs. There was an anesthesiologist and a nurse preparing him for the surgery; another nurse was helping a scrub technician set up the equipment for the surgery and the two surgeons were discussing the case. Pretty impressive. Including myself there were seven individuals besides the patient present for this surgery.

Lanky came up to me, "Ra, you really need to work on your punctuality. Did you get to review Dr. West's case in pre-op?"

"No, I barely got changed in time."

"Don't let that happen again. The patient is Dr. Peter West; he's a recently retired urologist who was diagnosed with pancreatic cancer. This surgery is the only chance at survival he's got."

"What size glove are you?"

I shrugged. "Medium?"

"Fuck man, don't you know your glove size? You look like a 7.5, I'll have the nurse pull that for you. Do you at least know how to scrub?"

"Yes," I lied. Sure I'd heard of scrubbing, the procedure of washing your arms from fingertip to elbow before donning a sterile gown and gloves at the beginning of surgery. I also read that it was complete nonsense; in other countries they just washed their hands and had the same rates of infection we did in the US, except here we spent a full five minutes scrubbing our skin with caustic disinfectants before *every* single case. But I thought better than to notify Dr. Lanky of this tidbit of information.

"There might still be hope for you. Go ahead and scrub, just don't use the middle sink, that's Robor's. I'll meet you back in here in a few minutes. Don't contaminate anything; everything that's blue is sterile."

I immediately headed out to scrub. After I took two steps I was stopped. "Hey, where do you think you're going?"

I turned, "Uh, to scrub."

"Other door over there; be sure you take a piss too. This case'll be at least 6 hours." At least the scrub tech didn't seem like he had a vendetta against me.

I managed to scrub and gown up without complication.

Once the case started, Robor stood to the patient's right and Lanky to the left. Behind Robor was the scrub tech, and I took up position behind Lanky.

This sucked; I was the shortest of the group, so even on my tip toes I could not see over Lanky's shoulder. This was how I spent the first two hours of the case, staring at Lanky's shoulder while they operated. Occasionally I'd get to see a piece of gauze doused with blood.

When a relief nurse came in to give one of the nurses a break, she noticed my precarious position and offered me a stool upon which to stand.

Amazing! My view changed dramatically. I was now looking inside Peter's abdomen. It was filleted wide open and I could identify the stomach, liver, both large and small intestines, and a sponge-like gray-green structure—the pancreas! They were just completing the Kocher maneuver. I was so enthralled I didn't even realize I was leaning on top of Lanky until he jabbed me in the stomach.

"Ra, hold this." Lanky handed me a metal retractor with which to hold the abdominal wall out of the way. My new mission in life was now to make sure the tissue I was retracting did not get in the center of the surgical field.

I must have done well because after 45 minutes of retracting I was handed a second metal retractor. This is how I spent the next two hours of the case, retracting tissues. My fingers, arms, shoulders, and back ached from the constant tension I was applying to hold back the tissues. But at least I was making a difference; I was helping to operate!

The enthusiasm of retracting is short lived, wearing off in about 15 minutes, after which the job became so boring that I started to doze off while standing on my feet.

My bladder also conveniently decided to remind me that it needed emptying. I soon realized this surgery stuff was for the birds. Who in hell, actually, who outside of hell, wants to spend hours upon hours in a cold OR standing on their feet elbow deep in blood and guts with no bathroom breaks, just to do another case after the first, day in and day out?

I kept trying to convince myself that even though my role was minimal, the muscle cramps were worth it; at least I was an active member in Peter's surgery. I wasn't.

A new nurse came in the room and announced, "Dr. Robor, the new auto-retractors are here."

"Great," the man actually spoke, "let's break them open."

As soon as he was handed the 'auto-retractor' I was relieved of my duties. Said device replaced what I'd been doing for the past three hours … talk about low man on the totem pole.

Worse still, Lanky took my step stool for himself, so I again got to stare at his shoulder.

Eventually the case ended, 6 hours 30 minutes after it started. The jargon used during the procedure was so intense I didn't even know if the case was a success or failure.

Robor immediately left the room and one of the interns entered to help close up the main incision. Once again I was left with a view of a shoulder, only this time the intern's because Lanky planted himself where Robor was standing previously.

After what seemed like an eternity, all the drapes and other sterile dressings were removed and Peter West was taken to the PACU to recover before being transferred to his hospital room.

My feet ached, my muscles hurt, and my bladder had grown to the size of a basketball; standing in an area of two square feet for over six straight hours in dress shoes is not the best use of my tuition money, at least in my opinion. On the bright side, I could use the bathroom now.

"Ra, go with Dr. Parker here to make sure the next patient is ready. I want to start the case within ten minutes so we can get out of here by 8 p.m. and do evening rounds."

This was not shaping up to be a good day.

I managed to see the next patient and micturate. And that's all I got to do before the second case started.

The second case was just like the first, only worse. Dr. Parker was in the room as well, so I got to stand behind *him* the whole six hours. And he was standing behind Lanky, where I stood for the previous case. I didn't even get to retract. The only 'operating' I did was to hand a couple bloody wads of gauze to the scrub tech for disposal.

The first couple hours were OK; I could at least hear them teaching Parker something here and there, so I learned a bit. By hour three, I was bored out of my mind. The teaching had stopped, and my view of Parker's back from about four inches away hadn't changed. Not to mention the room was only heated to 60°F and the mask was difficult to breathe through. Thus, I was shivering as well as hungry for oxygen.

At hour five somebody spoke to me, but it was only to tell me to step back because I was in the way.

The case ended at hour six and Robor left the room. I sighed in relief; I could finally see the abdomen. I even got to hoping that maybe I could throw a stitch or staple. That thought was short-lived.

"Ra, I'll close up here with Dr. Parker. Why don't you get the next patient prepped so we can start right away." Except it wasn't a question.

The third case was fortunately much shorter, just a splenectomy for the treatment of autoimmune hemolytic anemia—wasn't sure what that was, but it sure sounded bad.

The only benefit during this last case was that when extreme boredom settled in during hour two, the case ended. Thank goodness.

It was 10:00 p.m. My first day of surgery was half over, and all I had done the past 15 hours was stand stationary for three major operations, fill out paperwork, and urinate once.

Again, as they started to close, I was dismissed to go check up on the previous two patients before evening rounds. The only good news was that the other patients I saw this morning were no longer my responsibility. From now on, I was only responsible for patients whom I scrubbed in on during surgery.

By the time I'd located the rooms of the two Whipple patients from earlier in the day; my pager went off with a terse message: RM 643, STAT.

I took off running and bumped into Parker in the stairwell, me descending and him climbing. I guess he got the same page and had to leave the OR. "Move it man, we need to put in a chest tube." He seemed excited about the possibility of a procedure.

We arrived and there was chaos abounding. I don't know how, but Lanky was already here. I could have sworn it'd only been ten minutes since I left the OR. He was prepping to place a chest tube in an elderly female who appeared cyanotic and looked two solid decades older than her stated age of 68 years.

"Ah, the team arrives. Dr. Parker, come on over here." Lanky whispered to him, "Have you ever done one of these before?" Parker shook his head, negative. Lanky spoke even softer, "Well, you're up, gotta learn somehow." He proceeded to hand Parker the equipment.

As they prepped the patient for a chest tube on her right side, I grabbed her chart and began to read up on our patient.

Jane Dover was a 68-year-old female who was admitted yesterday for shortness of breath and found to have several lung lesions on her CT scan. They likely represented multiple foci of cancer given her greater than 40 year history of tobacco use and recent unexplained weight loss.

She was placed on supplemental oxygen overnight with the plan of obtaining a PET scan in the morning to continue the work up of her suspected cancer.

Twenty minutes ago she reported pain on her right side and shortness of breath that was worsening despite oxygen. A STAT chest X-ray revealed a right sided hemothorax, which was not present earlier that day and would certainly account for her symptoms. The most likely cause was that one of the cancer nodules had eroded into a blood vessel which had then bled, causing the lung to collapse.

The loss of her right lung was something she would not likely survive unless a chest tube was immediately placed to evacuate the blood and allow her lung to re-expand.

I recalled reading that placing a chest tube could be a very satisfying procedure, as patients experienced relief almost instantly, not to mention that it was a life saving procedure if it went well. But in a heavy smoker it could be quite tricky due to a very small and fragile lung, making tube placement critical and often times difficult.

Instead of holding Parker's hand and guiding him through the process, Lanky was just talking as Parker did the procedure by himself. I listened in; nobody else in the room seemed to be paying much attention to the procedure. The nurses were all helping hold Jane in position and administering medications or monitoring vital signs.

"Good, that incision size is perfect. Now expand it with the hemostats, excellent." Parker seemed to be confident in his ability, though I noticed that his hands were shaking. Likely due to either to nerves or adrenaline, I wasn't sure, but I'd be shitting my pants if I was doing my first chest tube without prior notice.

Lanky handed him a rubber tube clamped within the teeth of a large pair of hemostats. "Here's the chest tube, I want you to slide it in just above the rib like we talked about and then advance it forward and slightly downward; we should see blood come out almost instantly." Parker did as he was told and almost instantly dark blood began to flow out.

"Good work. Now go just a little further, good. Keep going. Yeah, just like that … a little bit more, you just have to be careful not to … FUCK!!"

Suddenly the right side of her chest deflated and the bleeding turned from a dark burgundy to a bright red.

Lanky literally shoved Parker aside shouting, "Occlusive dressing STAT. Get an OR NOW! We gotta open her up and get this fixed. Call Dr. Blake and have him meet us there."

The three nurses in the room dropped what they were doing and immediately began to wheel the bed towards the trauma elevators. Within 20 seconds the room was barren except for me and Parker. The others were well on their way to the OR.

I looked to Parker; he didn't seem that worried. He took off his gloves and was the first to speak. "Guess we should finish up rounds."

Maybe it was just me, but I felt that a modicum of emotion was in order. I know I'm not a doctor yet, but even *I* knew something really bad just happened. From what I could tell, the right side of her chest suddenly decompressed, meaning that the blood had to have gone somewhere. It clearly didn't come out of the tube, which meant it likely went into the abdominal cavity. The only way that could have happened was if the diaphragm got punctured during the procedure. The bright red blood that suddenly appeared was probably secondary to a laceration of the liver because the tube was advanced too far and too aggressively.

Translation: serious complication.

I wanted to ask him about this, but Parker was already out the door headed up to the seventh floor.

"Uhh, shouldn't we go to the OR?"

"No, Drs. Cooper and Blake will take care of it. Our job is to manage the patients on the floor." He clearly didn't want to talk any further about what happened.

I wanted to ask how he managed to rip through the diaphragm and tear into the liver, but I figured it was best to keep my mouth shut if I wanted to pass this rotation. After all, it was July, the absolute worst time to be a patient at any university hospital; that's when all the new interns start. Many studies have shown that the rates of death and number of complications that occur in July and August are significantly higher than other months, likely due to episodes as I just witnessed.

What really irked me was that Parker had no remorse about his actions; in fact, he seemed unfazed by the experience. If I'd done something to cause someone a potentially life threatening complication requiring high risk emergency surgery I think I'd be quite shaken up and seriously re-evaluating my life, and probably even considering another career path.

The lack of empathy pissed me off, coupled with the fact I had to refer to interns as "Dr." I decided surgery sucked. Surgeons live in their own little egotistical world—a world which has some of the highest rates of divorce, adultery, alcoholism, and other unsavory statistics. Surgeons also log in some of the longest hours of any occupation on the planet and take home paychecks with lots of zeros … somebody's gotta pay the alimony and child support.

Though I didn't know it at the time, I'd learned an important rule: in medical training, a lot of what you learn is what *not* to do and how *not* to act by watching others.

I tried to get a bite to eat, but the cafeteria was closed. The surgeon's lounge had already been raided and all that remained were some half eaten cookies and soda. Bon appétit … at least they were calories that'd keep my blood sugar up throughout the night.

Eventually I made it to Dr. Peter West's room, our first Whipple patient from the day, and knocked on his door. The lack of response clearly meant I should enter; hospitals have no sense of privacy. I was quickly greeted by a well dressed woman who looked to be about 50—either he robbed the cradle or she aged extremely well. Dr. West was sleeping and appeared quite sedated from his anesthesia.

"The good doctor's wife, I presume?"

"Yes, pleasure to meet you," she shook my hand, "Doctor?"

"No, name's Raj, I'm the medical student. I was observing your husband's case earlier today."

"Oh, nice of you to swing by. Bert stopped by earlier and told me the case went extremely well and we should know in a couple days if it was curative or not. Unfortunately, I've read all about pancreatic cancer and that poor Peter's chances are only 10% for a cure and living to see this month next year, given the size of his mass."

"Are you in medicine also?"

"Oh, heavens no. I completed my Ph.D. when Peter here was doing his residency in urology, what ... some 38 years ago? We married and I got pregnant shortly after I defended my thesis, and I have been a stay at home wife ever since, raising our three kids."

"One of the most educated moms to have never worked, huh?"

She laughed at the compliment. "Nah, I really only got the degree to keep myself busy because his hours at the hospital were so long. We lived in San Francisco at the time. He was at the SF General Hospital and I was at Cal. We met at UC Berkley, his last year of medical school and my first of undergrad, and got married his first year of residency. Bert Robor and Peter went to medical school together at UCSF."

"Dr. Robor is one of the best surgeons around for pancreatic cancer."

"Oh yeah, I've known Burt for years. Don't tell anyone, but Peter performed a prostate biopsy on Bert last year."

"Has Dr. West been retired for a while?"

"HA. A surgeon retire? We had grand plans of traveling the world and vacationing in luxury, but Peter always said we'd go later. Well, later never came and he was diagnosed with cancer just last month. Our dreams to travel and see the world never came true." She longingly stared out the window, clearly wondering what life could have been like.

"He's still working?"

"Well, once he got diagnosed I forced him to retire. He's been working seven days a week for 34 years. He started a group in Beverly Hills and owns a number of medical buildings and a couple of surgery centers. He was so successful he could have retired a decade ago. I think he just loves to work. He worked so much in fact that our youngest refuses to speak to him, and the other two hardly call him but once a year. I travel to see them and we're close, but they don't view Peter as anything other than an absentee father."

"I had no idea. I figured you'd have the perfect life and family."

"You are naïve, aren't you, my dear? I love the man, but he was just never there. Sure I could buy anything I ever wanted and the kids had top notch educations; he even set up a trust fund to pay for the education of his nieces, nephews, and grandkids. But that doesn't make up for the fact that he was simply never there. I delivered all three children alone; he was at work. I went to all the parent teacher meetings by myself. I was the soccer mom, tutor, chauffeur, basketball coach, bed time story reader, and daddy all wrapped into one. He was just the provider."

"I had no idea you could be married yet so alone."

"That's the life of a surgeon. He always loved the thrill of operating and saving lives. He was happiest when recanting stories of how he was able to completely resect a tumor, or restore urinary function, or correct erectile dysfunction and drastically improve the life of another. I guess I can't fault him for taking joy in the service of others. I just wish I was able to share some joys with Peter outside of medicine, but the time for that was always later …"

"I'm sure he's going to be in the 10% and beat this thing."

She nodded, acknowledging my attempt at empathy and reassurance. We sat in silence for many minutes and when Mrs. West started speaking, she told me about life as a surgeon's wife. No wonder surgeons had such a high divorce rate, they were never home and opportunities for affairs were plentiful. They also had the perfect excuse to cover up such rendezvous. They could always claim they were on call and a spouse wouldn't think twice about why they never came home that night.

The kids had some of the best clothes, fastest cars, and coolest toys in high school. College tuition was paid for and money was never an issue, yet they detested their father for not being a dad.

It was unsettling to learn that a surgeon could lead such a successful professional life yet leave much to be desired socially. Stupid me always envisioned a surgeon would be treated like a hero at home.

"My, look at the time, it's almost 2 a.m. I'm sorry for having kept you so long Raj. It was nice talking to you; I've been going through a lot lately. Please don't take anything I've said in a negative light. Medicine is a wonderful career and the opportunity to help others during their time of need is priceless, but everything in moderation and balance is best."

With that she kissed Dr. West on the forehead and left the room.

I saw Dr. Lanky charting at the nursing station, walking up to him I asked, "How'd that case go?"

"We lost her on the table. Bled out." He said it so matter-of-factly that you'd think he was discussing the weather.

"That's all?"

"What else is there? She was a smoker for a zillion years, she had cancer all over the place, she was going to die anyhow, and be miserable during chemo and radiation. At least Parker will never push too hard when he places a chest tube again."

I was at a loss for words. All I knew was that if I ever needed medical care it'd be through a private practice at a non-teaching hospital where my survival mattered more than somebody else's learning. It's no wonder medical trainees call teaching hospitals 'human wet labs'.

I decided to retire for the night when I heard Lanky's pager go off. I figured I best stay as I'm sure it was more work headed our way.

"Ra, come with me to the ER, there's a multiple shooting that's headed our way in a couple minutes. Three gangbangers apparently arguing over some drugs; one has multiple gunshots to the abdomen, another with a bullet to the chest, and the third with a shot to the arm."

We ran down the hallway to the trauma elevators. "I'll do the thoracic case with Dr. Blake; that guy has a chance of making it. The abdominal case is a goner, but he's still alive, so why don't you and Parker have at it? If nothing else it'll be good experience and there's no possibility of a complication. The arm guy can wait until later to have his bullet removed."

One look and I could tell that the guy with the abdominal injury was a goner; there was no point in even attempting to operate. His abdomen looked like Swiss cheese with bits of intestine and blood leaking out through several holes. Parker's rationalization was that the one good thing this guy might do with his life is provide us the opportunity to learn so that we can use that knowledge to help others in the future.

Even with a miracle, what were his chances of survival with an intern and medical student attempting major surgery? Turns out they were zero.

We got him to the OR, opened him up, and fooled around for about 45 minutes. We transfused him with 12 units of O negative blood before his heart finally decided to call it quits. Sure it was a great lesson in anatomy and fascinating to see how much damage four small .22 caliber bullets could do by bouncing around in an abdominal cavity. It definitely wasn't a great use of hospital OR time or resources. But I guess that's how surgeons are made. No wonder it costs over two million dollars to train a surgeon.

Parker was elated. He got to clamp the abdominal aorta, remove a spleen, cauterize a liver laceration, and then he even let me put in the staples to close our John Doe ... after we pronounced him dead on the table.

I don't know if it counts as *operating* after we've already declared the body a corpse.

I think all 12 units of blood ended up on our gowns, which were soaked with a combination of intestinal contents and blood. In fact, there was so much blood that it had soaked through my gown, through my scrubs, and onto my boxers. My shoe covers protected my shoes, but my socks were damp from fluids I didn't want to think about. I was gross, damp, and unhappy.

Despite being more blood soaked than me, Parker was high as a kite. The thrill of operating placed him on cloud nine.

I rushed off to the locker room to shower and decontaminate. It sucked; I didn't know I was even going to be on call, so I didn't have a change of clothes. I threw away my socks and boxers; I ended up free balling it in my slacks and wearing my dress shoes barefoot.

I finished showering, just in time to pre-round at 4:30 a.m. Dr. West was still in la-la land, and our other two post-ops were in the ICU due to delayed extubation and were somebody else's problem until they arrived on the floor.

Since the gunshot case was going to be a few more hours, the attending excused Lanky so he could round while Blake helped him finish the case. After completing rounds I figured our day was over given the new national rules set forth by the ACGME that mandated residents were not allowed to work over 88 hours per week or over 30 consecutive hours without at least an 8 hour break.

I was wrong.

There were six cases on the schedule for today: two large bowel resections, three gall bladders, and a Nissen fundoplication.

Lanky and Parker somehow had the energy and motivation to stay and assist for those cases. I was sent home after the first case at about noon. They stayed well past 7 p.m. or about 37 hours from when they stepped foot into the hospital the day before. They had only slept about two hours during that time. The kicker is that this is not an atypical day for surgeons in residency; they are often on call every three to four days and extraordinarily busy for most of their five to seven years of training.

I quickly learned that surgeons in training simply don't honestly report the number of hours they work.

Stats for my first day of surgery: length = 30 hours, patient deaths = 2, pairs of my boxers soiled by somebody else's bowel material = 1. Only 7 weeks and 5 days to go. A full month on this service and another month somewhere else.

I needed to invest in some more undergarments. That was my final thought before I fell asleep for a short afternoon nap of seven hours.

~~~~

"Good morning Dr. West," I said as I gently nudged his shoulder. He woke up with that look of haze one gets when they have been on high doses of narcotics.

"Huh. Oh, hi." His voice was coarse and weak, but it still had an intonation of confidence and authority.

"I'm Raj, I don't know if you remember me? I spoke with your lovely wife yesterday."

He was waking up now, and looking around as though seeing his room for the first time. But he quickly remembered where he was and why he was here. "Oh yes, medical student I imagine, short coat. Sorry, I don't remember you, but Bert had me snowed with narcotics yesterday."

We shook, and despite having undergone major surgery just yesterday, his grip was firm. "I just wanted to see how you were doing and how your night was."

"Well, I'm still here, aren't I? Must mean it was good. Are the pathology results due back today?"

"No, they're likely going to be back tomorrow. From what I understand your tumor was quite large."

"Yeah, tell me about it. I just waited and waited until the pain got severe enough to prevent me from operating, so it's my own fault." There was no remorse in his voice, clearly a man who took responsibility for his actions. I already liked him; he was honest and affable. Hard to believe he was such a workaholic that his children disowned him. None of the three had come to be with him after such a major operation.

"I heard you recently retired from doctoring?"

"Wait, just a minute there. I am retiring from being a surgeon and the practice of medicine, but I'll always be a doctor; that's all I know how to be."

Ain't that the truth. But I kept that thought to myself. "I'll just check your wounds and be back with the team when we round, if that's okay?"

"Hey, you're the Doc, I'm all yours." He winked.

Rounds went well and there were only two long cases with Robor today, so we were free to finish up evening rounds by 8 p.m. I swung by Dr. West's room to check up on him, and he was flipping through a medical journal.

"I thought you retired?" I asked as I pointed to the journal he was browsing.

"What can I say? Can't teach an old dog new tricks. I've been reading these journals for so many years I don't know what else to do with my time."

"Why not travel? Your wife says it's been something that keeps getting pushed off."

"Hard when I have 40+ staples that are barely holding me closed and potentially a cancer that's eating me alive from the inside."

"Excuses. Suppose the cancer is completely resected with clean margins. The staples will come out in a couple weeks and within a month or two you'll be good as new, and then what?"

"I like you kid, you don't bullshit, get right to the point. If the cancer is completely removed, I'll make you a deal, I'll do all the things that I said I would but ignored due to work."

"Ok, shoot."

"What you talking about?"

"Sorry, I mean fire off the things that you are going to do. I'll be your scribe. Talk is cheap, but if it's written I can hold you to it."

"You're serious?"

I nodded.

"I like you even more. Ok, let's go: 1) buy my wife flowers; 2) sit front and center at the NY Philharmonic for which my oldest son plays the violin; 3) first class trip to Europe; 4) an anonymous donation to the battered women's shelter in New York for which my daughter works. That's all I got for now."

"Good start. Seems like you've thought this through." I placed a little box next to each item on the list and taped it up on the mirror next to his sink. Then I took a photo of it with my phone and saved it in case I needed it later.

"In the last couple of days I've accepted that I've been living life for myself. I've been selfish and others have suffered greatly for my behavior."

"What do you mean?! You're a hugely successful surgeon; you've saved countless lives and helped thousands of others with their problems. That's not exactly how I'd define selfish. Am I missing something?"

"Sure, I did those things and many more, but not because I cared so much for what I was doing. It made *me* feel good. When I saved a life or cured a cancer, it was a huge rush and feeling of accomplishment. It made me feel larger than life. It was easy to get addicted to that feeling and forget everything else. I know I was a bad husband and father. I was never a dad. Sure I was respected and rich, but I was no different than your heroin junkie. I was in it for the rush, the feeling of power, and the thrill of success."

"But you gave all your time to help others during their time of need. I fail to see the selfish nature there."

"Here, let me put it in perspective. I love to operate, but I don't like surgery. What I love is that after surgery I get to walk towards a family who has been waiting for me for hours, literally sitting on the edges of their seats with anxiety that is palpable, fearing the worst and desperately hoping for the best. They await my arrival and then I get to break the good news to them. It's such a rush to tell a family their loved one is cured of a life threatening ailment; it makes your head spin. That empowering feeling became my addiction. Sure the money was good, but it was secondary. I was like a junkie getting paid for obtaining his fix. It was great; for years I earned seven figures. And once you have money, it's easy to make more. The real estate, surgery centers, medical corporations, and venture capitalism earned me more than my salary. But the money didn't do it for me; it was being able to play hero that I loved."

"Your passion for success motivated you to do excellent work."

"Sure, my outcomes were above average, even exceptional. But it came at the cost of my wife and children. Don't think I didn't know it; I was just willing to pay that price to make myself feel good. Not unlike a crack whore or meth head."

"So, now that you're done, won't there be a withdrawal? Alcohol and heroin addicts can die if they quit cold turkey."

"I might already be dead. My fate is in the pathologist's read."

"Fair enough. But as a surgeon, you know to expect the unexpected and always have a Plan B and even C; medicine is all about options. Let's assume you're cured ... for once you're on the receiving end of the news instead of delivering it."

"Well, my wife has put up with a lot. I think it's time I let her be selfish. I might even be able to learn how to have fun again."

"And the kids?"

"Well, one refuses to talk to me. In fact he said I was dead to him almost 15 years ago, so that might be a dead end road. The other two, I'll have to let them judge me on my actions; they speak much louder than words."

"I thought you said the donation would be anonymous, she might never know."

"She's a bright girl, she'll figure it out. Went to law school at Duke, got a high powered job at some NY firm, did it for a couple years and quit to work at this shelter. I think deep down inside she does it because she thinks I battered her mother with my absentee lifestyle. Thus, to give back to society she's helping out battered women who have nowhere else to turn. She helps with counseling, both psychological and legal, even represents them in court, anything to help them get back on their feet."

"Quite altruistic. You must be proud."

"You'd think I was, and deep down inside I am, but I never let her know it. I always pushed for her to go the corporate route and try for partnership at a big shot firm where she'd pull in the big bucks. I equated success with financial remuneration and emphasized that too much to my kids."

"Your son must be doing quite well, playing for the NY Phil. That's very prestigious."

"He's my oldest, very smart and talented kid. He played tennis and got offered a half scholarship to Stanford, but his passion was music. I insisted he attend The Farm and do either pre-medical studies or business and manage a hedge fund. My wife was sympathetic to his passion and was insistent that he attend Juilliard."

"Not a bad position to be in, choosing between two of the finest schools in America."

"Again, one would think, but I was so insistent that he not throw his life away as a hippy musician; we got into several fights. Eventually he sided with his Mom and bought a one way ticket to New York. He is much respected for his performance skills and is quite sought after by several professional orchestras. His dream is to become a conductor one day and I think he'll do it sooner rather than later."

"What about your other son?"

"Ah, Jeremy, the baby of the family; he's only 21 years old, a decade younger than his siblings and hasn't spoken to me for about ten years. He always hated how I wasn't around. One day I promised to see him play soccer; it was the regional championship game, but I had an emergency case come up and missed his game and the after party at the ice cream parlor. He always held it against me and refused to speak to me from that time onwards. It was an awkward five years living with him."

"You mean throughout high school you two never spoke?"

"Well, I'd speak to him, but he never responded to me. He'd talk to his Mom when I wasn't around and she'd relay his thoughts to me. But he never asked for much or caused much trouble. Between you and me, I think he was involved in drugs, but you'd never be able to tell by his school performance; he was a superstar student."

"He didn't get into any trouble?"

"No sir, he was always came off as a straight arrow. I think it was mainly because he was too smart to get caught."

"Better than the alternative."

"He skipped a couple grades. His reasoning was it allowed him to leave home that much sooner. I'd offered to send him to Andover or Exeter or any other boarding school of his choice, but his Mom wouldn't allow it; they got along fabulously and she didn't want him gone sooner than necessary."

"But he did leave for college at a young age?"

"Oh sure, at 16 he enrolled in Caltech and graduated with a killer GPA with a double major in math and physics. He was immediately given countless job offers. Took one for a government think tank operation, one of those 'I'd have to kill you if I told you' jobs with the highest levels of security clearance."

"I'd say on paper you have a dream life: beautiful wife, successful career, money galore, and three hugely successful children. But the fact that your wife generally leaves you alone even after major surgery and none of your children so much as visited indicates that the paper version is quite misleading."

"You don't know the half of it. I bought Jeremy a new car for his 16th birthday, and for getting into such a wonderful college, he got a new Porsche 911 Carrera. He never once drove it, and the day he left for college he just left a note on the window, 'return to sender.' That was the only direct communication I've had with him since the age of 11."

"What are you going to do for him when you get out of here?"

"Good question. I don't know that there is much I can do. He's pretty well taken care of from what I can tell. I know he tested positive for some illicit drugs a couple months ago, which is grounds for termination with his level of security clearance. But the powers that be just turned their heads and he's still doing whatever it is he does."

I was so engrossed in our discussion that I'd lost track of time. I was jolted back into reality when the whole team entered Dr. West's room for evening rounds. I was sure I'd get reamed a new one for slacking off, and I had no excuse, given the team had worked seven extra hours yesterday while I napped.

Before I could defend myself, Dr. West spoke up, "Ah, the whole team's come to pay me a visit. Must be a slow day in the gun and knife club, huh?"

"Hi Dr. West," Blake took the lead as the team filed into the room behind him. "Just wanted to make sure all was well and the med student wasn't causing any trouble."

"Raj here, he's absolutely delightful. I'm afraid I've kept him from his other duties recanting stories about my past. The mix of narcotics and anxiety of awaiting the pathology results after tumor resection surgery can do that to a person."

"No problem, Dr. West; he's as much a part of the team as any of us. If you need Ra's assistance at any time, just let me know."

"You guys have done a great job. Tell Bert I said 'Hi.' All is well here. I'm sure I'll see you all tomorrow."

Blake performed a quick exam and we all left Dr. West's room. Thankfully nobody realized the checklist note I'd taped up on his mirror.

"You're lucky he took responsibility for making you late Ra, otherwise that would have been your third tardy since starting this rotation," remarked Lanky.

I managed to make it through the rest of rounds without drawing any further attention. We all left the hospital together. I'd say it was a successful day; nobody died just so the surgical trainees could learn something.

~~~~

I awoke in a startle; I thought I was having a bad dream. Turns out it was the start of a bad day. The startle was from my pager going off. I must not have heard it the first time because there were two identical pages a couple minutes apart. Immediately I called back the number.

It was Blake. "Ra, we need you immediately. There was a nine car collision on the 10 Freeway this morning. Well, it happened about 15 minutes ago. Several surgical trauma cases are coming our way. We need everyone we can get in the OR STAT to help out. See you there in 15 minutes. I'll be in OR 10. Meet me there."

He hung up. I blinked a couple times to get my bearings, realizing I was still at home. Fortunately I had fallen asleep in my scrubs on the couch, so with some quick tooth-brushing and a splash of water on my face, I headed straight for the OR.

The life of a surgeon sucks.

The ER was sheer pandemonium. Every trauma bay and individual room was filled with somebody who was bleeding. The overhead loudspeaker was constantly requesting further medical assistance in the ER.

There was blood everywhere. In fact, if a patient wasn't bleeding they weren't even allowed to be in the hallway; they were relocated to the waiting area.

For the first time in my life I saw triage tags. They were only used in catastrophic situations; this must have been a serious nine car pileup.

I was trying to figure out where I was needed when the trauma doors burst open, and in came a crib followed by a gurney. The crib had a black tag on it meaning the occupant was no longer alive. The commotion was going on behind the crib. That gurney had a red tag, meaning emergent intervention required. There was a whole team performing CPR on a … person; at this time I couldn't tell if it was a male or female. Blake was heading up the effort when he caught my eye.

"Ra, help me here. Take this bag and ventilate her fast. Get her to OR 10 STAT; I'll meet you there. She's got a right pneumothorax, pelvic fractures, and severe lacerations on both lower extremities. We have a chance at patching her up. Get her intubated and tell anesthesia to pump her full of at least 6 units to start and we'll go from there."

I was just given my battlefield upgrade. Instead of being scared and trying to hide, I did as instructed. As scared as I was, the team of nurses, techs, and paramedics were looking for someone to lead, and that was me.

Her right leg was still bleeding profusely from a very deep laceration. "Somebody get a tourniquet on her right thigh," I shouted with authority as we maneuvered to the elevators.

To my astonishment, by the time the elevators opened up a tourniquet had been placed on her right thigh and the bleeding was significantly less. I could get used to this type of treatment.

"Give her a liter of normal saline and keep pressure on her wounds. Make sure she has a pulse and is getting oxygenated."

"Pulse is 130 and weak Doc, but definitely present," someone replied.

"Her left lung sounds are clear, and she has only trace cyanosis," another reported.

Turns out a trauma response team works great as long as somebody is present to lead it. Before I knew it, we were bursting through the doors of OR 10.

I gave the anesthesiologist a quick report and she immediately intubated our Jane Doe (JD) to obtain control of her airway. Next JD was given some powerful pain medications and muscle relaxants. While this was occurring the OR techs quickly cut off all her remaining clothing using their trauma shears. Simultaneously, the anesthesia resident placed an arterial line in JD's left arm, and the

attending placed a subclavian line on her left side after she was intubated.

Total time to do all this = 3 minutes.

Just as the first unit of blood was being rapidly transfused, Dr.
Blake walked into the room. His confidence immediately relaxed
everyone. Before he could speak, Blake was handed a chest tube
which he inserted with just a couple fluid motions. Within seconds,
the right side of JD's chest re-inflated and her color almost immediately transformed from a mild baby blue to a healthy pink.

"Well, that's one less thing to worry about. Pneumothorax is
fixed. Next we have to amputate that right lower leg; it's too mangled
to salvage. Whoever put that tourniquet did a great job, probably
saved her life," announced Dr. Blake.

And we went to work. Operating with a motivated and well-
trained chief resident was a totally different experience than witnessing a hack job performed by Parker. Within three hours we had completely assessed JD, corrected her right sided pneumothorax,
amputated her right lower leg, stabilized her pelvic fracture, and
sutured all her multiple lacerations.

Stripping out of our gowns Blake pulled me aside. "You did
good in getting her to the OR Ra. Without your quick thinking about
her bleeding leg she might not have made it at all. I think she's going
to do just fine with some time and rehab. We'll get her a great pros-
thetic leg and she'll be able to run a marathon in six months."

"Thanks." We walked out together, the sun just now starting to
rise. "Did you see that crib?"

"That was her daughter, only two years old. She was DOA.
Nobody had the heart to admit it. I was the one who tore off the red
tag and pronounced her outside. Sucked."

I didn't know how to respond, so I did what med students do
best and changed the topic. "Do you want me to go help out with
rounds?"

"Tell you what; Parker has been fucking up lately. Two people died on his watch. He needs time to cool off and get his head on right. Why don't you assist me today and I'll have him do the notes. He didn't respond to my page this morning, anyhow."

Assisting a seasoned surgeon was a world of difference compared to monkeying around with interns. Blake was all business and a great teacher. He let me see what was going on, and if I answered his "pimps" correctly he rewarded me by allowing me to place a few sutures and even close a large skin incision. At the end of the day with him I felt like I was actually learning and that this whole surgery thing might be something to seriously consider.

On a mild natural high from actually doing something, instead of just staring at shoulders, I was excited to round on my patients that evening and see how their days had gone. Presumably better than the young mother who had just lost her leg and her baby.

Nine made it to the OR last night, of which four died intra-operatively due to the extensive nature of their wounds. Another six didn't even make it to the OR due to black tags, and six others had less severe injuries. All this because a drunk driver that entered the freeway on an off ramp and hit several cars head-on. The cars thought they were doing the best thing by slowing down when they saw him approaching, but it turned out to be unwise because they were that much closer to each other upon impact. The fact that he was driving a huge SUV didn't help either.

Thoughts of so many people dying because of a reckless drunkard dampened my feelings, and I felt as though I could use some good news. My wish was granted.

I entered Dr. West's room and was floored to see dozens upon dozens of flowers filling up the entire space. Instead of hospital odor, the room smelled like perfume.

"Dr. Raj!"

"Hi Dr. West, I'm guessing the pathology results came back?"

He pumped my hand with vigor, "You betcha, and I bought my wife here some flowers to celebrate the fact that I had completely clean margins."

"I'd say you bought her a small florist *shop*."

"Well, 'go big or go home' is what they say, don't they? And from here on out, the Wests are going big."

Mrs. West started weeping again. She was sitting on the side of the bed with her husband and they resembled a happy newlywed couple. She leaned over and gave him a hug and peck on the cheek.

"So, back to the grind next week?" I jokingly (well, half jokingly) asked.

"No, I'm true to my word. Medicine was my profession, now Pauline is my life. We have a lot of fun to make up in the next few years. Hell, I just realized I hadn't taken a real vacation in the past 34 years, only trips to conferences that'd I'd call 'vacations.'"

Their enjoyment/elation/relief was palpable. She lovingly rubbed his head and he held her hand. It was moving to see how different their demeanor was compared to the past couple days. "So what's first on the agenda?"

"Well, Burt is a slave driver, he says I gotta stay in the hospital at least two more days and then I need to follow up with him for staple removal and post-op care routinely over the next two weeks. Then I have to watch my diet and take it easy for another couple of weeks."

"Not bad, you went from having a life threatening cancer 4 days ago to being totally cured. I'd say a month of recovery is reasonable."

"Every minute I'm not doing something fun I feel like I'm missing out."

"I thought you forgot what it's like to have fun?"

"Hmm ... that sounds like something I'd say doesn't it? Well, I'm going to have fun trying." He leaned over and Pauline was more than willing to accept a peck on the cheek.

"I notice that's a car magazine over there. You done reading the medical journals?"

"Well, we've both driven the same cars for the past ten years. I figured it's finally time we go from place A to place B in some style. Any recommendations?"

While medicine was my major, automobiles were my lifelong minor. I knew just about everything about any car manufactured since '93 and was always happy to share my knowledge. They were content to know that they had a resource to exploit for their purchase. We traded contact information and I got through rounds with my head spinning.

That was the first time I'd witnessed a miracle of modern medicine. To go from being given a death sentence to being cured was a rare occurrence, and to be a part of it made all those long hours and late nights of study worth it. I made a mental note that I'd have to reconsider surgery as a career path.

~~~~

That mental note lost some of its appeal when my alarm clock buzzed at 3:40 a.m. the next morning, though many would (probably correctly) argue it was still night.

Dr. West continued to recover like a champion, and that evening I found him walking laps around the nursing station and flirting with the young nursing students a third his age. I had to admit he was quite the charmer, and I could definitely see why his patients loved him. He had an endless supply of energy; his confidence coupled with the commanding nature he used in telling stories was so engaging, it was hard not to be drawn in. And a group of nurses has clearly fallen under his spell.

I ran into his wife gazing intently at her husband from near the water cooler. She was staring at him as only someone smitten can.

"He's quite the life of the party, isn't he?" I asked.

"That's the man I married decades ago."

"I'm glad he's back."

"Sure took long enough! I want to thank you for all you've done, and don't say it was nothing. I really appreciate how long you chatted with me the other night, and Peter said he'd had a couple engaging discussions with you, too. Though he wouldn't tell me what that note he tore off the mirror said. He just referenced a medical student, and you're the only one that's been around."

"It'd be better you experience that note than have me ruin what it said."

She patted my back and joined the group of listeners as Dr. West recounted how he treated a celebrity's erectile dysfunction before the advent of Viagra.

There was only one scheduled surgery the next morning, likely due to the fact it was Saturday, but surgeons didn't seem to differentiate between week days and ends.

After morning rounds the Wests were packing up. I caught them just as they were about to leave their room.

"And to think if I didn't come by you'd have left without saying goodbye."

"Hardly," replied Dr. West as my pager went off. "I bet that page is from this here nursing station. I asked our nurse to page you and check if you were free."

Indeed he was correct.

"We need all the manpower we can get. These flowers aren't going to move themselves." He winked at me.

"I'd be happy to help." And I started to scoop up some flowers.

"No no, put them down. I was just joking." I actually couldn't tell.

"I called you here because I wanted to thank you and give you a little memento of my, our, appreciation for your gentle nature and willingness to listen to a grumpy, old curmudgeon."

He handed me an envelope.

I tried to open it but he stopped me. "Not here, open it when you get home."

I tucked it in my pocket and insisted that I push his wheelchair to his car. Hospital policy forbids anyone from walking out of the hospital even if they are more than capable.

Once we arrived outside we were greeted by a handsome gentleman standing next to a SUV, though his expression was a bit dour. He warmly hugged Pauline and patted Dr. West on the back as he stooped down to the wheelchair in one of those pseudo-hugs.

"Raj, meet my oldest son, Jamison."

We shook and helped the West's into their car. Despite beating cancer, Dr. West still had a long road of recovery ahead of him, especially if he was going to save his family. I wondered if he'd really keep me posted. After all, talk is cheap. Actions are what matter.

Chapter Four:
Myiasis

"YO, DOC, I bet you ain't ever seen nothing like this!" the paramedics shouted to Peters as they wheeled in another patient into the overcrowded ER.

We were in the midst of a heat wave with the fifth consecutive day over 100 degree weather, and the ER was packed beyond the normal bursting.

It's typical to have all the rooms, sans trauma bays, filled in the ER with an equal number of patients in the hallways and chairs—which is to say over 40 active patients at any moment. Today we introduced the *double park*.

Most "hallway" patients are just what they sound like, a gurney filled with someone that is ill, but not critically so, that is "parked" in the hallway. Today we double parked the hallways, making it so tight that unless your BMI was less than 25, you weren't going to make it through without getting a little too cozy with any number of the homeless derelicts littering the hallways.

The homeless generally show up to the ER on the hottest days of the year due to the lack of air conditioning on the streets. But they aren't dumb; they claim chest pain, not dehydration. If one is dehydrated, they get IV fluids and are out the door within the hour.

The chest pain must be taken seriously and requires at least seven hours of evaluation until the labs are confirmed as negative. By that time the sun is setting, the temperature is manageable, and the liquor stores are open for business.

The cost to evaluate somebody faking chest pain in an ER setting can range anywhere from five to ten thousand dollars, depending on the hospital. It'd be cheaper to put up the city's homeless in the Ritz Carlton during the dog days of summer.

"Guys, I'm a bit tied up with this chest tube right now. Just park her in the hallway over there, and I'll meet you in a bit," answered an overworked Dr. Peters.

I watched in confusion as three paramedics, two firefighters, and Detective Higgs all wheeled the patient past me. Unless she was Nancy Reagan or a serial killer, this was way too big an entourage. Something was going on.

Upon closer examination, everyone wore a smug expression, and the firefighters were giggling like schoolgirls, not acting macho like their pro-wrestler physiques resembled.

Curiosity kicking in, I decided to follow and see what was going on. The bum who I was about to assist with the bedpan could wait. One whiff and it was obvious his clothes had been serving the bedpan's function for some time now.

Just as I turned the corner in pursuit of Higs, I heard the characteristic splash of fluid hitting tile floor. At least housekeeping would get paid to clean up his mess. My tuition dollars were better used to investigate what was going on elsewhere.

The paramedics parked our mystery patient's gurney along the wall, as Dr. Peters had ordered, and took to slapping each other on the chest and grinning stupidly. But they quickly straightening up as I approached and made eye contact. Soon they formed an impenetrable barrier around the gurney, preventing me from taking part in the excitement.

"Hi, Detective Higgs." Hearing my salutation to the boss only heightened everybody's suspicions about me. They continued to stare me down, nonverbally communicating, loudly and clearly, that I was not wanted around.

"Hey, buddy, you're the med student from that baby shaker case, aren't you? I'm sorry; you're going to have to remind me of your name." Hearing Higgs acknowledge my existence caused the five human pillars forming Hadrian's Wall to slacken. They still wouldn't grant me access to their patient though.

"Rajen."

"That's right. Are you still working with Dr. Peters?"

"I finished that initial rotation. Now I'm back for my second two weeks in the ER. Then I move to the inpatient ward upstairs, but I'll still be around the ER for admissions."

"You remember that case of the shaken baby a couple months ago right?"

"Oh sure! How could I forget that? It was my first patient."

"Well, the legal shit is still going on … that fake father, what was his name, the dude who was nuts and thought the baby was his?"

"John," I offered.

"Yeah, well, he was proven insane. Got some real trust issues, that one. He still thinks the baby is his despite a DNA test confirming with 99.99% accuracy that it isn't. Got admitted to one of those psychiatric hospitals where he supposedly had a full breakdown. I think they're still putting him back together. Probably will take years to fix his loose screws."

"What about the guy who actually shook the baby? And Juanita?"

"Well, the Mom used the age defense and they tried her as a child instead of an adult … why, I don't know! But she got like four years of jail and some serious mandatory counseling and community service. I figure with good behavior she'll be out in two years. Can still go to college if she gets her head on right and takes birth control.

"The baby is a vegetable and blind, but her body's working. Got a good 70 years ahead of her in a nursing facility that you and I will be paying for."

"Sad."

"Worse is that we could never get a lead on who actually shook the kid. Juanita only knew him as "J" which was apparently a fake street name and nobody knew who he was. Her child's real father is still in jail, and he claims he knows nothing."

"So that's it?"

"Not completely. Mom filed an appeal, so that's got to be dealt with before this case can be put to rest."

I was staring curiously at all the guys around Higgs that were listening in on our conversation.

"I figure you're wondering why all of us are here? And trust me; it's not cause of the aroma. It's amazing how the ER smells worse than an abandoned urinal once it gets over 100 degrees outside."

I couldn't help but wonder how many medical student tuition dollars were given to the hospital only to participate in bedpan duty. Hell, nurses didn't even help with bedpans anymore. They had their CNAs do the dirty work. Some CNAs even had MAs do *their* dirty work.

Dr. Peters walked over to Higgs with a clearly feigned look of surprise in seeing the big man. "OH, I hardly noticed your entrance. You guys were about as stealthy and subtle as a sonic boom. The six of you blitzkrieg through the ER, cater to a single gurney, and yell out to the attending without checking in. You don't need to be a sleuth to guess something's up. Shit, half the ER is wondering about your cargo. I'm just going to drop off this specimen and I'll be back in a few minutes." She left towards the laboratory at a brisk clip.

"Yeah, on second guess, the VIP entrance might have been bet-ter," muttered one of the paramedics.

"So you going to let me in on the situation or does the medical student get sent away for coffee rounds?" I asked the group.

"I don't think this is for medical students," one of the paramed-ics volunteered. "Jack here lost his lunch on scene at the nursing home; luckily he made it to the sink. I bet they're still cleaning it up."

"Gentlemen, let's be professional here. He is going to be a doc-tor soon and needs to know what he will encounter in the future," offered Higgs. Then he winked and the wall parted, allowing me a glimpse of what lay on the gurney.

One thing was immediately certain; she didn't command such a convoy due to her social status. Her odor was unique, like that of decaying flesh, but not of rot. Akin to raw meat that has been left out too long mixed with sweat. Overall, slightly more tolerable than the stench of stale urine permeating the rest of the ER.

Most disconcerting was the sound … a sort of squishy-slurping, as though passing several spoons through a thick macaroni salad. I quickly localized the sound to the head of the gurney.

I glanced quickly and noted that she was covered with a sheet all the way to her neck, and even then only the left side of her head was exposed. Her skin, or what little of it I could see, revealed that she hadn't showered in some days, judging by the amount of caked on sweat and grease clinging to it. Her hair would have made Einstein jealous. The right side of her face was covered with a large abdominal pad dressing taped onto her skin. This is from where the sound ema-nated.

I moved closer. As soon as I realized what was going on, I fell backward onto the floor and felt my breakfast coming up. I managed to squelch the heaving, but not before some of my gastric contents escaped via my nostrils onto my sleeve. Damn, did that burn.

Once I got to my feet, I realized that I'd drawn the attention of everybody in close vicinity. Looking around I was greeted by laughter and two of the firemen taking pictures of me with their phones. Wiping my nose and regaining my dignity I returned to our patient's bandaged head.

That's when I discovered that the dressing was *moving*.

And escaping from the bottom edge of the dressing near her right jaw were not-so-small white maggots. They looked like they wanted to crawl towards her eye.

One of the medics gloved up and lifted up the dressing. I don't know what hit me first, the stench, sound, or my partially digested breakfast. Housekeeping would certainly earn their keep today.

Her entire right eye was missing. Her orbital cavity was instead filled with dozens of crawling maggots where her eye once used to be. The squishing sound was even louder with the dressing removed. The light must have scared them because they all seemed to want to take shelter within her orbit and down her right nostril.

"Alright guys, you had your fun, cover her up until Peters gets back. I'm gonna love to see her expression when she sees this," boomed Higgs from behind me, handing me a towel to clean up.

"What the hell is going on??" I asked nobody in particular. "That was the most disgusting thing I've ever seen in my life."

Just then Dr. Peters arrived and took in the scene: two paramedics standing at the head of the gurney laughing, me cleaning up my sleeve, Higgs shaking his head in amused dismay, and the firefighters standing against the wall trying to look professional.

"Raj, you ok? What the hell happened?"

"Nothing, breakfast didn't sit too well with me."

"Higgs, what did I tell you about picking on my students?"

"I warned him, Doc, but he insisted on being part of the team. Handled it better than I thought. Jack over there lost his lunch and

Sam had to leave the room. The medics have been having a field day with their damn camera phones."

"Ok, guys, what have we got here?"

One of the medics came over, "59 year old female, history of squamous cell cancer of her right eye. She refused treatment on two separate occasions. Her nursing home called us to report a 'moving dressing' over her right eye, not specifying any further and requested immediate transfer to the ER. And here we are."

Peters gave the patient a once over and quickly gloved up and walked closer. She was immediately drawn to the dressing on the right side of the patient's face. Of course now it wasn't moving, guess all the maggots were trying to hide from the recent light exposure.

"Ma'am my name is Dr. Peters, what is your name?"

"Be … Be … B … Beatrice," she whispered. "Are you going to give me more milk for my eye?"

I had forgotten that there was a patient under there. I hadn't even attempted to talk to her or try to build any rapport.

Peters was now surrounded by the whole team, everyone just waiting to catch her expression when she realized what was going on.

"Do you know where you are, Beatrice?"

"Yes, at the hotel. I was told if I leave the nursing home I'd get more milk. You know I have cancer on my right eye. But I've been giving it milk for the last three months and its getting better I'm sure."

"Well, I'm going to examine your right eye now. Please don't move."

Beatrice nodded and a small maggot fell out from under the gauze just as Peters was about to un-tape it. It bounced on the floor and began to writhe away. Peters knelt down to examine it and stood up to face Higgs.

"What did I ever do to you to deserve this? I bet she has a raging myiasis, probably even lost her right eye, huh? That's why the dressing was moving? Let me guess. She stays in some shithole nursing home where they didn't properly care for her wound. The heat wave and invasive cancer were perfect for the flies to lay their eggs and PRESTO. Do I even want to take a look?"

Everyone was amazed at how she put the entire story together without even removing the dressing, but they were also sad that they didn't get the look of shock they were waiting for. Higgs broke the silence. "Damn, see, that's why she's the Boss. You know you do, Doc, you like the sick shit."

"Higgs, I'm gonna get you for this, don't you forget it." The gleam in Peters' eyes was real, and the cogs were turning. This was not going to be forgotten and Higgs would repay with ample interest. I secretly hoped I'd get to be there; not much shook the behemoth.

Peters quickly lifted up the dressing and moaned in disgust as three of the dozens of maggots fell off Beatrice's face and plopped onto the gurney. One bounced and continued its descent, writhing in mid air, only to splat smack onto Peters' new Ferragamos.

She managed to keep down her breakfast. Glancing down and assessing the irreparable damage to the costly suede pumps, she threw Higgs the coldest of stares I'd ever seen. Peters then promptly reapplied the dressing to cover the maggot farm, and swiftly excused herself, exuding nothing but the highest degree of professionalism and aplomb to all around. Managing to shout as she turned the corner, she yelled, "Rajen, get her a STAT head CT scan and call the ophthalmologist ... and get psych involved too."

This sure beat bedpan duty and homeless usher. I called the consults, got Beatrice ready for her CT scan, and decided to help with her transport to escape the odor of the ER. The stench of maggots gnawing on cancer still beat the stench of homeless in a heat wave.

Upon her return from Radiology, Beatrice was placed in a private room. Apparently a face full of maggots, or vaginal bleeding (the other, more common diagnosis that was not evaluated in a hallway), was what one needed to get out of the hallway and into an actual room.

Higgs and his buddies had apparently moved on to other duties. They were no longer around when I returned, and Peters was busy with a minor trauma from a motor vehicle accident that had just come in.

Before I could find something else with which to occupy myself I saw an overly energetic resident rushing to the central ER desk, taking care to skirt hallway obstacles and avoid stepping in an undesirable puddle which was still present. I heard him ask the charge nurse for the eye patient.

She pointed in my direction and he headed off towards me. As he approached all I could make out on his badge was that it said "Ophthalmology," which made sense given he was asking for the eye patient.

"Hi, Dr. Sun, I'm ..."

"Call me S. We're on the same team; the doctor stuff is for egos and patients. You the med student on this case?"

I nodded, "Rajen." Declaring his nickname odd, I decided to stick with Dr. Sun.

He nodded back and proceeded straight to Beatrice, gloved up, and removed her dressing.

"HOLY FUCKING SHIT ... what did you get yourself into this time, Beatrice?"

I stood in shock; this wasn't how a physician spoke to a patient. Or at least not how we were taught to speak to patients. I'd never encountered other physicians speaking to patients in such a casual manner, but I'd also just come off a surgical rotation in which I had to refer to my colleagues as 'Doctor.'

This was the moment in my training marking my initiation into the dark side of medicine. The side that only practitioners know of, well hidden from the public eye. I didn't know it yet, but I soon learned that physicians used profanity in ways that would make sailors proud. Only makes sense given the stresses of making life or death decisions on a daily basis.

"Is that Dr. Sun? I've been using my milk like I told you; I think I can see better now and the cancer is almost gone, isn't it?" She spoke with marked lucidity in a nonplussed way given that her eye was missing and a maggot just fell out of her right nostril.

"Dude, Rajen, did you get a look at this? This is the nastiest thing I've ever seen! Get your camera.

"Beatrice, I'm going to take some photos of your face if that's ok with you? I just need you to sign these forms." Dr. Sun thrust some forms for Beatrice to sign and proceeded to take videos and photos of Beatrice from all angles.

"Rajen, I'm telling you, this will make for a fucking awesome grand rounds or medical student case presentation. Hell, if you're interested we can probably publish it. I've never heard of a case of such fulminant orbital myiasis in the developed world."

I wasn't sure what to do. Nobody had treated me as a colleague before and never had I witnessed the use of such colloquial language in front of a patient. I just stood and took it all in. But he seemed competent and involved in her care despite his language and laissez-faire attitude.

"Myiasis?" I finally asked.

"Oh, sorry for the jargon. Just the twenty dollar way of describing an infestation due to maggots." He continued to snap some pictures and videos.

"Well, Beatrice, thanks for the photo shoot. Now we should get you cleaned up and see what's going on here. Do you know how this happened?"

"What's happened, Dr. Sun? Can I have some milk?"

"Haha ... okay, Beatrice, I guess I'm not going to get much of a history from you. Can you read these itty bitty letters for me with your eye?"

Remarkably she read the 20/20 line with her left eye and followed commands just fine, never arguing or causing trouble. The joys of the pleasantly demented.

"Alright, Rajen, let's get this mess cleaned up and see what we got here. Can you get me a Yankauer suction setup? I'll get us some gowns and forceps and all the specimen collection shit the pathologists want. Meet you back here in five minutes?"

"Sure."

With a mission, I took off immediately in no apparent direction, with the only problem being I had no idea what a Yankauer was. Luckily, I ran into the charge nurse around the corner and asked her.

"What you need that for?"

"Uh, Dr. Sun asked me to get one for him."

"Ah, you met the eye doc? He's a good guy. You could stand to learn a lot from him. He's one of the few that loves what he does and teaches anyone who shows interest, not just fellow physicians. He even lets students help out with procedures and examinations. You working on the maggot lady?"

I nodded and she led me to the storage room, raving about the eye doc and handing me several pieces of plastic equipment.

"Good luck, let me know if S needs anything else. And don't mind that I won't be stepping into the room."

I headed back to Beatrice, learning that despite his foul tongue and overly casual style, Dr. Sun was one of the most published residents in the university and loved by nearly all.

Beatrice's room had been converted to a mini operating theatre with drapes all over Beatrice, a bright overhead light, and numerous tools and containers. Dr. Sun stood at arms, all gowned and gloved, waiting for me.

"Great, good work, you got all the right stuff. Most students get anything but what is needed. Here, let me show you how to plug it all in."

He went on to show me how to setup a Yankauer. Apparently it was a suction device used for aspirating fluids by anesthesiologists and surgeons. Turns out I'd used them before during major surgeries, but it was just always referred to as 'suction.' The maggots wouldn't slurp through the Yankauer tip I'd brought, so we modified the apparatus by cutting the tubing to create a large bore suction hose, akin to a hand held vacuum.

All gowned, gloved, and masked up we set to work slurping up maggots from Beatrice's right orbit. The suckers were smart and sensing something was happening, tried to burrow deeper into her tissues. But Dr. Sun outsmarted them by having me pour sterile normal saline into her orbit to flush the maggots out. Apparently they couldn't breathe underwater. They slowly surfaced and we slurped away for a good 20 minutes. They passed through the tubing just like tapioca boba balls with a little "plop" as they splashed into the collection container where they writhed in the blood-tinged saline, like little fishes out of water, until one by one they just floated.

When we were down to the last few maggots, we stopped with the suction and switched to forceps to procure a few specimens for the pathology and microbiology departments. The famed Dr. Debakey (inventor of the forceps we were currently using) must never have envisioned his tissue forceps being used like this.

After getting a couple specimens, Dr. Sun asked me to come closer and handed me the forceps.

"Ok Rajen, your turn. Gently grab the little suckers and place them in the formalin vial. Don't squeeze too hard; they tend to squish and squirt some white spooge-like shit." He pointed to his gown as some of the whitish discharge had splattered across his chest.

I grasped the forceps and realized this was the first time I was going to do a procedure, even if it was to collect a maggot from a person's half eaten face. I also realized that I had a tremor. Well, either that, or acute onset Parkinson's. I prayed it was the former and just due to nerves, else I'd have no potential career as a surgeon.

Guiding my hand, he assisted me in grasping and collecting a maggot. I placed it in the formalin and labeled it. There were only two left and I grabbed the next one on my own. I reached and grasped the last one. But before I could put the specimen in the container I felt another hand squeeze around mine. Then I felt a "pop" and something splattered my forehead and hair.

"Sorry dude, I couldn't be the only one with some splash damage!"

"Ewww!" I reflexively dropped the forceps and ran for some towels to wipe away the maggot innards.

The charge nurse and Dr. Sun were by the door laughing themselves silly. I guess it could have been worse, at least the mask and eye shield protected me. I finally felt like I was part of the team instead of just hoping to be noticed.

"Here, babe, let me help you." The charge nurse wiped the goo off of me and collected the specimens.

"Thanks, Lorraine, appreciate you taking those to Pathology for me," said Dr. Sun as the nurse disappeared down the hallway.

"I owe you S, for not making me assist in that mess. Do me a favor and take the student out for dinner; he deserves it after that."

We disrobed and threw away all our personal protective apparel and finished up our paperwork.

"So you know her?" I asked Dr. Sun.

"Beatrice? Yeah, met her about eight months ago in eye clinic. I helped with her biopsy. Squamous cell carcinoma of the right orbit. It was pretty large, and we told her we needed to exenterate her right eye. That's taking out the eye, skin, and superficial bone. And doing so would have saved her life. With some plastic work and an ocular prosthesis she'd have looked almost the same as before surgery. Of course she declined; instead she decided to treat herself with topical milk therapy."

"She can do that?"

"Well, I thought she was nuts, so we admitted her to the hospital and got a psychiatric evaluation ... twice. Both times the attending faculty said she was capable of making her own decisions, and we couldn't force her. Well, now you see the results. She was in a nursing facility for palliative care as the cancer had spread to her brain and who knows where else. She refused testing and routine evaluations."

"So what's next?" I asked.

"I'm guessing you called a psych consult?"

"Yeah."

"Cancel it, no need to waste their time. She's DNR. And on palliative care, doubt she'll be around more than a month or so anyhow. Now you'll get to see me be a bully; we'll call in the ENT guys and have them take her to the OR to clean up the wound and dress it properly. They're gonna be thrilled. But I figure there is nothing for us to do. Hell, the eyeball is missing, can't fix what ain't there."

Psych was happy to have the consult called off. ENT was pissed at having to come in and fought Dr. Sun against the consult, refusing to see the patient, claiming it was not their area of expertise.

"Dude, you don't have to tell me you're not coming in. Tell Peters, she's on today. Let me get her for you." Dr. Sun spoke politely to the ENT resident knowing that he was going to win this little battle by enlisting the name of the supervising physician.

"Wait, Peters wants the consult?" inquired the ENT resident with sudden renewed interest, knowing that an attending was involved and he was now no longer just being beckoned by another resident.

"Yep, hold up, she's coming over to talk to you."

"No, no, it's cool. Tell her we're happy to help and I'll be there in a few minutes. I'll book the OR, too, so she doesn't have to bother." Amazing how quickly things were accomplished when the appropriate authority's name was dropped.

"Wow, I thought he wasn't going to come in the way he was talking to you earlier," I sputtered as soon as Dr. Sun hung up the phone.

"Rajen, medicine is a huge fucking pecking order about who has the biggest penis ... or ovaries ... whatever your reproductive organ of choice. While on the surface we have to make it seem like we're all here to help each other out, it's really just about who wields the power—at least in academics or at university hospitals. In the private world everybody's willing to help out because they all get paid."

We left Beatrice alone with her dementia, to whichever happy corner of her subconscious that it takes her, and found Dr. Peters to sign out. We also informed her that ENT was on the way. Dr. Sun was very precise in his wording about how they were happy to see the patient at her behest. She simply nodded and continued to proceed with the lumbar puncture she was performing to evaluate a patient for possible meningitis.

Dr. Sun peeled off and hurried down the hall. He turned when he realized that I wasn't following and hollered, "Hey Rajen, you did great today. If you keep up that attitude, you're gonna be a great physician." And with that confidence boosting remark, he was off.

I stood there, strangely content that I'd helped make a difference in somebody's life even as a lowly medical student. Maybe this whole medical thing wasn't such a bad idea after all.

My afterglow was short lived as I felt something slimy in between my fingers when I placed them in my right side coat pocket. I knew without having to look down that Dr. Sun had left me a little present from our recent patient. Holding my hand out in front of me, there was the last little maggot from Beatrice, squished and sliding down space between my middle and ring finger. The trail of slime on my fingers glistened in the fluorescent light of the hallway.

I scurried to the nearest sink and thoroughly washed my hands … thrice.

~~~~

Having nothing else to do, I decided to check the ER patient 'board' (which is really a huge digital flat screen of all the active patients) for something interesting. As I was perusing the chief complaints, Dr. Peters came up to me and handed me an envelope. "Raj, this came in for you a couple days ago. You did good today. Why don't you take off early and take a nice long shower?" We looked at each other and just laughed. I'd never have guessed that I'd be assisting in maggot removal on the job.

"Thanks, Dr. Peters."

I hurried out of the ER for fear that Dr. Peters might rescind her offer allowing me to leave only halfway through my shift. Once safely outside I took the envelope she'd handed me. It was from Peter West, with a return address from New York.

Dr. Peter West was a cancer patient I'd helped care for a couple months ago. He'd survived pancreatic cancer thanks to a successful Whipple procedure. I'd almost forgotten the generous gift he'd given me upon his discharge from the hospital. He gave me two first class tickets from Los Angeles to New York with open travel dates good for one year and a gift certificate good for two tickets for center orchestra seating at the Avery Fisher Hall, where his son plays in the Philharmonic.

It was a very generous gift, likely worth more than my car.

With renewed excitement I opened up his envelope and found a single color photograph of Dr. West, his wife, and his son all standing around the conductor of the New York Philharmonic with huge smiles on their faces. I guess he made good on visiting New York to attend one of his son's concerts.

I flipped the photo over and found a short note, "A wise man once told me that 'talk is cheap.' Next up is Europe."

I was impressed that he even remembered who I was. Dr. West was clearly a man of his word, making good on his promises to me of enjoying life after surviving cancer.

Chapter Five:
High Five

"DR. MOK, THAT was an excellent presentation. You have come a long way since the beginning of this rotation."

I was flabbergasted. A compliment from Dr. Clyde was rare, and now I'd received two in the past month. It certainly added a bounce in my step that entire day. It's true; all it takes to make a med student's day is a simple compliment; frequently the lack of criticism or anger also suffices.

This was supposed to be my last day on the ICU rotation for the year, but I got suckered into trading rotations with Cathy because she begged and really wanted to do another elective rotation. Plus, she paid me $1,000. Thus, I'd be taking her spot and doing *another* month of ICU.

I pretended it was a huge ordeal for me, but in reality it worked out in my interest. Now I wouldn't have to do any ICU time next year and could just pick some sissy rotation where attendance was optional and explore the L.A. happy hour scene. The cash didn't hurt either.

The only common factor this month would be that Dr. Clyde would be the attending physician for the next two weeks. Otherwise the faces of the ICU would change tomorrow and it'd be a whole new team.

"Hi … Raj?" came a hesitant voice from behind me.

I turned and was treated to a pretty face with a shy smile attached to a petite frame with long, straight black hair. Her name badge identified her as Cindy Lee, and the long white coat indicated she was a fully fledged MD, and not a student. I instantly hoped she'd be my resident on the new rotation starting tomorrow. If so, I really came out the winner. Before answering I also took note that her left hand was ring-free.

"Yep, the one and only." I managed to dorkily reply.

"Oh, great, nice to meet you," said Cindy, introducing herself and shaking my hand. "I've heard you've done quite the job impressing people in the ICU and wanted to come by and say hi. We're going to be on the same team starting tomorrow and I was wondering if you could update me on our patients if you have a second?"

Finally, a small dream comes true, with the beautiful Cindy to lead me; the next month was surely to be great!

It wasn't.

~~~~

The meeting with Cindy went well. She was to be my intern on the new team and was nervous about doing the upcoming month in ICU, as she'd never rotated in the critical care setting before. She managed to skip out of those rotations during her training at NYU School of Medicine. She was also new to California and didn't have many friends here. At the end of our conversation, I made the magnanimous gesture of taking on the responsibility to show her around L.A. Even better, she accepted.

That's how we ended up getting lychee martinis just down the street after work and got to know each other. She even treated, maintaining that interns at least made an income versus the debt incurred by med students.

I liked her even more.

She was a gorgeous girl who wanted to spend a few years training in L.A. before heading back to New York to become a Cardiologist. Her inspiration came from her father who immigrated to the U.S. from Korea and worked double shifts in the cardiology ECHO laboratory. It was there he met Cindy's mother, an X-ray technician at NYU, the same hospital where Cindy was born and educated. And also the same hospital where both her parents were treated for cardiac arrest and where they both ultimately passed away within two months of each other last year.

She was actually to do her residency there, but needed a respite from the place due to the recent forlorn memories.

If only she had remained in New York. Perhaps, then she wouldn't have contracted HIV and dropped out of medicine altogether.

~~~~

"Dr. Lee, what are you doing here? It's not even 6 a.m." I asked of Cindy upon entering the ICU. I was accustomed to being the first to arrive, not being greeted by senior members of the team.

"Rajen, good to see you. Thanks for your detailed update yesterday; it made rounding so much easier this morning. I hope you don't mind. In order to get more acquainted with our patients, I wrote the notes for today already."

Needless to say, I was impressed. Cindy was not only chipper; she did all my work for me *before* I even got to the hospital, and thanked me for it to boot.

"Wow, most residents come in 'bout six a.m. or later. We don't start call until seven a.m., and rounds don't begin until 7:45."

"Yeah, I like to come in early and be on top of things. I figure that makes the day run smoother. Besides, medical students shouldn't have to come in any sooner than us interns. What do you think we get the big bucks for, sleeping in?"

I never thought such creatures existed in medicine: genuinely nice and with a willingness to help out.

"So I guess we're on call today; hopefully we get something interesting. I'd be happy to show you the New York style of patient management. It's much more rigid than the laid back Cali style I've seen these past few months."

I nodded and we completed the orders: electrolyte replacements, ventilator modifications, x-ray review, and other errands for our five patients.

Dr. Clyde arrived at 7:45 a.m. sharp and rounds commenced. After quick introductions, I learned our junior resident was Sheila Khan and our senior resident was Jack Flanders. Both seemed as though they wanted to be anywhere except here. Though rumor had it Jack was quite brilliant, insightful, and a master of short cuts. I'd never met Sheila before.

Rounds were uneventful and Dr. Clyde sat us all down in the ICU conference room to review how he liked the ICU to run. Just as he began his discourse, Jack's pager chirped. It could only be one thing: our first admission.

"Jack, why don't you kindly give the information you jotted down to Dr. Mok? He already knows how the ICU runs here. He can get started on the patient in the ER until we're done."

We were all amazed that he knew it was an admission and in the ER. I doubt he heard what had transpired during the phone call. Seems as though omniscience comes with experience. Nobody questions Clyde; he's simply never wrong. That's why he's Director of the ICU.

I grabbed the bullet-pointed note card. It didn't give much information, but it wasn't Jack's fault; there wasn't much known about our patient.

Bed 2
JD, 30ish ♂
↓ W. Hollywood
104°F
A & 0 x 1
AMS

I headed out the door and was impressed by how succinct, yet organized Jack was. In just a few words he managed to summarize that our patient was located in ER bed 2, he was a John Doe, appearing to be in his thirties, was found down in West Hollywood with a high fever, was alert and oriented only to one of the four common questions (person, place, time, and event) asked to a patient when initially triaging them. The reason for admission of our JD was 'altered mental status.'

The typical individual who meets this description is somebody who is heavily inebriated and slept the night in an alley after some heavy partying.

If the fever is higher, in the 106 degree range, ecstasy is the prime suspect. It can literally melt one's brain due to high fevers if taken in large enough quantities. A lower fever could be anything from dehydration to an infection by any number of pathogens.

"Blllluuuggh." It didn't take a rocket scientist to figure out the origin of that noise. It was followed immediately by a splashing sound of something viscous yet chunky hitting the floor. If the sound didn't give it away, the smell did.

Our JD just vomited all over the floor next to his bed. Another good reason never to sit down on any floor space in the ER. Ever.

JD didn't look so good. His skin was pale with a slightly green hue. He was covered in oily sweat with specks of his recent upchuck all over his face and chest. Despite this, one could tell JD took care of his physique; he was quite the specimen with all his muscle groups well-defined and a trim waist. He clearly wasn't a stranger to the gym.

Just like you can't judge a book by its cover, don't try to assume anything about a patient by their external appearance. Just because JD appeared fit did not preclude any number of medical conditions. The fact that he just lost control of his bowels and soiled his jeans reinforced that something was seriously wrong with him.

But it did provide some insight into whatever was going on, namely, it was bad and moving fast. The ER team rushed into the room and began a repeat evaluation before I could even get gowned and gloved up.

One of the nurses yelled out to the nearest attending, "His pupils are fixed and dilated and he's not responding to pain."

The ER attending, someone whom I didn't recognize, rushed over in his blood streaked scrubs and took in the situation. "Any results from his toxicology screen or CT scan yet?"

"Tox is pending, CT scan of his head showed no herniation but radiology suspects some kind of infection based on a possible abscess. Unfortunately, they said the scan quality was extremely poor due to motion artifact. Lungs were clear."

JD began to seize.

"Get the crash cart. We're going to intubate and then perform a LP. MOVE people! I want to get this done in the next five minutes."

The crowd dispersed with vigor, as they now all had something to do. The attending positioned himself at the head of the bed in preparation for the intubation when a cough of blood escaped from JD's mouth followed by a gush that immediately covered his face, neck, and continued to flow onto the gurney. The attending wasn't fazed at all; nor did the added blood change the appearance of his already soiled scrubs.

I guessed JD must have bitten off a good portion of his tongue as he began to seize, because the blood kept pouring out of his mouth with no indication of slowing.

The convulsions began to subside after about 15 seconds, which is when everybody regrouped with all the equipment that the attending had requested.

"Crash cart's here doc, you ready?"

"This is a fucking mess. Get me suction, STAT! Then a 7 French tube with a straight scope. Go ahead and give him some heavy sedation and induce paralysis. If I don't get it on the first try we're just gonna trach him."

The equipment materialized out of nowhere. The suction cannula was placed in JD's mouth, which was now more like an erupting volcano spewing hemoglobin everywhere. Somehow the attending was able to locate the pharynx. But from where I was, all I could see was blood and more blood.

He plunged the tube into the middle of the eruption. He connected it to a bag and began manual ventilations.

"I got breath sounds, Doc. You're a magician, how the hell did you get that tube in?"

The question went unheard; the attending was too focused on what to do next.

"Connect him to the ventilator. Place him on his right side and get him prepped for the LP."

About 20 seconds elapsed and a voice rang out, "He's all ready for you, Doc."

"Next time make it faster. Get the manometer set up, I want to measure his opening pressure."

With the efficiency that only comes with experience, the attending plunged the long needle deep into JD's lower back, through his spinous processes, and into his spinal canal in one single fluid motion. Slightly turbid CSF began to gush out.

"Connect the manometer!!"

The pressure measuring device was immediately connected to the needle in an effort to determine the opening pressure of the CSF.

The only problem was the pressure was so high that the CSF coursed up through the first manometer and erupted through the top like Old Faithful.

"HOLY-FUCKING-SHIT … attach another one on top of this one now!"

A second one was quickly affixed and the pressure measured.

"God damn! The pressure is 68!" exclaimed the attending. "Give me five tubes. I'm gonna collect the samples, and we'll pray he doesn't have a continued leak or herniation with that pressure. Where's the ICU team?? I want him out of here yesterday."

While he was collecting the samples Cindy arrived at my side.

"Hmm … that doesn't look so good. I'm guessing he's our admission?" asked Cindy.

I gave her a quick rundown of what had taken place so far.

"What's your diagnosis, Dr. Mok?"

"Well, there're only a couple things I know that can cause a CSF pressure that high along with a fever and seizures. And given he didn't have any signs of tuberculosis on the lung scan, I'm going to go with Cryptococcal meningitis."

"The accolades I've heard about you have just been validated."

The pandemonium around JD had calmed down now and one of the nurses was calmly cleaning him up in preparation for his transfer to the unit. The attending was headed towards us. He had so much blood on him that the only part of his name badge I could make out was Dan.

Cindy was quick to greet him. "Hi, uh, Dr. Dan; we're here from the ICU."

"Pleasure, I'd shake, but I think you'd prefer I decontaminate first. I don't know what half this shit is that splattered on me." He proceeded to scrub his arms in the sink while talking. "Well, I can't tell you much. You must have heard the LP fluid was dirty and the pressure was sky high. He seized down here and bit off about 20% of his tongue. Somehow we managed to intubate him. He's paralyzed, sedated, and all yours." With that he rushed over to attend to his next bloody mess. Literally.

If nothing else, Dr. Dan was competent and efficient.

"I saw ENT on their way over when I was coming down. I'm guessing they are going to fix his tongue so he doesn't exsanguinate before we even get him to the unit. So what do you want to do for this guy?" asked Cindy.

"Well, I already checked his belongings. I found a driver's license that says Jacob Winters. If that's him, he lives in Santa Monica. I also found his cell phone; it only had four numbers on speed dial, "Claudia, Rachel, Patricia, and Amber." He'd called Claudia several times during the last couple days. His phone didn't have the typical "Home" or "Mom" or "Dad" entries in the directory.

"My guess is he was partying all night in Hollywood and passed out from the festivities. The names are either his drug dealers or booty calls. Ecstasy overdose can certainly cause hyperthermia and seizures in a young healthy guy and isn't uncommon in this area.

"Thus, we should follow up on the drug screen and get an MRI of his head to evaluate for Crypto." Cindy nodded her approval.

"I'm assuming routine labs and cultures have been drawn, but we should double check to make sure. Let's see if we can get the MRI done now; it's on this floor and it'd be easier than transporting him back down from the ICU later. Anything else you can think of?"

"Yeah, let's start him on Amphotericin B." Too bad it's such a terrible medication. It has horrible side-effects. Some of the worst are renal failure, liver failure, blood dyscrasias, cardiac arrhythmias, heart failure, rigors, headache, and death—to name just a few. "Perhaps we could also add a couple broad spectrum antibiotics as well as large amounts of IV fluids."

"Good show, Dr. Raj."

"I suspect he might have HIV or AIDS. But I don't think we can test for that without consent. And while he's like this with no family present, our hands are tied."

"We can deal with that later. Let's see about this MRI first."

He arrived in the ICU three hours later. ENT had managed to suture up his tongue and packed his mouth with some gauze. The MRI "wet" read was consistent with a florid Cryptococcal cerebral infection complete with several abscesses and associated meningitis.

We got him situated in the ICU with an isolation room, ventilator, his medications, and ample IV fluids.

I tried calling the number on his license, but it was a cell phone with no greeting. Having no next of kin or emergency contacts, it was just a matter of 'hurry up and wait' for Jacob to either wake up or go to sleep permanently.

Finishing up the admission paperwork, I ran into Jack and told him about the case and how we couldn't ascertain his HIV status until he woke up.

"That's bullshit man; you can easily figure out if he's got the 'HI-5' without his consent. You just gotta order the right tests," winked Jack.

"I don't follow. Federal law states that we *must* have patient consent to order HIV testing or share results of such testing."

"Exactly, you have to have consent for *HIV* testing. But I never said to order an HIV test. Just order a HIV viral load and CD4 count. Neither test requires specific consent. If he has a positive HIV viral load and low CD4 count, you can essentially make the diagnosis of

HIV or AIDS. Gotta think outside of the box, my man." He patted my back and took off to wherever he was headed.

Now I knew where Jack got the reputation of being clever and knowing how to get out of work.

But what he said was brilliant. If we did what Jack recommended we could get our answers and circumvent the whole consent issue. Sure, it was a little shady, but it was very legal and would help us with JD's management and care. At least that's how I rationalized it immediately before I ordered the tests.

The tests would take at least 24 hours to perform. In that time Jacob continued to steadily improve throughout the day such that he was starting to wake up and respond to pain. To help decrease some of the cerebral edema caused by the infection steroids were started the following morning. The result was quite profound. By the end of that day Jacob was responding to verbal commands and trying to pull out his endotracheal tube.

During evening rounds Dr. Clyde decided we'd leave Jacob on the ventilator overnight and extubate him first thing in the morning if he continued to show such dramatic improvement. His labs had not returned by the time we rounded.

I completed my work and was ready to head out of the hospital. The rest of the team had already called it a night long ago, except for Cindy who was double checking her orders. Figuring I'd keep myself busy until she was done and walk out with her, I decided to check up on Jacob's labs once again. BINGO, the results were in, less than 36 hours after being placed.

Jack was one sharp cookie. Jacob did, in fact, have a severely decreased CD4 count of 36 and a raging viral load of over 110,000 HIV RNA copies per milliliter of blood.

"Eek, you scared me," I manly whimpered. Cindy had startled me by tapping my chair while I was engrossed with Jacob's lab results.

"Whatcha looking at there?" She asked.

"Guess what? Jacob is, in fact, HIV positive. Take a look at these values." I nudged the monitor in her direction.

"OH WOW, his viral particles are having one big party. That certainly explains his Crypto meningitis. Though he doesn't have that characteristic look of someone with HIV wasting syndrome, nor that lipodystrophic look that people on anti-HIV medications develop from fat redistribution."

"In other words Detective Lee is saying he's never been on a HAART treatment protocol?"

"Doesn't look like it. Anyway, let's get outta here. It's already 9 p.m. and we gotta be back too soon." We headed out of the ICU and before going 20 feet, our discussion was back to medical topics, and Jacob in particular.

"How do you think he got AIDS?" I asked, "He seems like such a normal guy."

"NEWS FLASH, normal people have sex and do drugs! Take your pick. It's one of those two. The era of HIV from blood transfusions died in the mid 1980s, and I doubt he was but a toddler in those days. And if he had contracted it then, he wouldn't be around now without being on treatment."

"Think he'll make it?"

"I suppose if he really gets off the ventilator tomorrow and continues to recover well, he'll do just fine. Once he gets on a HAART regimen, his CD4 count will essentially normalize and he'll easily have a good 30 years or more to live. You know, these days it's rare to die of HIV/AIDS or its associated infectious complications. Most people with HIV die of something unrelated to the actual disease itself."

"I read that somewhere. I guess it's fascinating because this is the first time I've seen AIDS diagnosed."

"Technically we haven't diagnosed it yet. But I hear ya; it can be exhilarating. Just remember, he's got enough viral particles flowing through him to infect everyone in the hospital several times over. You have to treat him like a biological weapon."

"Good point, I'll make sure to double glove. Do you think he knows what he has?"

"I'm sure. He's probably known for a while but was in denial, probably why he never sought medical attention. I just hope he hasn't *knowingly* ruined anybody's life by fucking around without protection. He's a good looking guy and girls aren't going to think twice about shagging him."

"I guess I never thought about that."

"About shagging a guy?"

"Perhaps I should think about it. It's too hard to meet a decent girl in this city."

"I don't believe that. You're a good looking guy; you must have to run away from the girls chasing after you."

"Now you've proven that you're delusional."

"Most delusions are based on some kernel of truth."

"Then I should take advantage of your current state of mind. Would you be interested in further exploring your delusions over dinner sometime?"

"What an interesting proposition ... I look forward to it."

"Ditto." I began to blush, but before I had the opportunity to screw up this harmless flirting, we entered the parking structure and headed our separate ways. The good news was that I'd see her again in a mere eight hours.

~~~~

I arrived in the ICU to see that Cindy was already there. Seeing me enter she rushed over and immediately started to update me on Jacob.

"So last night your friend tried to pull his ET tube out again. Apparently his sedation got a little light and he woke up enough to start tugging on it. He did that despite being on high dose narcotics, telling us he likely has a history of drug use. If you or I got half the dose he did we'd be out for a solid 48 hours. Anyway, he pulled the tube so hard that he partially dislodged it, and the resident on call decided it was safer to extubate him; repositioning the tube wasn't possible.

"Once Jacob got his voice back he was extremely rude to the female nurses and required sedation to shut his ass up. He should be waking up soon. Would you mind interviewing him this morning? I think it'd be easier if you talked to him given his chauvinistic behavior. I'll take care of all the other paperwork on everybody else."

"Sure, I can help out with that stuff, too."

"No, just take your time. I know you were excited about your first AIDS case, so go slow and learn as much as you can. You have almost a full hour to chat with our friend."

This was sure shaping up to be a good month; a whole hour with a patient without having a dozen other things to do was a rare treat. I made a mental list of what I knew before I entered Jacob's isolation room. He had AIDS, possibly previously undiagnosed, meningitis which almost killed him, a history of drug use, and likely a penchant for sex and partying given where he was found down.

I reviewed his vitals before entering his room. Jacob seemed to be doing better, his temperature was just below 100°F, the other vital signs were essentially normal with good oxygen saturation on nasal cannula and only a mild tachycardia.

His labs were another story. The drug screen was positive for opioid derivatives, ecstasy, cocaine, and alcohol. Cindy was right about the drug use. His blood cultures were negative, but his CSF cultures were positive for Cryptococcus. Speciation and drug sensitivities were still pending.

With technology and lab testing, speaking to a patient is almost unnecessary in modern medicine.

I put on my personal protective equipment in the anteroom of Jacob's isolation chamber, which consisted of an N95 face mask, eye shield, gown, and gloves; being that they were all disposable, this meant that the mere act of entering Jacob's room cost about five dollars every time somebody went inside. Jacob was asleep but easily aroused when I nudged his shoulder.

"Good morning, Jacob."

I waited for a response, but he just shifted position and rubbed his eyes, trying to sit up.

"Just relax, let me help you. I'll elevate the head of your bed for you so you don't have to strain yourself. There, how's that?"

"Who are you?"

"Name's Raj, I'm the medical student on the team taking care of you."

"What?"

"Do you know where you are?"

"Naw man, I don't remember much. I remember some hottie here a while ago. I tried to hit on her, but she got real mad at me. I realized something wasn't right. Next thing I know I'm talking to you."

"You are in the hospital, in the intensive care unit to be exact. You've been here for the past two days."

That got his attention, and he sat bolt upright. "SHIT, where's my car and clothes?"

He looked around in a confused manner taking everything in and began to reach for his IV line. I stopped him and did my best to comfort him, but his agitation grew.

"Jacob, listen to me for a second, try and relax ..."

"I can't relax! I'm late for work; they're gonna can me if I miss another day. I need to get out of here. Shitshitshitshit ... where are my clothes?"

"Take a deep breath and calm down, I'll answer all of your questions. You are in a hospital."

"I can't calm down, damn it! I need to get outta here and get my car and get to work. Fuck, you don't understand, I'm going to lose my job if I miss another day." He was throwing off his sheets, searching the room for something, I presumed his clothes.

Obviously the nice guy routine wasn't going to work with Jacob, so I decided to give him a dose of reality. "Your clothes have been incinerated and your wallet confiscated. But after all the blood and puke you got on them no dry cleaner would've touched them. You had a seizure in the emergency room and bit off a piece of your tongue."

"Shit, really?" He stuck out his tongue; he had two small sutures on it. Apparently a very small cut on the tongue could cause a lot of bleeding. I'd have sworn he bit half of his tongue off down in the ER given the profuse amount of blood that was gushing from his mouth. "No wonder my tongue itches."

"You really don't remember pulling out your breathing tube last night?"

"What you talking about?" Confusion began to take over, and with it curiosity. Jacob began to calm down. I think he was starting to realize the gravity of his situation and that he wasn't going anywhere anytime soon. "Ok, ok, back up. I've been here two fucking days?"

"Well, closer to 50 some hours. I'm not exactly sure when the ambulance brought you into the ER, but close enough."

"Ambulance?"

"Yeah, you were found down in some alley in Hollywood. Lucky for you a kind passerby called it in and you were brought here. Once in the ER you had a nasty seizure. That's when we discovered you have an infection in your brain caused by a fungus. Hence the yellow IV solution you're getting."

"Oh snap. Yeah, it's coming back to me. I was partying at that new club, Drai's or something, up in Hollywood … and … oh man, I was getting close to scoring with that blonde hottie. Damn, I forgot her name. Hopefully I got her number. She was so fucking hot and bothered, I wasn't sure if we were going to make it to my car. Actually, we weren't, that's why we went to the alley, figured nobody would mind if we had a quickie there. Know what I mean? That way I wouldn't have to deal with her the next morning either. The girlfriend can smell when another woman's been in my bed." And he winked at me as if we were in some sort of fraternity together sharing our exploits of the previous evening.

"You must have been partying pretty hard if you passed out."

"Nothing out of the norm." He was starting to become much more coherent and interested in the discussion. Jacob clearly thought a lot of himself and clearly had some narcissistic tendencies. I decided to run with it and see what I could learn.

"What does that mean?" I inquired.

"You know, same ol', same ol'. Had some drinks and did a line or two of coke so I could party longer. Then my buddy and I met a couple of chicks who were definitely down to have a good time. They were even more interested when they found out we had some coke. Both helped themselves to a healthy dose and then were all over us on the dance floor. When I mentioned I had some E, their eyes lit up. After we all dropped a pill they were as good as ours. I mean these girls were horny even *before* the ecstasy." He paused, and then completed his thought, "Damn! I wish I was around to see what she was like after the E."

"Your urine also tested positive for narcotics."

"You checked my piss?!" He calmed down almost immediately realizing I wasn't trying to be confrontational. "Guess it makes sense to check it out when I can't tell you anything, huh? I pop some pills here and there. Nothing too crazy, usually just Percs. Oxy if I can score it, but it's tough to come by these days and costs a mother."

"That's Percocet and Oxycontin, I presume? What about heroin?"

"Nah, never tried that shit, I don't like needles. I just stick to the pills. My buddies smoke heroin, but the vapors don't agree with me. Besides the black tar just ruins anything it comes into contact with. Destroys furniture, which is bad for both business and pleasure."

"What do you mean?"

"I help run a very successful interior design company, so looks mean everything. Can't win over a client if you have tar under your fingernails or heroin streaks on your walls. I'm the best designer they've got. I would have been partner in the corporation last year, but my irregular hours don't sit well with everyone on the board. But they all know they need me. I bring in the big Hollywood contracts."

I had no reason to think Jacob was lying to me; he was pretty forthcoming with his drug use and it was all consistent with his toxicology results. He really loved talking about himself. As interesting as his drug and employment history were, I was ready to take it one step further and delve into his sexual history and HIV status.

"Do you have any other medical conditions I should know about?"

"Apparently I've got a fungus in my brain. Strange since I've never even done 'shrooms. Is that how somebody gets a brain fungus? From eating those magic mushrooms? I always knew it fucked with your mind."

I wasn't sure if he was serious or just messing around, so I decided to keep it professional. "Certain mushrooms are certainly hallucinogenic, but a *Cryptococcal* brain infection isn't from eating mushrooms. Most people get it by inhaling aerosolized spores from bird droppings."

"So you're saying I inhaled bird shit?"

"Well, we all do it simply by breathing. It's just that people don't get infections unless their immune systems are severely compromised."

"What are you trying to say?"

"I know you have some other medical problems."

"Look at me, would you?" Jacob flexed his arms showing off his well formed biceps. "Do I look sick to you? I work out and exercise, even do a little modeling on the side. I'm healthy. I ain't got no medical problems. NOW, when can I get the hell out of here?"

"Why are you suddenly getting defensive? Our goal here is to help you get better, and to do that we need to know your whole medical history."

"Well, I'm telling you I ain't got no other medical history than what I just told you. Now can you tell me when I can get the hell out of here?" He was starting to get confrontational. I could see it in his demeanor. He was tense with his jaw clenched and his hands balled up as though he was ready to rough me up. Though I had little to fear, if he got himself worked up to the point of getting out of bed he'd likely suffer a severe headache and send himself into a fit of seizures.

Instead of patronizing him with the typical line of 'calm down' that so many doctors use, which only serves to further rile up patients, instead I decided to buddy up with him to see if I could get any more information. I'd just feed into his narcissism.

"Jacob, I know you don't want to be here; hell, I wouldn't either. You've been through a lot in the past couple days and come out of it like a champion. Most people in your situation wouldn't have even made it to the ICU, if you know what I mean. And the strength it takes to pull out a breathing tube is just incredible."

"Damn straight, I didn't even feel it come out." His jaw slackened and his fists uncoiled. My plan seemed to be working, so I continued to feed his ego; after all, medicine is about building rapport, not friends.

"Incredible. You must have a pretty high pain threshold. I'm assuming it comes from the hours that you obviously spend in the gym?"

"Interesting, I never thought about it that way. I guess as I build muscle I'm probably also building up a higher pain tolerance. Makes sense, more muscle means more tolerance for pain. I bet that's how I can do lots of things that my other friends think are too painful, like eating hot sauces and lifting heavy stuff."

"You might be onto something." God this guy was so full of himself; it was amusing. At least he was starting to warm up to me. Now I could get to the heart of the matter. "Do you remember anything else about the night when you were found passed out in the alley?"

"I told you all I remembered."

"Is it common for you to party like that and hook up with random people?"

"Hey hey, I don't hook up with random people, only chicks of the most attractive variety."

"Must be pretty easy for you to get girls, huh? They love bad boys who workout."

He was getting into the conversation. He clearly enjoyed speaking of his exploits. I, on the other hand, was starting to get sick. He was committing manslaughter if he knowingly had unprotected sex with others while being aware of his HIV status.

"Single chicks are no problem. But I like to go for the ones who are with other guys. There's a challenge to stealing another man's old lady for a night."

"That's a dangerous game. If one of the girls was to get pregnant, they could trace the child's DNA back to you and nail you for child support or even go after your corporation. You must use some sort of protection, no?"

"Used to, but stopped last year. Figured I'll only be young once and it feels so much better without a cover on Jacob Jr."

"Aren't you worried about getting HIV or Hepatitis C or some other STD?"

"Not really. Why are you asking all these questions? If you want to hook up, I know some pretty ladies who'd love to have a doctor. But those dates aren't cheap, if you know what I mean?"

"Thanks, but I'll pass. I have somebody I'm interested in already." Guess Jacob supplemented his modeling and interior designing income with some pimping on the side. I was about to start probing him about his HIV status when Cindy entered the room.

"Helllllloooooo, nurse! Here to give me my sponge bath?" Jacob was clearly interested in Cindy. And who could blame him? She looked good, especially since she wasn't wearing a gown or mask. Like many docs, she ignored the personal protective equipment requirements. She'd also had a lot more experience with AIDS than I did, so she likely knew what was and wasn't really needed.

"No. It's Dr. Lee. I'm Raj's boss on the team managing your care," she said with authority as she showed Jacob her ID badge.

"Well, if you're free for dinner later, you know where to find me."

"I'm busy." Redirecting her attention to me, "Dr. Raj, did you confirm with him about any illnesses he has, or might have contracted, that can account for his weakened immune system?"

"Uhh, umm, I was …"

"WAIT … are you saying I'm sick with something else? Is that how I got this fungus infection?" Jacob cut me off and was angrily staring at Cindy.

"Well, I was speaking to Dr. Raj, but yes, that's what I'm saying. There were some lab tests we got back that indicate your immune system is not as healthy as your appearance would belie."

"What are you trying to say, Cindy?"

"It's Dr. Lee. What I'm saying is the infection you have in your brain typically occurs in people who are significantly immune-compromised, meaning in those with weakened immune systems. It can be due to many things such as genetic immunoglobulin abnormalities, cancer, previous organ transplantation, or AIDS."

He again started to get agitated. Sitting up and leaning slightly forward, the muscles in his jaw clenched and his eyes squinted ever so slightly. He did not like where this conversation was going. "Well, I'm the exception to the rule, none of those in this body," he said as he gave himself a very approving once over. "Does it look to you like I have a genetic problem?"

"Well on examination you don't have any of the scars that recipients of organ transplants usually have. However, that doesn't preclude any cancer for which you may be under treatment or infection with HIV."

"I don't take any meds. You already checked my piss, so you know what all I've used recently! I've been honest with Raj here, ask him. What *exactly* are you getting at, Missy?"

"I'd like to test you for HIV." I cringed as she said it. I'm sure Jacob wouldn't take nicely to being confronted so bluntly by a female. I was definitely starting to get male chauvinistic vibes from him.

"I don't have no HIV!" The too quick and overly emphatic reply implied that he had something to hide. Though technically he was right, given his low CD4 count and an opportunistic infection with *Crypto*, he had AIDS, not HIV, but I'm fairly sure that's not how he was thinking.

"Then you won't mind us testing you? With modern technology we can just take a small droplet of blood from your finger and have the results within 20 minutes. If we can exclude that condition, we can focus on other causes of why you have a fungus infecting your central nervous system and get you better that much faster."

Jacob was not taking kindly to Cindy's in your face style of doctoring. He was turning red with rage and repeatedly opening and closing his fists. He was used to being in the position of power and I don't think he liked the role reversal and feeling of impotence he was experiencing. His only options were to lash out or admit defeat.

"This is bullshit! I'm outta here, you can't keep me here against my will, and I *know* you cannot test me for HIV without my consent. Give me the AMA forms. I want to sign out of your nuthouse."

"Jacob, you seem to know a lot about hospital protocols for somebody who's supposedly so healthy with no medical problems. Care to tell me how you know that we can't test you for HIV or that you have to sign special forms if you wish to leave a hospital against a doctor's advice?"

"I know my rights. Besides it's all over the news about how health protection and anti-discrimination laws prevent testing for HIV and other genetic conditions without explicit written patient consent." Jacob said this smugly, clearly thinking the verbal jousting was now in his favor.

"I suspect that you already know what the results of your HIV test will show."

"Yeah, they'll be negative, Miss Lee."

"Interesting, given you have an extremely low CD4 count and a very elevated HIV viral load." I shuddered as she said it, fearing he might physically lash out at her. The New York style of patient care was much more confrontational than the laid back buddy-buddy California style.

"WHAT ... THE ... FUCK? You can't know that, I never said you could test me."

"We didn't test you for HIV. We simply counted specific blood cell types in your body and checked for replicating viral particles. Nowhere does it state that consent is needed for those tests. Especially from somebody who is found unconscious and almost dead upon arrival to the ER. We ordered those tests so we could save your life, which we did, might I add. You should be grateful we checked.

Otherwise your diagnosis might have been delayed and you'd be in the morgue instead of talking to us."

Jacob was livid. Standing ramrod straight right next to his IV poles which were infusing into him the very chemicals that were keeping him alive, he looked from the hanging IV bags to Cindy and then to me. I can only imagine what was going through his head. He had just been called out and proven to be a liar. Worse yet, Cindy wasn't done.

"Jacob, I know what you're thinking. You want to lash out against me because I spoke the truth. I'd strongly advise against that, not only because it will get you thrown in jail, which it will, faster than you can imagine, but also because we are here to help you. In order to help you we need honesty and cooperation. You seem like a bright guy, and with the right care you can live a long healthy life."

"I don't need your help; I was doing just fine on my own. Just treat this fucking infection and let me out of here. I have shit to take care of. You're just a doctor, you can't tell me what to do. Just do your job and quit preaching to me, you little bitch."

Wow, I'd never seen such insolence on the part of a patient before! But Cindy was nonplussed and took it in stride; she'd seemingly been down this road before.

"Listen Jacob, I've only treated you with respect and been forthright with you. I expect you to show me the respect that I deserve. However, it doesn't seem like that's going to happen, so let me lay it out for you. I believe you know about your HIV status, and if it turns out that is true, and you've been having unprotected sex with other individuals, male or female, without informing them of your infection, you are guilty of manslaughter and a slew of other charges that only a lawyer can tell you. I already know about the numbers on your cell phone. It won't be hard to get a court order to contact said individuals and ask them about their sexual relations with you and their knowledge, or lack thereof, about your condition."

That was my cue to grab Cindy and run out of Jacob's room. As the door was closing behind us I heard a loud crash. It was one his IV poles smashing into the door followed by a solid kick that must have dented the inner door of his room. As we ran out of the second door I intentionally kept it open. Doing so ensured the inner door leading into his room was locked. Because he was in an isolation room, both doors could never be open at the same time. One had to enter into the anteroom allowing the door through which he entered completely close before the other door unlocked and could be opened. Had I let the outer door close behind us, he'd have been able to exit and follow us in his rage.

The charge nurse saw what transpired and immediately called security. Two officers and Jack materialized within seconds and we explained to them what had just transpired. The security officers called for backup and conferred with Jack about what to do.

"Yeah, we'll need to let the attending know, but I think we should make sure the patient is calmed down before trying anything. Raj, good thinking on locking him in there. There's no knowing what he'd have done if he escaped. If he doesn't calm down I think we'll have to put him on a psych hold as a danger to others. Let's give him some sublingual Xanax and see if he relaxes a bit so that we can reason with him."

Security nodded their approval with Jack's plan. Jack turned to Cindy, "What the hell did you do to get him so agitated suddenly?"

Cindy, having composed herself stood her ground. "Well, I confronted him about his HIV status. He was clearly lying about his knowledge of his disease and wasting everyone's time. Worse, he knew he was infected and he's sleeping with unsuspecting people on a regular basis after giving them drugs to get them aroused." Turning to me, "Yeah, Raj, I heard a large part of your interview from the anteroom. You did a good job, but I couldn't stand to hear any more of that jerk talk about his 'Jacob Jr.'"

Jack looked at us with a look of approval if I wasn't mistaken. "Cindy, I'm the one with a rep for pissing off patients, but I think you might have just stripped me of my crown. I don't think you did anything wrong per se, and we did had the right to search his belongings, including his phone, when he was unconscious as part of our effort to save his life. When you testify, just say you were searching the phone for an emergency contact or next of kin, not for girlfriends.

"We still don't officially know if he has HIV. BUT, if we put him on a psych hold, he loses his rights and we can test him that way. If he turns out to be positive, and if we can prove he *knew* about his disease while he was fucking around without telling his partners about it, we'll have to get the police involved. I know just the detective to call. I'll get on it. You guys debrief Clyde; this *might* even get a reaction out of him."

We turned to leave and Jack called out to us as a passing thought, "Guys, make sure to document the hell out of everything on this case, its serious CYA time. This is going to get messy."

~~~~

Dr. Clyde was doing a lot of silent nodding as Cindy and I filled him in on what happened in the ICU conference room. He'd occasionally ask a question here and there, but he mostly just listened. He commented after our story was finished. "Well, we obviously can't go through his phone now. How do you know he has at least four girlfriends Raj?"

"Well, I just went to the 'favorites' section on his phone and there were four female names there. So I took a picture of them with my phone, along with their phone numbers. Most people keep important numbers under that heading. You know, like 'Home' or 'Mom' and typically a few best friends."

"So you don't know that they are his girlfriends per se. You just know there are four female names on his quick dial list? They could be red herrings, i.e.—he might refer to his mother or sister by their first names."

"Yes sir, Dr. Clyde." In all honesty, that thought had never crossed my mind, but was very rational of Clyde to conclude.

"Certainly we can say that going through his phone was required emergently in an effort to locate a contact that could provide further medical history critical to saving his life. Thus, looking through his phone is kosher. Also, there are two separate female nursing notes commenting on his rude and crass treatment towards them. That helps demonstrate his poor regard for both women and authority. Make sure you both document exactly what transpired this morning as well as his aggression when requested to comply with standard medical testing and care."

Dr. Clyde straightened up in his chair, stretched his arms, took off his glasses, rubbed his eyes, and threw his spectacles across the table. Staring hard into the distance at nothing in particular, he finally spoke, "Well, what we have here is a ... how do I put it? A mess."

After several moments of uncomfortable silence, Cindy was the first to break it, "Well, we didn't technically do anything wrong." I always find it amusing when even the nicest people refer to a situation with "I" when things go well and either "we, us, or team" when something is awry. One of the easiest ways to exude humility in medicine is to always use the third person—for both *good* and bad.

"No, nothing was wrong. Perhaps not handled as tactfully as possible, but we're not in violation of any laws or hospital rules. In fact we saved his life and his recovery has been fantastic, so that's the upside. The downside is this has become a very touchy case. He's likely to sue us for some cockamamie reason or other, either discrimination or maltreatment or God knows what else. The other, more pressing issue is that he's likely going to continue to infect other innocent people with HIV as soon as he gets out of here. It's definitely a gray area. We have to report cases of HIV/AIDS, but technically we don't have the diagnosis confirmed. The question is where to go from here?"

More awkward silence as we all pondered his question.

This time I broke the silence. "Why don't we get an ethics consult?"

"Yeah, that's a great idea." I was happy with Cindy's enthusiastic support.

"Normally I'd agree, but due to the economic downturn, that position was dissolved about a year ago."

So much for my brilliant idea. I figured I'd throw out another one. "Can't we just scare him into getting tested for HIV, or strong arm him somehow?"

"Well, from what you've both told me, he's too smart for that and knows his rights. He's demonstrated his knowledge of how to work the system in his favor. Also, fear is a poor motivator in medicine. Just look at the continued rates of smoking and obesity despite widespread public awareness of lung cancer and the risks associated with being overweight."

"Perhaps we can place him on a psychiatric hold and then test him?" Cindy added.

"I was thinking about that, Dr. Lee, but what are our grounds for placing him under a 5150 hold? We can't place him on a 5150 just because he got a little upset and ran at you two. We have patients threatening to attack staff and physicians all the time. Calling security is all a first time offense warrants unless there is any form of physical harm; in that case a patient simply goes to jail."

We were getting nowhere fast. Stuck in a limbo of stupid laws requiring us to heal someone who had no qualms about ruining the lives of others. That's when I noticed an ephemeral glint in Dr. Clyde's eyes. I knew he'd come up with something. I just didn't know what. He'd been doing this for decades, but the current situation seemed to stump even him. His next words were a testament to his brilliance, though I didn't realize it at the time.

"Well, I think perhaps we should all take a step back and let Jack handle this case for a while."

"But Dr. Clyde, I feel quite comfortable managing AIDS, and we had plenty of tough patients in New York ..."

"Thank you, Dr. Lee. I have no reservations about your knowledge, credentials, and ability; but I think given his aggression towards you and other females, it is safer if you allow Jack to assume care over Jacob beginning immediately. I'll be available for consultation should the team need my input; otherwise I think in Jacob's management, less is more. Thus, we need not formally round on him any longer."

"But ..." Cindy tried to argue, but the decision was clearly final.

"Thank you for your time and for informing me of this situation, Drs. Raj and Lee."

That concluded our meeting, and completely changed the course of events in Jacob's management.

~~~~

I ran into Cindy the next morning looking through Jacob's chart. "Hey, I thought you were off the case?"

"I am, but that doesn't mean I can't still follow what's going on. We're all on the same team after all. Actually, Dr. Clyde didn't say you were off the case. He just said that it was to be handled by Jack. My evaluation is shot to hell, but it doesn't mean that you can't still learn from Jacob. He's an interesting case, both medically and socially, plus you have the most rapport with him."

Great, just what I wanted, to have more work. Don't get me wrong, I don't mind learning, but I also don't mind going home earlier and having to see one less patient, especially a pain in the ass patient like Jacob. But of course I couldn't actually *say* that, it would mean my evaluation going to hell, too, and other unpleasantries such as not passing the rotation, getting a good residency, fellowship, job, etc. So of course I had to seem excited by agreeing with Cindy. But I also couldn't risk pissing off Jack or Clyde. "Sure I'd love to follow Jacob, but you heard Dr. Clyde; he's Jack's case now."

As if on cue, Jack entered the unit and bee-lined straight into Jacob's room.

"See that's what I like about you Rajen, always willing to do what it takes to learn. I'll talk to Jack and see if you can still follow Jacob. I'm sure he'll appreciate the help, and then you can keep me posted on his status."

"Uhh … sure, I'd love to help out. It's almost like a soap opera in how this is unfolding." Little did I know it would be more of a murder mystery soon enough.

"Sure is, that's why I love medicine, always interesting and unpredictable. Oh, here's Jack coming our way. I'll ask him if you can continue to follow this case so you don't have to ask."

Before I could thank her, though that was the last thing I wanted to do, she broke off and intercepted Jack.

"Hi, Cindy."

"Hey, Jack. I had a quick favor to ask of you."

Jack was busy scribbling in Jacob's chart, clearly trying to avoid doing any extra work or favors. But Cindy seemed oblivious to such subtle clues as Jack turning away from her, sitting down, and continuing to write. But she just stood there and quietly waited. Eventually he responded, "What's up?"

"I was wondering if Raj could still follow Jacob with you? After all Clyde said for me to be off the case, he never said anything about the med student. Also, Raj was the first one to see him in the ER and diagnose him. Plus he's built some good rapport which will be very helpful ..."

"Sure, no prob, I'll let Raj run point and I'll assist."

Convincing Jack was much easier than Cindy had anticipated.

"Hey Raj, why don't you come here and look over these orders with me, huh? Thanks for your concern Cindy; we'll keep you posted. See you at rounds."

Cindy nudged me as though we'd accomplished something great as I walked past her towards Jack. In reality all she accomplished was creating more work for me. Granted she was nice, but a bit clueless.

Jack tossed me the chart, "Look over these orders and meet me in the cafeteria. We'll discuss the details there. Don't bother with a physical exam; he's comatose."

I shuffled through the chart. Apparently after our little confrontation last night Jack was able to calm Jacob down enough so that he agreed to remain in the hospital and complete his treatment. Jacob also began to develop some tremors and was started on high-dose IV diazepam; that'd certainly explain why he was comatose. He also signed the consent form for his HIV testing which was drawn last night.

I was completely confused. Just yesterday Jacob was refusing to be tested for HIV while about to attack me and Cindy and storm out of the hospital with a life threatening infection. Now, by some miracle, Jack had convinced him to remain in the hospital for his treatment as well as agree to being tested for HIV. I clearly had a lot to learn about the art of medicine. Knowledge could get you but so far, there was no substitute for human interaction, or manipulation, as I soon learned.

"So what'd you think?" Jack asked before I could even sit down with my bagel in our secluded corner booth of the cafeteria.

"About what?"

"Raj, you're not an idiot, don't beat around the bush with me. About Jacob, who else?"

"Oh, well, I guess after you gave him some time to calm down, you were able to reason with him and get him to agree with getting tested for HIV. I noticed you started him on IV Valium. I presume that was for alcohol withdrawal? The timing makes sense, it's been about 72 hours or so since he was admitted to the hospital, assuming he hasn't drank since he's been here; this is when an alcoholic would be expected to start withdrawing. I'd say you caught the withdrawal early, potentially saving his life."

"And how did you put that little story together?"

"Well, we know how he almost attacked us yesterday; security was called. He was notified that if he kept up this behavior he'd be placed on a psychiatric hold under which he would lose his rights and be tested for HIV regardless of this wishes.

"After hearing that he must have calmed down, allowing you to talk some sense into him. Clearly logic and reason prevailed. The alcohol withdrawal was likely coincidental, but good thing you noticed it, instead of whoever was on call. Besides, it's all consistent with his presentation; he's a drug addict who was way drunk when he came in, so a history of alcoholism is not surprising."

"And you'd swear to that under oath?"

"What are you getting at?"

"It was a simple question."

"Uh ... yeah, I guess. It's the truth and all documented after all, doesn't take a rocket scientist to figure it out."

"Are you pro-life or pro-choice?"

"Pro-choice, but what does that have to do with Jacob?"

Ignoring my question Jack continued his questioning. "Are you familiar with the trolley thought experiment?"

"Yeah, the one where you're in a position to pull a lever which changes the track a trolley is on? If you don't pull the lever the trolley runs over a family of four killing them all. But if you do pull the lever only a single individual is run over and killed. Basically a question of sacrificing one to save many and the dilemma of whether the failure to make a decision is the same as being proactive?"

"That's the one. So, if it was you, would you pull the lever to save the family?"

"Sure."

"Ok, tougher situation. What if you have nice gentleman who you've known professionally for some time with end stage cancer with metastasis to bone. You *know* that shit hurts like a mother. Say he used to be an active guy with a great family, but over the last couple years of chemo and radiation he's pooped out and always in pain. He's so weak that he's essentially immobile, and not anything close to the vivacious character he used to be. In essence he's already dead, but technically he's alive and in constant pain, so much so that he's unable to do anything he used to find joy in.

"Understand that his family still takes excellent care of him, but he's gone from being breadwinner and head of household to completely dependent and occasionally incontinent. He's told you in complete lucid candor on more than one occasion that he wishes to die. He's at peace with himself and has led a good life. What do you do?"

"Well I'd offer hospice or palliative care options, either in home or at a skilled care facility."

"Raj, do I look like a dung beetle? Cause you're feeding me a lot of shit. Do you help this nice gentleman commit suicide or not? He's not going to a home or anything else; he has a great family. He feels like a burden on them and you know for a fact that he's only going to get worse with time."

"Then in a word, yes, I'd help him." I instantly thought of Duane Little.

"You know that committing suicide, or assisting one to commit suicide, is a criminal offense?"

Finally I saw where Jack was going with all this ... he wanted to feel me out before he let me in on some kind of secret. I bet it had to do with Jacob.

I have to admit he piqued my curiosity and I wanted to know more, so I played along.

"Well, two things then, there's the issue of getting caught, which can easily be avoided, and the second is whether it is actually assisting in one's suicide," I said, my turn to be vague.

"What do you mean about actually assisting in suicide?"

"Well, suppose the aforementioned gentleman has signed a DNR form; that clearly means that if he stops breathing our hands are tied per his request. That document is perfectly legal. Now suppose his pain is so severe that very high doses of narcotic medications are required for alleviation of his pain. Such high doses, in fact, that his breathing is arrested before his pain is controlled. That way he legally gets what he wants."

"But if it's still you giving the medication, aren't you technically a murderer then?"

"Fine, put him on a PCA pump and let him push the button to keep increasing his medication dose until he is either comfortable or stops breathing. That way both the choice and action is his, and we are only carrying out his wish for no resuscitation."

"BINGO! That's thinking outside the box! More importantly, it's perfectly legal. Not bad for a third year med student."

"I get the feeling this was some type of test?"

"Let's just say you passed."

I stared at Jack quizzically. He continued, "Raj, there are good doctors and nice doctors. You're destined to be a great doctor. You've shown that you can make the tough decisions and stick to your guns. Your answers are definitive and your thinking is both clear and logical."

Jack continued, "I know you like Cindy, but she's the proverbial 'nice' doctor. Meaning she's warm and fuzzy and patients are going to like her personality. She's more interested in where a patient went for vacation and how their family is doing, rather than making the tough decisions specialists are paid to make.

"Don't get me wrong, she's a great person and very competent, but she's definitely the primary care type. She gets too emotionally attached to patients and takes things too personally.

"You have to remember that *patients are not your friends!* Nor is your goal to befriend them. Patients are simply *not* meant to be your friends. You are a professional and they are seeking your services, expertise, and opinion in a time of need—nothing more."

I just nodded until Jack was done, and then asked, "That's fine and all, but how does this all relate to Jacob?"

"Always cutting to the chase, another sign of a specialist. That's where I was headed with all this. Clyde basically put me in charge of Jacob's care because it's a sticky situation with no easy answer or way out. He needs somebody who is not afraid to do what needs to be done to get some results. Consider this case your initiation into one of the unspoken realms of medicine, except I'll openly discuss it with you. Of course if you mention it to anyone else, I'll deny it."

I wasn't sure if I liked what I was hearing, but I was definitely fascinated about yet another subculture of medicine. It felt like politics, where what is stated is not necessarily what was actually said.

Jack continued, "So what actually happened last night was that Jacob was acting completely immature and hostile. Annoying maybe, but nothing for which we could have *actually* placed him on a 5150 hold. Our threats to do so were empty and unfounded.

"So it was either let him leave the hospital AMA and infect other innocent people and ruin their lives like a serial killer, or think outside the box. I noticed, in his fit of rage, a twitch in his leg. Given his documented substance abuse history and elevated liver enzymes, I deduced he might have been withdrawing from alcohol. Thus, I started him on IV Valium. While the Valium was kicking in and he was in la-la land, I snuck a consent form under his pen and told him to sign for HIV testing. He readily agreed. Of course he'd have agreed to live on Mars at that time too, but that wasn't what I asked. And if you look clearly at the times on the notes, the consent was signed a full 15 minutes *before* the Valium was administered. Again, it's all about what's documented; what really happened is irrelevant."

I wasn't sure how to respond. There was something so wrong with using power like that to coerce somebody into doing something they didn't want. It was not unlike using GHB as a date rape drug or sodium amytal as a truth serum to obtain information via enhanced interrogation techniques.

"It's going to take some time to get your head around this new way of thinking and patient management, but you'll learn. After all, the story you told me earlier is what the chart indicates occurred. What I just confided in you now was what actually transpired. Of course, if you tell anyone there's no way to prove your story. And just FYI, keep in mind that it's illegal to record conversations about patient care unless you have a court order prior to the time of recording."

I just stared blankly, trying to process what I'd been told. My immediate interpretation was that medical charts are not necessarily what they appear to be. Sure there is a lot of documentation, but there's a lot that goes on in between the lines.

"Think of it this way Raj, if we'd let Jacob walk out last night, he'd call up one of his girls and have unprotected sex or share drug needles with her. She'd be unaware that she's infected and the cycle would just repeat. More and more people will become infected all BECAUSE Jacob is aware of his condition but REFUSES to notify sexual partners as *required* by law.

"So you tell me who's the good and who's the bad guy in this scenario?"

He went on, "That's why Clyde put me as lead on this case. He knows I can get things done that most others have a very hard time with. He also doesn't want to be involved because of liability reasons … the joys of academic medicine. As residents we're totally protected by virtue of our training status and humongous malpractice insurance. So he'll support us to an extent, but try not to ask him too many questions. You'll just end up getting answers you might not want."

My brain was in information overload mode; I couldn't grasp what was happening. Jack seemed to realize this and started on his breakfast, allowing my brain some time to process. Eventually my dendrites and neurons rebooted and I could again form a thought.

Essentially we were taking care of a potential murderer who was more than happy to leave the hospital and continue on with his life, not caring for the lives of others. On the other hand, he *might* not know he was a murderer if he didn't know he had HIV. Also, what if he never actually infected anybody else? We were making a lot of assumptions without data to back up our conclusions. We were basing our opinions of Jacob on emotions, not from objective data.

Once I formulated my thoughts I summarized them for Jack.

"That's why I like you Raj, you're practical. I agree with you 100% … while we're pretty sure he knows that he has HIV or AIDS, we aren't certain. Thanks to his consent, *we* now know of his diagnosis."

"How does that help us?"

"In many ways. We have to report it to public health authorities and they might question his sexual partners. However, if he doesn't volunteer contact information about his partners, there's nothing further we can do. Also, if he infects any further individuals going forward without telling them of his disease status, that's certainly

grounds upon which to take legal action. But that'd require us to follow him at all times, not very practical."

"I don't know about the future, but what about the people he
already infected? He's so smug about it."

"Whoa, hold up there. You're being emotional now. What people? Do you know of any? I sure don't."

"Well, there were those four numbers in his phone. Can't we just
call them and ask them if they knew he had AIDS or have been
tested?"

"Sure you can, if you want to go to jail."

"Huh?"

"You can't just call up somebody's contacts without their consent or look through their personal belongings without the appropriate search warrants or psychiatric hold."

"Great, the 5150 again. Why don't we just put him under hold
and call them up?"

"Dude, you're going in circles here. No reason to put him on a
psych hold."

"Fan-fucking-tastic! So basically our job is to help him get better
and let him go so he can do whatever the hell he wants, and he's off
the hook? All he has to do is notify future sexual partners of his HIV
and he gets a free pass for all his previous infractions? He's not
responsible for the lives he knowingly destroyed?"

"Pretty much." He said it so simply that I knew there must be
more. "He might not have known in the past. All we can do is document we told him during this hospitalization. Innocent until proven
guilty remember? Been a law for hundreds of years."

"But … there's gotta … I mean …" I wanted to say something
else, but I was at a loss. Wasn't involuntary manslaughter a charge? I
guess the girls on his phone would have had to have died of HIV,
and somehow it'd have to be proven that they were knowingly
infected by Jacob. That was nearly impossible.

"This sucks." My brilliant conclusion sounded pretty lame, especially when said out loud.

Jack leaned in closer; there was a glint in his eyes. He lowered his voice to a conspiratorial tone, "Well, if you're interested, there is something we can do."

Ah ha, this was it! I knew there was more than meets the eye.

Of course I was now committed after he whet my appetite. But I didn't want Jack to think I was too eager, so I tried to play it cool, "What do you mean?"

"Well, remember how I said Clyde had me take over this case 'cause I get things done. Well, I'm proposing you help me take care of this case, if you're up for it. Otherwise you can back out now and plead the fifth should anything happen or anyone question you."

I didn't like the sound of that, but curiosity had already won me over. I knew it was likely an emotional response, but I figured, worst case scenario, I could always plead I was a med student. I didn't have a medical license or anything else to lose.

"I'm in."

"Well, you know how I said we can't call the numbers on Jacob's phone now that he's alert and oriented?"

"Yeah."

"Well, I already called all four of them when he was in the ER. I left messages saying that his life was imminently in danger and they all called back. So now that the lines of communication are open, all we have to do is convince them to get tested for HIV. If they're positive I'm sure it won't be hard to professionally imply that recent sexual contact might have caused their infection. They will naturally assume it's Jacob and he'll be cornered."

I was taken aback by Jack's foresight and how he'd taken the initiative to call the numbers I'd retrieved. And thus, our plan to fight fire with fire was born.

~~~~

"How'd it go?" I asked Jack.

"Well, he was pretty pissed that I tested him for HIV and even more pissed that his test came back positive, though he wasn't surprised—just angry. Of course he calmed down when I showed him his signature on the consent form."

"Guess he couldn't argue that, huh?"

"He claimed it was forged, but I showed him the witness signature, date, and time. He said he didn't remember signing, but I simply countered that he didn't remember coming to the ER either. That shut him up. Pretty easy. How about you, any luck?"

"Definitely. I followed up with all four 'girlfriends' that you'd called earlier. Since then they have all called Jacob and he's refused to allow any to visit. But I planted the seed that they might have some kind of infection due to their recent close contact with him. I was very vague just like we rehearsed. They are all coming in this week for a full physical exam. I placed them all in different clinics; I figured it'd look suspicious if they all saw you. They'll be sure to get tested for HIV and other sexually transmitted diseases."

"Nice work."

"Dr. Flanders," one of the nurses shouted out. "Isolation room two is complaining of chest pain and shortness of breath."

We looked at each other and both rolled up our eyes. Jack said, "Why don't you help out Cindy and I'll take care of our friend. She's on call tonight so I want her to get done with her work so she can catch a few winks before the pain begins."

Who was I to argue with that decision? Cindy was just finishing up her notes for the evening when I came by. Even in scrubs and after a 12 hour day she still had a vitality that was infectious.

"Anything I can help with?"

"Oh, hey, Raj. Sure, I could use some company for dinner, if you got the time?"

Gee, that was a hard question. Though I might have blushed. "I'm all yours." Now I definitely blushed at my stupid response and rushed to try to cover it up. "We better hurry; the cafeteria closes in like five minutes."

"I was thinking we could leave the hospital for a bite. The ICU is completely full, so we don't have much to worry about acutely."

I liked what I was hearing, and we were off to a delicious dinner at the gourmet Subway down the street.

It was nice to chat about topics other than medicine for a while. We covered recent movies, celebrity sightings, hiking trails, and favorite foods. We were just taking our last bites as Cindy's pager went off. "Good timing, at least we made it through dinner."

I couldn't quite make out the whole conversation she was having due to the traffic noise as we were walking back to the hospital, but it sounded like Jack giving her an update on Jacob.

"Well, it appears as though your first HIV case just got more interesting. I guess you know that Jack somehow got him to agree to HIV testing, quite impressive how he got that done. Anyhow, he just became febrile with chest pain and shortness of breath. Jack thinks he might have some sort of bacterial sepsis and perhaps pneumonia—not surprising given how low his CD4 count was. The chest pain is probably just from some pleurisy; it got better with IV Toradol and his initial cardiac enzymes were negative."

"Why didn't we catch that earlier?"

"Well, he probably had a low grade PCP when he was admitted and the steroids that he was placed on to treat his brain swelling caused it to get worse. No big deal, we'll just start him on some appropriate antibiotics and get a chest x-ray. The chest pain is likely nothing, but given his young age, we'll stop feeding him and get him a cardiac catheterization tomorrow if his enzymes bump up. The fever is concerning; he must have something active going on for his limited immune system to get all riled up."

"Wow, you sure know your AIDS." Not the best line to use on a girl to express your interest in her. Luckily she wasn't offended by the comment.

"We saw a lot of it in New York. What pisses me off is that all this testing costs a ton of money, and Jacob wasn't the least bit appreciative. Has he been better lately?"

"Not really, he was pissed off about the HIV results and hasn't been allowing any of his 'girlfriends' to come visit."

"He's just an unhappy person, but, then again, he's going through a lot." She didn't know the half of what he was about to go through, I thought to myself. She continued, "Why don't you talk to him about our plan of getting blood cultures and treating his pneumonia? I'll go write the orders."

I entered Jacob's room after donning my cap, gown, gloves, and mask, even more important now that he had a suspected pneumonia. My guess was that he had acquired a MRSA infection either due to an abrasion from falling down in the dirty West Hollywood streets or from the hospital itself, where the bacteria was ubiquitous. While I had hoped that my last patient with MRSA did well, I had no such kind thoughts about Jacob.

Duane, my last patient with MRSA, was still in the hospital a full three months after he had a terrible MRSA infection and developed a horrific complication from the treatment in which his skin literally peeled off. I hadn't checked up on him in a while and added it to my list of things to do.

"Knock knock," I verbally announced to indicate my presence.

"What do you want now?" grumbled a voice from under the covers. His tone indicating he didn't want to be bothered.

"Hi Jacob, Raj here, remember me from the other day? Jack went home for the night and I just wanted to let you know what the plan was."

He removed the cover from his head and I saw that his whole face was glistening with sweat. The monitor beeped and informed me that his temperature was close to 102°F, and his breathing a bit shallow with poor oxygen saturation for somebody who was supposed to be getting better. In a nutshell, Jacob was one sick cookie and about to go downhill fast if we didn't do something.

He looked a little paler than when I had last seen him. His hair was matted down with a combination of grease and perspiration. But he still wanted to be anywhere than here. "I'm betting you're going to steal some more of my blood and tell me I still can't go home?"

"If you mean take a sample of your blood for laboratory evaluation in an effort to help you get better, yes." Not even a vampire would want to suck his blood given all the pathogens having a party in his circulatory system.

"Whatever man, not like you guys care what I think or want." He was starting to get under my skin; he still had no appreciation for anybody else other than Jacob. I took a breath and calmed myself; there was no point in letting him get to me. That was his goal after all. I just had to keep reminding myself of that and remain professional.

"I see you haven't eaten your dinner. It might be a good idea to eat some of it now because I'm going to have to keep you NPO after midnight tonight. We might have to perform a cardiac catheterization tomorrow morning to make sure your chest pain wasn't caused by something serious, like a heart attack."

"If I wanted to eat my food, I would have eaten it. In fact why don't you take it with you on your way out?"

I wanted to remind him that was housekeeping's job, but I bit my tongue. "Sure, no problem, we're going to get those blood samples and X-rays, and start you on another couple antibiotics—Vancomycin and Bactrim—they can be toxic to your kidneys so I'm going to increase your IV fluids." I was very well acquainted with how life threatening Bactrim could be.

"Yeah, yeah. Also, tell them to stop transferring calls to my room. Just take down the messages and read them to me when you get back." He buried his head in his sheets, indicating our conversation was over.

Another deep breath and I left his room carrying out his uneaten dinner tray.

I touched base with Cindy and since all was quiet we retreated to the lounge to grab a snack and chill out until we were paged. Amazingly there were no pages that night, allowing Cindy to be well rested for the worst morning of her life.

~~~~

Because it was Jack's day off, Cindy and I were in charge of Jacob. Given we already had a plan that Jack approved of, we didn't mention anything about him to Clyde on rounds.

"Dr. Lee, isolation room 2 is complaining of being hungry again." Announced one of the nurses who saw us nearby working on some orders.

"Well, his repeat cardiac enzymes were elevated, so he'll need a cardiac cath today. Do you know when his cath is scheduled for? Wasn't it supposed to be early this morning?" Cindy asked the nurse.

"Yeah, it was, but there were three code whites. All three cath labs are open and are running way behind, they had to cancel all routine stuff. The cardiologists reviewed his EKG and because it didn't have any acute changes he won't be able to go until sometime early this afternoon."

"Raj, would you mind telling him?"

"No problemo, I'll notify him about the delay."

I entered Jacob's room to find him sitting up in bed and looking annoyed while furiously surfing through channels. It's impressive how the hospital affords extended cable service and flat screen HD televisions for ICU patients. Yet that still wasn't enough to please Jacob. As soon as I entered he barked, "Why the hell are you starving me?!"

I wanted to counter that he brilliantly refused his meal last night after my advice to eat up. But he did look quite ill last night. In fact, he looked significantly better this morning; much of his color had returned and he was no longer sweating. I figured his improvement in health had reminded him of his empty stomach.

"Sorry about that, Jacob, there were some emergent cases that required immediate attention and your procedure has been delayed …"

"So that's what it is, huh? Skipping over me because you don't take my symptoms seriously?"

"That's not it at all; we take your symptoms very seriously. Hence we got you scheduled immediately."

"Harrumph … some immediate. You guys are the worst businessmen; can't even keep an appointment. If you were my clients I'd fire you."

Oh believe me, the whole ICU staff wanted to fire him.

"Well, we're in the business of saving lives, and the fact that you're talking to me and asking for food is a testament to the excellent job we've done. Left to your own vices, you'd have died a few nights ago when you partied too hard."

"Hey, fuck you, man! You're just doing your job. Don't patronize me by pretending you care. Go check how much longer the wait is for my cath. And while you're at it, tell the nurse I want my bed made and a new hospital gown."

The nerve he had. I didn't say anything else and snuck out to report back to Cindy.

There wasn't much else we could do; he was inconsolable and unreasonable. I mentioned sedating him until his procedure. That's what Jack would have done, but Cindy was absolutely against it, stating that there was no medical reason.

Apparently, maintaining our sanity didn't count as a good enough reason. I figured his sedation would prevent the headaches everyone taking care of him would suffer from his attitude. But that was not a 'medically indicated' reason for sedation.

It was a particularly busy day in the ER, and another two emergent code whites came in before Jacob could be catheterized. He was getting increasingly agitated as the hours passed. By early afternoon he had called the nursing station over a dozen times, initially demanding updates and later cursing at the staff about their incompetence.

The charge nurse eventually paged Cindy, after the second time she was cussed out, asking for advice on how to manage Jacob's uncivilized and now potentially threatening behavior.

Cindy gave me a quick update and I immediately thought about how Jack would handle the situation. Instead of attempting further reasoning, he'd just call risk management and notify them of the situation. That way it'd be documented and become somebody else's problem. Thus, that's what I mentioned as a proposed plan of action.

It was quickly vetoed.

Cindy asserted that she could 'polite yet sternly' inform Jacob about the delay and calm him down.

"Wouldn't Valium or Xanax be easier and safer?" I asked.

She gently punched my arm, "You're so cute." I didn't mind the flirtatious contact, but she clearly didn't take my suggestion seriously. Thus, I pressed forward, "No, I'm serious."

"I don't think that's necessary. He's just a little hungry, apprehensive, and tired of waiting."

"Precisely what Xanax will help with, no? Besides, he was using profanity with the staff; that's not our responsibility to deal with. We should just notify the legal team about his inappropriate behavior. Maybe they can sue him," I joked.

"Come on, Raj, back in the day docs dealt with all this stuff. It shouldn't be a problem."

I quit arguing knowing I'd lost. But I definitely saw what Jack meant about Cindy wanting to befriend patients. Perhaps she was overly eager to compensate since her initial interaction with Jacob was rather unfavorable. I just backed off and let hear lead the charge.

"Let's go talk to him. We can go together."

I shrugged and gowned up to talk to Jacob for the fourth time that day. Freaking twenty dollars spent on just me seeing Jacob today. This time he was more agitated—the medical way of saying 'pissed off.'

Cindy took point, and immediately she made the fatal flaw of starting off with an apology, giving Jacob the upper ground right off the bat. "I'm sorry for the delay, but there have been a lot of emergencies today. You are next on the schedule. It shouldn't be too long now."

"NOW! My procedure has been delayed for over seven hours! I was scheduled for 8 a.m. It's after 3 p.m. now. What kind of a joke are you running here? Starving me on top of everything. This is bullshit."

"There is no reason to be angry. We have kept you updated and even changed your sheets and given you a new gown as you requested. We have been nothing but professional and your rude treatment of the staff is …"

"My rude treatment? Have you looked at your staff?? They are a bunch of fat fucks. They should be the ones dieting, not me! Why don't you keep them NPO? They could stand to lose a few pounds. Instead you starve me so you can watch and laugh at my suffering."

"I assure you it's nothing like that. We are doing our best to ensure you get better. The fact that your fever is reduced and your energy improved is proof that we're making progress."

"Why the hell are you here, anyway? Where's the other doc? He's smart; he's the one who started me on these medications. You're just taking his credit." I could sense that Cindy's resolve was fading and emotions were taking over. Not a good sign, we needed to exit his room STAT.

Jacob was just trying to get a reaction, and Cindy was about to give it to him.

"Jacob, this is your last warning, I need you to calm down or I'll …"

"Or you'll *what*?" He slammed his palm into the wall for emphasis. "Nothing is what you'll do." Jacob was feeling empowered now, feeding off the fact that Cindy was powerless and throwing empty threats in his direction. "Just like you've done nothing all day. You don't need an MD to starve people; you can just go to Somalia and stare at all the hungry people you want if that's what gets your rocks off."

Oh boy, this was not a good situation.

Cindy was turning red with anger. That was my signal to get the hell out of there. I grabbed her arm and dragged her out of the room. I pantomimed a phone and mouthed 'risk management' to the charge nurse. She took my hint and began to dial.

A small group had gathered as we stormed over to the central work area. Cindy ripped off her mask and threw it down. "Can you believe him?! I was just trying to reassure him and explain … and he cussed me out and told me to go to Somalia! The nerve."

"Hon, you don't need to be dealing with that," one of the nurses said. "You're a professional not a punching bag. Just let him go home and have his MI there while he's too strung out to call 911." Nods and mumblings of approval followed.

"Sir, you cannot be here, please shut that door immediately!" We all turned to see a respiratory therapist rushing over to where Jacob was walking out of the second door of his isolation pod and entering the common area.

This is where Cindy and I vastly differed.

I grabbed the nearest phone and dialed security.

She rushed over to try and confront Jacob.

"Jacob, please return to your room, *now!*" She shouted as she rushed over.

Time seemed to slow down for what happened next.

Jacob grabbed his IV pole and slammed it to the ground. Next he ripped out the large IV going into his hand and flung it to the side. A huge gush of blood escaped forming a large arc of deadly red droplets in front of Jacob. The problem was Cindy was in the center of the arc and it splashed across her face, in both her eyes, and into her open mouth as she screamed in response to the incoming blood. She fell to the ground in an effort to duck, but it was too late. The blood had already made contact.

I suddenly had a flashback to Dr. Dan from the ER when we admitted Jacob. I made a mental note to notify him of Jacob's HIV status. But I recall he was well covered and shouldn't have gotten any splatter on his actual person like Cindy just did.

Thank God, I still had on my mask with eye shield. I rushed over to Cindy's side and pulled her back to the work station. Jacob stood there with blood dripping from his hand as everybody backed away.

He was a walking biological weapon that could erupt again at any moment.

The scene was surreal, like a showdown in the Wild West. But instead of a gun there was a stream of blood dripping from his hand. Before he had a chance to draw and splatter anyone else with a stream of blood, security and risk management burst into the unit.

It was the first time I'd seen a firearm drawn and pointed towards a patient. Only, it wasn't a firearm, it was a Taser, and there was no hesitation like you see in the movies. The officer didn't ask him to raise his arms or get on his knees; he just took in the scene and shouted for everybody to get back ... then he fired.

Two small metal darts with wire tails buried themselves in Jacob's chest. He looked down, but before he could comprehend what was happening, I heard the sizzle of electric current which instantly caused all of Jacob's muscles to contract simultaneously. His eyes rolled up in his head and he fell forward, hitting the ground with a dull thud.

Once the threat was neutralized, everybody rushed over to Cindy to ensure she was OK.

She wasn't.

Cindy was a mess the rest of the day between emotional duress and the myriad of testing performed by employee health services. It's no surprise she didn't come to work the next day.

I hazarded a phone call to her despite Jack's advice to let her recover; he'd heard that she wasn't taking anyone's calls.

She took my call and I consoled her for 45 minutes through several episodes of sobs and silence. I did my best to reassure her. But she was extremely distraught over how she got a mouth and both eyes full of highly contagious HIV infected blood. Which makes sense; I'd certainly be unhappy about it too.

We both knew the risk of infection was somewhere in the range of about 1/100, or less, that she actually contracted the virus. But the disquieting thing was that his viral load was so high. Thus, even a tiny amount of his blood would harbor many more infectious and virulent HIV particles than somebody who was well treated. Therefore, we estimated her risk to be somewhere about 10%, worst case scenario. Unfortunately, a medical literature search revealed that HIV infection through infected fluid-eye contact had been reported to cause infection in previously HIV negative individuals.

What affected her most was that she would not know if she was positive or not for a full 6-8 weeks and would have to take prophylactic HAART medications during that time of uncertainty.

The Chief of the hospital and CEO granted her as much time off as she needed without any penalty of being held back. It was a small consolation. Or at least I thought of it that way—Cindy not so much.

Jack came up to me later in the afternoon, "Where were you? You called Cindy, huh? She answer? What's going on?"

I filled him in and he nodded in silence. Then he looked up as though he had an epiphany, "Oh, I almost forgot to tell you, all of Jacob's 'girlfriends' showed up to their appointments and got tested for HIV. They were pissed at why we were testing them out of the blue; supposedly they were all in a monogamous relationship with him … fucking jerk."

"Do we know the results yet?"

"I put them in as routine, so as not to arouse suspicion with STAT requests. Results will be in tomorrow, though I talked to Drs. Donner and Blake, they both said the girls were already starting to point fingers at Jacob. They all know of his hospitalization and are very upset at why he hasn't been returning their calls. Naturally they assume he has something to hide. And being called in for testing of infectious diseases only heightened their suspicions."

"We should just tell them about Jacob."

"OH we will," Jack confided in me as he put his arm around my neck and walked me out of the ICU. "You want to continue to help me in Jacob's management?" He whispered once we were outside and halfway down the long hallway.

I figured his statement had multiple meanings, but I wanted nothing good to happen to Jacob, and didn't mind being involved if I could help retaliate for what he did to Cindy. "I'm in."

"My boy! You realize what I'm talking about right?"

"Uhh ... I guess we still have to treat the jerk and get him out of here ASAP."

"You are right on both accounts, we must treat him and get him out ... but there is nobody to dictate how we treat him. And last I checked 'mistreat' contains the word 'treat.' And when you say get him out; I hear any way possible, including the ninth floor."

The ninth floor was a joke among medical professionals here because the hospital only had eight actual floors. Thus, the ninth floor came to mean discharge to the powers that be, resulting in the body being taken to the morgue in the basement.

I admit I should have been appalled, but I liked where Jack was going. Technically, he was also right. We'd still treat Jacob and get him out of the ICU, just not in the conventional way of thinking.

"So, what's our new treatment plan?"

"Well, it's complicated, but I already got the ball rolling. His recent culture results show MRSA bacteremia. Bad, but I went down to the lab and had his sample re-evaluated; there was also a gram negative bug that showed up. Strange how that happened, the microbiologist was sure it wasn't there before, but added an addendum to his report. Translation, Jacob needs another antibiotic."

"Gentamicin?"

"Bingo, you're good at this game. So yeah, we add that to his regimen. Now he's on three *highly* nephrotoxic drugs: Gentamycin, Vancomycin, and Amphotericin B, but needs them all to survive. The Gentamicin will also make him deaf if it's not dosed right."

"But the pharmacy doses his meds; they're super anal about peak and trough levels."

"True, but they don't personally draw the blood with which levels are calculated. All we do is start drawing the blood ourselves. It's easy; we draw from his PICC line when the infusion fluid is going in full tilt."

"Clever. The specimen is already diluted and we can still document it was drawn through the same line as all his other specimens."

"Nobody has to know that the fluid infusion was not shut off at the time of the lab draw. Besides, it's just assumed that it was done," Jacob winked.

"Even if his kidneys are shot in a matter of one or two days, that's not a big deal is it? Won't they just put him on dialysis? And isn't toxicity from Amphotericin B pretty easy to notice?"

"I think I saw him twitch again; bet his alcohol withdrawal is coming back. We gotta put him on high dose Valium again. His stupor and somnolence will hide most of the acute toxicities."

I still wasn't in love with the plan and voiced my concerns, "Worst case scenario he ends up deaf and on dialysis. Now he's a huge drain on society, but can still live for years on end. Though I doubt he'll get a kidney transplant given his history of drug abuse." I wasn't convinced Jack's plan was a good one.

"You're right, so that's where we come in ... this next part is a bit shady, and I need your word that you won't tell anyone."

I didn't like where this was going. I think Jack was making the transition from more passive to active infringement on Jacob's life. On the other hand, Jacob actively decided that the girls he infected were not deserving of a full and disease-free life. That thought, along with Cindy sobbing on the phone, triggered my decision to join Jack to the end. "I'm in, I promise."

"You're a rare find, Raj. Ok, here's how it goes down. We're both on call tomorrow. We tank him up with all his meds today and tonight, and then draw the diluted blood specimens for the lab ourselves. Tomorrow, when we're on call, we push a shitload of steroids into his system. That, in addition to his other anti-infective medications, will cause his potassium levels to plummet, sending him into cardiac arrhythmia."

I sighed, "But a code team will respond immediately, identify the problem, and resuscitate him."

"Who's the leader on the code team tomorrow night?"

I finally got it; Jack was brilliant. "You are."

"Bingo."

"You're scary. Even if they do an autopsy, they'd expect to find steroids and all the drugs in his body anyhow. Checking levels for most drugs will be useless given all the medications pumped into him during his Code Blue. It'll be an open and closed case, his cause of death will simply be reported as due to AIDS related complications and cardiac arrest."

"Not to mention his history of drug use. Just another junkie biting the dust. He should have never fucked with us. Just should have been a good patient and allowed us to fix him up. But he's getting what he deserves, just without the hassle of a judge and jury."

"We're essentially saving the taxpayers hundreds of thousands of dollars."

And so I rationalized the demise of Jacob. To us he was getting what he deserved. He knowingly put the lives of five girls at risk of AIDS and likely countless others who we just didn't know about. He had no remorse or guilt over what he did. Why should we think twice about our plan? Yet, I thought over it several times and feared my actions tomorrow would haunt me for years to come.

I wanted to say that it was difficult and highly risky to carry out Jack's plan, but the reality was that it was a piece of cake. Everybody in the ICU wanted Jacob dead, and we were just carrying out their unstated wishes.

That day both Jack and I stayed late and made sure we over-dosed him on all his medications as we'd planned. We drew the labs ourselves. Just as we thought, the pharmacist was concerned that the levels were way too low and increased his doses. About midnight his labs were due again after the dose increases. We just happened to still be around the hospital and were nice enough to allow the nurse taking care of him to take a break while we kindly drew his labs while checking up on him.

Jacob was more than happy to comply. He was so sedated on Valium that he could barely open his eyes, much less respond to our questions.

An astute pharmacist would have noticed the medication levels were way too low at about 4 a.m. when we were home, but we prevented this by writing so many 'pharmacy to dose' orders on our other ICU patients that the pharmacist was overwhelmed and unable to check levels until we arrived at the hospital at 5:30 a.m.

The covering resident was relieved to run into Jack, "Oh wow, you're here early."

Jack said, "I couldn't sleep and thought I'd round before breakfast; everything ok?"

"Not really, your isolation patient's Vancomycin and Gentamicin levels are sub-theraputic despite high doses."

"Really? That's strange. I'll take it from here and look into it."

"Thanks, man, nothing else overnight."

I sighed, not realizing I'd been holding my breath. This was too easy; nobody was even suspicious of anything. Only I seemed to think this strange. Jack seemed totally relaxed, like he'd done this many times before.

We walked into Jacob's room and Jack yelled out, "Hey DUMBFUCK, you still with us you piece of shit?!"

No response.

Jack turned to me, "Well, I guess he's still a bit sedated from treatment for his alcohol withdrawal."

I looked at Jacob's urinary catheter; the fluid was dark brown and there was almost no urine production overnight. Jack saw me looking and commented, "Yep, his kidney's are shot. I doubt they are working but five percent of what they should; he's gotten enough drugs to shut down the kidneys of three people."

With that we left Jacob's room and allowed the pharmacy to further up the doses for all his antibiotic medications.

I followed Jack into the call room and saw him place a tourni-quet on his arm and jab a needle into a large bulging vein! "What the hell are you doing?" I asked.

"Getting Jacob's morning labs." He looked at me like I was a retard. "Why do you think I asked you to come in this early? We have to prove his kidney function is normal, so I'll send down my blood in his chemistry tube. Lucky for us, different tubes are required for all the various tests he needs. The other tests can be his real blood. But my blood will indicate his kidneys are functioning just fine."

Wow, it was that easy to fake blood results for a patient? Just send down any random tube of blood with the correct label and that was as good as law.

Jacob's morning labs showed that he was still sub-theraputic on his medication levels, but his kidneys were functioning just fine. Nobody noticed that his urine output was essentially zero. A quick instillation of saline into his catheter collection bag made the urine level appear normal. Because no urinalysis was ordered, the fluid was simply measured and discarded.

The afternoon was uneventful, and Jacob pulled me aside after lunch.

"Here, put this in your pocket. At 8 p.m. tonight Jacob's going to need another lab draw for his medication levels. I want you to draw his labs and inject this entire syringe into his IV after you get his blood sample. Then meet me in the ICU lounge."

"What's in the syringe?"

"Enough steroids to arrest the immune systems of half a dozen guys."

I quickly shoved the syringe it into my pocket and forgot about it as I busied myself with menial tasks throughout the day.

An hour before show time I was getting nervous and decided to look up the lab results of Jacob's female friends.

What I saw shocked the hell out of me … three of the four were positive for HIV. I pulled up their detailed health questionnaires and found that all four were HIV negative within the last two years due to required testing for life and disability insurance. Furthermore, one was a lawyer, one was a medical student, and the other two were in college. Only one of the college girls tested negative.

I just knew Jacob was responsible for those three getting infected. My blood boiling, I knew what I was doing was the correct thing. This murderer didn't need a judge and jury, he just needed an executioner. Lucky for him, we just happened to be on call tonight …

~~~~

Just before 8 p.m., I started chatting with his nurse and mentioned that I was going to check up on him. She was more than happy to oblige an eager med student's offer to help with Jacob's lab draw for the evening.

I gowned up to enter Jacob's room. He was so sedated that he was drooling on himself. He looked pathetic and had a faint odor of ammonia, likely from his recently failed kidneys causing a buildup of the toxic waste product of metabolism. Or was that due to liver failure? I wasn't certain, but he probably had both from the ridiculous doses of medications he was receiving

As I stood beside Jacob I tried to arouse him with a sternal rub. No go, he was out. I drew his blood into the correct tubes. Next, I unhooked the bag of Amphotericin B from the IV infusion machine for a minute and squeezed it with all my might before re-connecting it. That infusion was supposed to go in over three hours, not less than two minutes. That alone could be enough to potentially kill somebody. Finally, I injected the steroids through his IV and casually walked out of his room and handed his nurse the blood for his p.m. lab draw.

I did not pass go, nor did I collect $200. I beelined for the ICU conference room to find Jack casually drinking a coffee.

"Hey, what's up Raj, all well?"

I was amazed at how calm I was. I had no mixed emotions or feelings of remorse over what had just transpired. "All's good in the hood," I replied, and sat down by Jack to watch the Lakers play against the Celtics.

We watched half the game in silence, and during the beginning of the fourth quarter our code blue pagers went off, announcing that ICU isolation bed two had stopped breathing.

I jumped up; Jack reached his arm out and threw me back in my seat asking, "What's the rush?"

We got up a full minute later and walked over to Jacob's bed. The majority of the resuscitation team had already arrived, but Jack instantly assumed the leadership role and asked for a report.

One of the interns yelled out, "Apneic with slightly elevated BP and what appears to be fine fibrillar V-Fib. One of the resident's is about to start a femoral line. We just started chest compressions and artificial respirations."

Jack then assumed care, "Forget the femoral line, he already has a PICC. Get whatever you need from there.

"Give him some atropine and bicarbonate IV NOW. Then get the shock paddles charged up and ready to shock at 200 joules."

"Medications in," somebody replied.

"Paddles ready," somebody else yelled after stripping off Jacob's gown and applying the appropriate goo to the paddles and placing them on his chest.

"Everybody clear! Shock."

A quick seizure coursed through Jacob's body, and he was again still.

"No pulse, resume CPR," Jacob yelled. He glanced at me, we both knew that this was an exercise in futility; his potassium must have been so low that only divine intervention could bring him back from wherever he was headed.

Jacob waited 30 seconds before barking out his next order, "Repeat the shock again at 300 joules."

Same result.

We repeated it again at 360 joules twice; still he was without a pulse.

"Ok team, stop all resuscitation measures. Time of death 9:28 p.m." announced Jack. The team quickly dissolved leaving only me, Jack, and the charge nurse in the room.

Jack pulled the sheet over his face and nodded to the charge nurse and we left the room.

"That's all?" I asked.

"May he go to hell," Jacob replied, a sound of satisfaction in his voice.

The rest of our call night was much more relaxed.

~~~~

Nobody ever questioned the cause of Jacob's death. Though when I told Cindy about it a couple weeks later, she wasn't at all relieved or happy like I thought she might be. I think she was even saddened that he didn't make it.

She didn't have that burning desire for revenge, the 'eye for an eye' mentality that had burned within me and Jack. She was a good person to the core.

I never saw Cindy again. She didn't return to complete the year, and through the grapevine I heard that she withdrew from the residency program and returned to New York. I called her several times, but the calls were never returned and her voice mail was eventually full and not accepting any further messages.

A couple months after Jacob's death, I came across the following article in the *New York Times:*

Physician-in-Training Found Dead in NY Apartment

By: Bill Blanek

New York Times

NEW YORK, New York — A 28 year old female was found dead inside her Upper East Side apartment yesterday morning. The body was found by the apartment manager when a neighbor reported a foul odor emanating from 35th floor unit. Police have not yet released a name.

She was found dead on her couch. The Medical Examiner's initial evaluation indicated that she died approximately 4 days prior to being discovered, based on the condition of her body. The cause of death is likely secondary to an overdose of several prescription sleeping medications combined with alcohol, both of which were found on the adjacent table.

Further details will follow upon completion of the police investigation. "We have no reason to suspect any foul play at present," said Detective Jansen, who is leading this investigation.

A short suicide note was found by the body, indicating that the individual's entire life savings, a sum of nearly $3 million, is to be donated to the AIDS Health Foundation "… to help find a cure for this condition, so that an innocent life might be saved in the future."

The deceased was supposedly a physician-in-training according to the neighbor, but this has not yet been confirmed.

Chapter Six:
Holey Man

HE KEELED OVER while reaching for the handle of the new German sports sedan he had recently bought outright. Feeling light-headed, he wasn't sure if he should drive or not. Moments later, he didn't even know if he'd make it to the driver's seat.

On his knees with beads of sweat forming upon his brow, he was barely able to raise a shaky hand to open the door of the sleek 500+ hp sedan. It was his pride and joy. An even more prestigious ride than his former boss had in his garage.

Using the handle for support he pulled himself off the ground. He wasn't in the best neighborhood and showing any signs of weakness would quickly get him mugged and his $150k car jacked.

A wave of heat coursed through him and he nearly fell again from the weakness. Despite the warm weather, he was shaking from chills.

Patting his right pocket, which was bulging from a wad of Bennie Franklins, his stamina suddenly increased, the diaphoresis subsided, and he managed to slump into the cockpit, realizing it was all worth it.

Business had been booming recently. His referrals kept increasing and repeat business was at nearly 90 percent. He'd even recently considered using business cards. But he thought better of it. His business was best done discretely with a very select clientele.

Perhaps a rate increase was in order. He simply couldn't keep up at the pace required of him. And bringing on a new associate wasn't so easy in his line of work.

No, he'd definitely have to increase his rates, perhaps just for new clients initially. It'd likely be a moot point; money wasn't such as issue for most of those he serviced.

It was nearing sunset in his former stomping ground, East L.A. While he'd love to cruise for a bit, he had an 8:30 p.m. engagement in Beverly Hills. It was already the eighth client of the day, and his was a predominantly night business.

In addition to the Beverly Hills appointment, he had four more West L.A. engagements before calling it a day. Of course another client might call anytime.

Perhaps a personal assistant was what he needed to bring more order to his life. A good assistant who could keep her mouth shut would cost him some big bucks, but business was just too good right now to be stuck dealing with phone calls and schedules.

As it was, he hadn't had a day off in over 3 months. Sleep, when he actually obtained some, was frequently interrupted with phone calls and requests for urgent meetings. The very nature of his business hinged on customer service, punctuality, and complete and utter confidentiality. Thus, a call going to voicemail was lost wages. As his former bosses always used to say, "If you ain't working, you ain't earning"—a creed he now embraced wholeheartedly.

Arriving 20 minutes early, "J" as his clients knew him, parked on the street a block away and reclined back in his plush leather seat. He welcomed the much needed respite.

The pain in his right lower abdomen returned as soon as he stopped driving. It intensified and was followed by a wave of nausea. Cringing, he popped three more Advil. He couldn't be in pain for his rendezvous.

The pain had been steadily increasing over the past three days. The fevers started only yesterday but had also been increasing. Advil was losing its effectiveness and barely took the edge off. But the real problem was the sweats; the rest he could handle. He needed to be suave, prim, and proper for his clients. Especially for the Westside clientele. His old stomping ground near Skid Row had less discerning tastes.

J took his mind off the pain thinking how much better his life would be once he moved out of Huntington Park, the shithole where he was born. It was bordered by the illustrious South Central Los Angeles on one side and Skid Row on the other side. It managed to combine the least appealing aspects of both.

One day he'd show everybody at home that he wasn't a nobody loser like they all thought. Right now J had enough cash to get a small pad in Beverly Hills. If business continued like it was, in a couple months he might even be able to spring for a house on Rodeo Drive itself! The problem was he'd have to buy it outright. His credit score was nonexistent, and he'd long since maxed out any credit card someone was dumb enough to give him.

As his appointment time neared, J washed himself with a towel doused in Evian. He donned a new tailored shirt with those stupid French cuffs he could never understand; designer slacks, shoes, and a cashmere sweater rounded out his attire.

Grabbing his fully stocked valise from the trunk he strode to the mansion's gate at 8:29 p.m. where he was greeted by the butler. They walked in through the side entrance avoiding the main entrance's surveillance cameras. J's clients usually didn't want any records of his visitations.

With his recent visions of grandeur and mansions, J thought he'd try increasing his prices right now. Peter Winnick was a long term client and CEO of some big corporation. If he didn't like the price hike J might lose some business, but he wouldn't mind a short break right now either.

"Ahh, welcome back, J, punctual as usual," greeted Peter. He was a dashing man of about 50 or so, a good 20 years older than J. His clients varied in age from about 35 to almost 80, with professions ranging from celebrity to scientist. While some were noble professionally, all morality was extinguished the moment they made an appointment with J.

"Great to see you again, Peter, it's been a while."

"Yeah, well the wife's been in town this past month and work's been busy. She's gone to her parents in New York for the weekend, and she took the kids. So I might need another … consultation tomorrow if you have time?"

Peter quickly ushered J in to minimize any peeping toms from seeing anything they shouldn't. Walking briskly past the library, through the long hallway, into the reading room, Peter was barely able to contain his anticipation.

"I'll see what can be arranged to accommodate your request. However, before we go any further, I must inform you due to a serious increase in business and the limited nature of my time and services, the rates have doubled. I hope you …"

"No problem." Peter handed J some bills from one pocket and peeled off another five hundred dollar bills from his billfold, handing them over without thinking twice. "The usual before we get down to business?"

"Hell yeah, I'll take a double." The rush had gone straight to J's head. He'd just doubled his price and Peter didn't even bat an eyelash. If all his clients were like this, he'd be moving into town sooner than he imagined.

Peter returned carrying two snifter glasses containing more than a dollop of Macallan 25. Peter was now shaking with anticipation and clearly wanted to get started right away.

Handing J the glass, they toasted and quickly downed their drinks, bastardizing the nearly hundred dollars of amber colored liquid they just consumed, which should have been sniffed and savored, not shot. But such was the nature of the supremely wealthy. Time was money, and J was more than ready to get down to business.

"Why don't you just use the bathroom here, J, so we can get started right away," instructed Peter, with a glazed look on his face, like a puppy dog ready to pounce on a long-awaited treat.

"Sure thing, Boss." J entered the bathroom, which was about half the size of his current apartment. He placed his valise on the ample countertop and removed his supplies. His abdomen was starting to get a little more tender, so he popped another three Advil. The next 15 minutes might hurt more than normal given Peter's obvious expectancy.

Finishing his preparations, he closed up his case and exited into the reading room where Peter was already standing at attention on the couch and ready to begin.

J put down his valise, untucked his shirt, and before he could even fully lift up his sweater, Peter was already ravenously underway.

~~~~

J arrived at his hovel, if one could even call it that, at just after 3 a.m. He parked his ride in the underground storage area for which he paid dearly every month. The dumpster had to be displaced to accommodate his Benz, else it'd be car-jacked within the hour if he left it on the street.

The effort required to extricate himself from the cockpit caused him to grimace. His abdomen was now throbbing and much more tender than it had been during the evening.

He barely made it up the three flights of stairs; only thoughts of dollar signs kept him going. J had progressively charged his clients more and more after he saw how easy it was with Winnick. His last client didn't even balk at the two thousand dollar price tag. And that visit only required 20 minutes of his time.

Getting in bed was a chore due to the pain; any sort of movement seemed to aggravate it. The only thought keeping J from passing out, from both exhaustion and pain, was that he had made nearly fifteen grand today, almost double what his previous best day had been. With renewed thoughts of riches, and an additional handful of Advil, J allowed sleep to envelop him until his 10 a.m. rendezvous with Winnick.

J awoke at 7 a.m. in a cold sweat with shaking chills and severe abdominal pain, so bad that he couldn't even sit up in bed.

He reached under his shirt and found his stomach burning hot and damp to the touch. Rolling out of bed, he bent over and dry heaved for almost ten minutes, sending his head spinning and making his vision blurry.

Slowly regaining composure, J realized he needed something stronger than Advil. J crawled over to his three-legged dresser, held up with the assistance of a cinder block, and opened up his sock drawer. There was a small Altoids tin in the back corner, but the white powder inside wasn't the residue of breath fresheners.

J tapped some of the powder onto his dresser and did a quick line of coke. He immediately followed it with a second and a third. As the rush hit him, his eyes glazed over, and the pain was no longer so much a part of him as something that existed in the periphery of his consciousness.

He much preferred the uncut pure white coke favored by the rich Hollywood crowd than the tan powder cut with battery acid he used in his past, especially now since he could afford the good stuff without having to steal it. It was much better than the black tarry heroin that he started on many years ago, though discolorations on his white walls were still reminders of his past.

Strangely enough, now that he was earning, his drug use had gone way down. He preferred to be alert and oriented when visiting clients, preferring them to be the junkies. It gave him the advantage of negotiating better rates. Not to mention having his faculties together to evade a hairy situation when one arose, which thankfully was not as often as he expected—and much less than when he used to deal drugs for his last boss.

Once again feeling in control, J packed some of the powder in a small vial, figuring he'd need it to get through the day. He already had nine meetings scheduled, with a few more that were likely to call.

With dollar signs running through his head, J got in the shower and decided today he'd wear a power suit with his best tie and shoes, appropriate attire for the increased wages he was about to charge everyone on the docket for the day.

As the water cleansed away the salty residues of his night sweats, J looked down at his abdomen and realized it was redder than yesterday and a whitish discharge was present in the lower right quadrant. His abdomen also seemed to be bloated and quite tense when he pressed his finger against it.

The coke certainly augmented his ability to deny that anything serious was occurring; deciding that it was just gas from what he ate yesterday, he donned his attire.

Bending down to put on his slacks was wrought with agony. His stomach felt like it was going to explode and his belt required two fewer notches than normal. Promptly deciding the best remedy was more inhaled confidence, J helped himself to another line and rushed out the door, but not before ensuring the contents of his valise were in exact order.

Arriving at his car, he found it covered with trash and debris all over his hood and some thick brown syrup streaked his windshield.

Apparently, somebody didn't realize the trash canister was now in the alley and used his car to rid themselves of their refuse.

J made a mental note to get the lock on the door changed, cursing as he picked the trash off his baby. The wipers made easy work of the syrup, or whatever the hell it was. The fact that the trash contained baby diapers was not encouraging.

Driving today was not as easy as yesterday. His abdomen throbbed at every bump on the road, and that was with his upgraded suspension set to luxury, where one could traverse a speed bump without noticing.

At a stop light J felt something damp on his stomach. Looking down he realized that he had soaked through part of his shirt. His face felt hot and his eyelids burned when he closed his eyes. J kept driving, but soon he became nauseated and almost vomited. Only fear of ruining his leather upholstery prevented the bilious fluid from escaping his mouth. Fortitude won and he held it back, burning on its way back to his stomach.

Immediately after arriving in Beverly Hills, J knew he had to do something. Inhaling another dollop of coke, the obvious answer was that he should look for real estate that he could buy to move out of his shithole. He likely got some stomach bug from one of his skanky neighbors.

While exiting his sedan and retrieving his laptop from the trunk, J realized his shirt was soaked through in the lower right quadrant with a milky white fluid. It couldn't just be from sweat. He stripped off his shirt and redressed himself from his valise, donning a new piece with those stupid cuffs his clients favored.

Tightening his buckle sent a pain so severe though his body he involuntarily convulsed and dropped to his knees. This time the bile exited and splattered all over the sidewalk. His vision was double and he was shaking as though plunged in a freezer.

All J could do was pull out his cell phone and dial emergency before another wave of pain took hold of him so violently that all his nerve endings fired at once and sent him flat on his back. His head hit the ground with a dull thud, and blood began to flow freely from his scalp. But J didn't notice, having already lost consciousness moments before.

~~~~

The hot tub's temperature was perfect and the jets just right. Even better was the ice cold beer that never seemed to end. The only annoyance was the bloody ambulances or fire trucks screaming by every five minutes, seemingly louder every time. Great! As if on cue, another one went screaming by. What the hell! It didn't just pass by, it got louder and louder and then just stayed; it must be right outside my apartment.

Damn it! It was my alarm clock and I was a good four snoozes past my 4:30 a.m. wake up time. I had to forego my shower this morning just to get my ass to the ICU in time to figure out what happened with my patients overnight.

I hoped a couple died; that way I might be able to get my work done on time without having to admit I was late.

Switching rotations and giving up my easy radiology month for another month of ICU was not the most brilliant move on my part. At this point I'm not even sure why I did it. I'm sure some deep-seeded part of my id or ego, or whichever part is responsible for prudent decision making, thought it'd be better to take on another "real" rotation so I could be a better doctor, instead of having hours of free time to go drinking in some of L.A.'s hottest bars.

Seven straight days on ICU, from 5:30 a.m. to about 9:00 p.m. and what did I have to look forward to? Another six days of the same before this rotation finally ended.

"Hey, Raj! Dude, did you have a rough call last night?" Asked the amazingly effervescent and always smiling Jenny as we passed each other in the hallway. Thank God she was going in the other direction and I didn't have to endure any further questioning about how my night in bed at home was nor explain why I still looked like crap.

"Something like that." I muttered in reply and I half walked/half ran down the endless corridor to the infamous ICU looming ahead with its two sets of behemoth doors and myriad of precautions, clearly letting all know something wicked this way comes.

Rushing to the census board I was instantly greeted with bad news; there was only one death overnight and it wasn't one of mine. All six of my patients still occupied ICU beds.

Grabbing a stack of progress note paper I quickly began rummaging through labs and overnight events, trying frantically to mentally recreate what happened overnight so I could present it cohesively to the team. After that, I'd be asked questions I couldn't answer, and we'd come up with a plan for the day. Same old.

It'd be great if I had anything remotely interesting; instead I had four patients whose average age was 96, all circling the drain. The fifth was an uninsured, non-English speaking AIDS bomb who was so infected with every pathogen known to humanity that he had a negative pressure isolation room requiring full blood, fluid, and respiratory precautions every time anybody went into the room.

To round out my docket, I had a 22 year-old attractive Princeton graduate who was applying to medical school but was hit by a drunk driver while she was walking to her car after her volunteer shift at the hospital. Now she lay on a ventilator with a tracheostomy, completely paralyzed, unresponsive, with a shaved head from the placement of her ventricular shunt last week. The pain I saw every time I looked at her was gut wrenching; it was such a sad story, and I had already seen too many of such.

Somehow I managed to finish all my notes and infuse myself with a dozen ounces of Pepsi before rounds began.

"Since we're on call today, I'll try to make rounds brief so we can handle the new admissions. Hopefully we get a few during the day today so the medical students can be actively involved." These were the first words uttered from Dr. Clyde, our ICU attending.

Damn it, I'd forgotten it was our call day. Things just kept getting better.

Clyde was one of those remnants from days long gone. He was the consummate physician, tall with grayed hair, always punctual with a starched white coat, slacks, tie, stethoscope, and a highly professional demeanor. His wrinkles didn't make him look old, only more distinguished. And his eyes held that kind of warmth which put families at ease even when he was delivering catastrophic news.

"Dr. Mok, why don't you present Mr. Martinez to the team?" It wasn't a question, though; being the Director of the ICU, Dr. Clyde always got what he wanted. But it was nice of him to ask.

Great, I was the first to present, and I was the only one in scrubs. Everybody else was well dressed, while my coat was wrinkled with a few odd stains on it. I was so over being in the ICU for two months straight. Shuffling through my notes, I got started.

"I'll just briefly recap for the team, as we're all well acquainted with Mr. Martinez. He's a 42 year old male with AIDS who was admitted to the ICU 27 days ago. He has a viral load of 250K, CD4 count of three, an ANC of 15, profound anemia, cryptococcal meningitis, CMV retinitis, oral thrush, *Pneumocystis jirovecii* pneumonia, a multi-drug resistant strain of *Tuberculosis*, Kaposi's Sarcoma on his chest and back, microsporidial diarrhea, severe cachexia from AIDS wasting syndrome, and florid onychomycosis." Wow, I managed that all in one breath and sounded somewhat organized.

"He continues to do poorly, failing to thrive and barely communicating. His PICC line was recently infected and required replacement by radiology due to poor vascular access. He cannot take in oral food or liquids; thus, he is being given total parenteral nutrition, this being day number 22. He has stage 2 decubitis ulcers over his sacrum.

"Overnight there were no acute events. His oxygen saturation is only running at 89% even on 12L/minute of oxygen with a non-rebreather mask. It appears as though he will likely require intubation and artificial ventilation soon. His hematocrit remains at 18 despite nearly daily blood transfusions.

"Ophthalmology reports that he has lost almost all vision in his right eye, but they are starting to make progress on his left eye with twice weekly intravitreal injections. He might be able to retain some useful vision if he stabilizes.

"Renal reports that poor perfusion and toxic medications have overwhelmed his kidneys and he will likely begin dialysis in the next couple days. Other services should provide their recommendations later today."

Phew! I survived that presentation. I wiped the sweat off my brow preparing to be slaughtered with questions. Instead everybody just stared at me contentedly.

"Well done, Dr. Mok. What is your plan for Mr. Martinez today?" Clyde actually inflected his statement, indicating it was a question. He only did that when he was impressed or teaching some-body a lesson by being rhetorical. I hoped it was the former.

"Well, I think we should essentially maintain the status quo and continue with all his current medications despite the nephrotoxicity. We should plan to intubate him in the next day or two before he completely crashes. We should also discuss his situation with the family. Given his grave prognosis we should strongly pursue a possi-ble DNR order, if the family is reasonable and willing."

"Any other information, or should we proceed with Dr. Mok's plan?"

The chief resident, Jack, piped up, "I spoke with the family yesterday and they wish to continue at 100% efforts for as long as it takes. They still seem to hope that he might recover and one day return home and possibly go back to work. They got quite upset when I insinuated neither of those were reasonable, or even feasible, goals."

"And so it shall be; he might occupy that room for many weeks before something overcomes the miracles of modern medicine." All the while Clyde was shaking his head, clearly in disagreement of the family's wishes. "Dr. Mok, please see that we continue to do all we can. Ok, let's move on."

And so went rounding for the next four hours.

Alas, it was finally time to get some food. Just as we regrouped to grab a team lunch, the Chief's pager went off, followed by a team groan.

"Hey Rajen, why don't you take this hit. It's some dude found down, next to his car. He's in the ER, bed 3. Call me once you get a handle on the situation," instructed Jack as he returned from answering the page.

"You got it, boss, hopefully it's something interesting." I replied with feigned enthusiasm, all the while cussing out the son of a bitch in my head for no good reason other than it made me feel better. Nobody had replaced Cindy, who was still on medical leave; and the work seemed to have increased with a commensurate decrease in morale.

Forgoing food, I headed straight to the ER, soon to learn that interesting doesn't always mean good.

~~~~

Walking into the ER, I was happy to see that it was relatively quiet except for some commotion in one of the trauma bays. Heading in that direction, I bumped into Dr. Peters.

"Rajen, good to see you. I'm guessing you're up here for bed 3, right? I'm glad it's you; I'm a bit tied up with this trauma. We might have to do a cardiac massage in a minute here. Please go ahead and get things started. Just order whatever you think is appropriate, here's my badge. You can use it to access the computer for the orders and ..."

"Dr. Peters, we need you now!"

She tossed me her badge and rushed into the ruckus as the wall of people opened to let her in. All I glimpsed was a squirt of blood that hit the ceiling before the gap was closed and the team returned to their frenzied work.

It was quite trusting of Peters to give me her badge. Hopefully it meant she liked my performance over the past year. I felt quite empowered knowing I could order any test in the whole hospital's armamentarium for this guy, from simple blood tests to highly specialized MRI scans. My mood lifting, I searched for his chart to get started.

The chart didn't contain much information beyond the paramedics' report. A 34 year-old Caucasian male was found down next to his car, I found it odd that the report mentioned the car next to which he was found down, a heavily modified black Mercedes Benz CLS 63 AMG. I figured they'd be busier, I don't know, say saving his life and trying to get him here, instead of taking note of his car.

I shuffled through the chart and was able to learn that his name was James Downs, and apparently he was in the process of dialing 911 for assistance when he lost consciousness not far from here in one of the nicer neighborhoods. EMS was able to use GPS to locate him because his phone remained connected with their switchboard despite his consciousness being disconnected.

James was profoundly hypotensive on scene with a blood pressure of 64/42, heart rate of 148, and short, rapid breaths at 40/minute. He had sustained a scalp laceration which was oozing heavily, and he was very febrile at 103.9°F. Nothing else noteworthy was found during the primary survey.

The paramedics placed him in a rigid cervical collar, placed an occlusive pressure dressing over his scalp laceration, started 2 large bore IV lines though which he got a liter of fluid on scene and another en route, and placed him on oxygen via face mask. They closed his car's trunk, reporting it was empty, and brought his brief-case with him. The contents remained unknown because it was locked. The car was also locked, and they didn't have time to search for a key.

Not bad given their total time on scene was just over four min-utes. Travel time to the hospital added another five minutes. Since arriving here he had a quick examination by Dr. Peters, if you can call it an exam. She cleared his C-spine, allowing his collar to be removed, and, well, that's all.

Guess the rest was up to me.

I walked up to James' bed and found what I'd expected, a very fit and well-dressed man who was barely conscious, with a couple empty bags of saline and a head dressing that was beginning to soak through with blood. Laying on a gurney with the head elevated a bit, he had some blood splatter on his shirt, and his face was glistening with sweat.

Something wasn't quite right; healthy guys don't just pass out for no reason. I scanned him again from head to toe while standing at the foot of his gurney, carefully looking for anything amiss.

This time I noticed bags under his eyes indicating he might be fatigued, not uncommon for a hardworking professional. There was some whitish debris on his face and nose, either dust from his face-plant on the roadside or cocaine; the latter was not uncommon amongst the rich yuppie crowd seen here.

His shirt was nearly soaked through from his copious perspira-tion. Looking at it more closely is when I noticed there was an odd bulge underneath the lower right portion of his shirt. His lower extremities appeared fine except for some tears in his slacks by his knees, presumably from his fall.

While I did have Dr. Peters' badge, I did not have her presence or garner any interest from the nearby staff to assist me with my evaluation of James. Besides, everybody was still busy helping out with the exsanguinating trauma case.

"James, can you hear me?" I asked. He didn't respond. I tried again louder, still no response. I tried yet again almost yelling.

"Yes, I can hear you! But my name ain't James," came a smart aleck response from the bed next door.

Ignoring the comment, I donned some gloves and gently shook James' shoulder. No response. A firm sternal rub didn't arouse him either. Given that no ribs cracked, I pushed even harder, digging my knuckles into his flesh while I rubbed forcefully up and down on the center of his chest. He grunted and tried to brush away my hand. His eyelids fluttered for a second and he turned his head to the side and was again unresponsive.

Well, at least I established he was alive and responded to pain.

I hooked James to a blood pressure cuff and oxygen sensor. While the cuff was inflating I checked his temperature. Shit, he was burning up, 104.1°F! At least his BP was a little better at 90/64, his heart was a healthy 124 beats/minute, and his oxygen saturation was 99% on 10L oxygen.

I bolused him another liter of normal saline and took a step back to decide what to do next. He must have an infection somewhere giving him this incredible fever. If he was sweating this much and working long hours, he could easily have passed out from hypovolemia.

I'm guessing the powder on his face was from cocaine. The problem (besides the fact that it was cocaine) was that it's one of the most powerful stimulants known to man; thus, whatever was making

James so somnolent had to be pretty damn severe. I had better hurry the hell up and figure out this mystery before Peters realizes the idiot I am, or James dies.

Interesting how my motivation was to impress Peters, above all else. Sometime over the year I'd transformed into caring more for my evaluations than my patients, but in either case the goal was saving lives. Snapping back to reality instead of introspection, I decided I needed to draw some blood for some basic labs and cultures.

I also wanted to check him for any illicit substances. There were two ways to do that: either by blood or urine. Given he wasn't awake enough to give me a voluntary piss sample, and there wasn't a nurse around to catheterize him, I'd send off for the blood version of that test. Sure I could catheterize him myself, but shoving a tube into a sleeping dude's penis, through his entire urethra, and all the way to his bladder wasn't something I was keen on doing.

Grabbing blood Vacutainers and culture vials I got ready to draw blood, when I realized I knew nothing about this guy. What if he had AIDS, Hepatitis C, Kuru, or some other strange infection?

I defended myself by putting on another set of gloves and a face mask with shield to minimize any risk of splatter. I learned my lesson about taking personal protection *very* seriously.

The blood draw went well … on my sixth attempt. James' veins weren't so good due to his dehydration. His BP was slowly dropping and his temperature increased by another tenth of a degree.

I labeled the blood and logged in to the computer with Dr. Peter's ID badge. Wow, with just a few clicks I had all the tests I wanted ordered, and many more, just because it's so easy to click away. No wonder the cost of medical care is skyrocketing, with the ease and availability of testing, nobody has to think about what's needed. Just order anything you want and figure it out later.

Now the fun part. I bubble wrapped and placed the blood specimens into the little missile shaped pneumatic carrier tube and punched in the code for "blood lab." There was a buzzing noise while the plexi-glass missile got moved into position, and with a muted "swoosh" it started its journey through the labyrinth of pneumatic tube passages concealed within the hospital walls. I must admit, it was fun to click the big red STAT LABS button too, ensuring that all the labs get done within the hour at only quadruple the standard exorbitant cost.

The only thing left was to actually examine the patient, and that task could only be accomplished with the assistance of trauma shears. The use of trauma shears is an empowering experience for medical students. There's something intensely personal and strangely satisfying about rapidly cutting off a complete stranger's clothes in an effort to try and save his or her life. It's almost like removing somebody's identity.

Clothes can tell you a lot about a patient, especially in a situation when the patient is so obtunded that a history cannot be obtained. James clearly spent a great deal of money on his wardrobe. Ferragamo shoes, Gucci belt, Prada shirt, custom tailored wool slacks, and pearl cufflinks … none of that stuff is cheap. His watch alone, a Piaget, might be worth upwards of ten thousand dollars—leaving me wondering about his source of income.

I gently removed his shoes, belt, cufflinks, and watch, placing them in a bag. The slacks and shirt wouldn't get such service because trying to wiggle him out of them could aggravate some hidden injury, resulting in more harm than good.

The shears made easy work of his tailored slacks and revealed boxers underneath, Dolce & Gabbana. His legs were hot to the touch and extremely dry, consistent with dehydration. Before attacking his shirt, I give him another sternal rub. He moaned and quickly returned to his slumber. I tried again, this time his eyes fluttered open and he murmured something barely audible.

"What was that James? Are you in pain?"

He nods.

I step back, wondering if perhaps he's so lethargic because he's in so much pain he physically can't endure being awake. In addition to hanging another liter of saline, I gave him 5 mg of morphine through one of his IVs, hoping to take the edge off any pain he might be experiencing.

In the few minutes it took me to get the saline and morphine, the bulge in his abdomen almost doubled in size. James suddenly looked like he was in his third trimester of pregnancy.

Without wasting time I grabbed the shears and rapidly cut his shirt off down the middle.

Involuntarily, I gagged and fell backwards. Thankfully there was a wall there, else I'd have been on my ass.

I thought Ms. Maggots was bad, but this was on a whole new level.

James had a bag stuck to the swollen, red, and juicy skin in the lower right quadrant of his abdomen. Except the bag was over-inflated and about to burst open, filled with a thick white-yellow discharge, like shaving cream mixed with egg yolk.

It took me a while to figure out what it was until it suddenly dawned on me. It was a colostomy bag that was full of pus and rapidly expanding. Essentially like a popcorn bag, but instead of containing goodies, his contained some blood, colonic contents, and a shitload of pus. I'm talking half a liter here.

The adhesive used to hold the colostomy bag to his skin was coming lose and some pus was oozing onto his skin and dripping off the side of his abdomen onto the gurney.

His abdominal colostomy wound had the telltale signs of infection. It was warm and likely very tender; I'd check that later when he was more awake. The edge of his colostomy, a surgically created opening in which one end of his colon is connected directly to his abdominal wall (like a two inch belly button that spews out diarrhea all day) was very red and angry in appearance.

I stood in shocked amazement; I'd never seen anything like this. I just watched, mesmerized, as the bag continued to dehisce from his skin, allowing more and more pus to escape.

Soon the bag came completely loose and slid down the right side of his abdomen, bounced on the gurney, and crashed onto the floor creating a huge splatter. I tried to turn my head, but not in time. A stream of hot gooey slime splashed me across my left cheek, eye, and hair. Scared to turn back, I rushed to the sink and washed my entire head with hospital grade antibacterial soap. Thankfully my glasses protected the stuff from getting in my eye! Thoughts of Cindy filled my brain. Who knew if this guy had AIDS or Hepatitis C? With renewed vigor I scrubbed my face a fourth time, removing several superficial layers of skin.

Hazarding a look down, through very blurry, irritated, and disinfected eyes, I discovered my scrubs, both top and bottom, were sprinkled with a healthy amount of the pus. My shoes fared even worse; they were caked with the thick yellow discharge. My outfit was destined for the hazmat container ASAP.

Walking back to James' room, I saw that the wall and floor to his right was quite splash-damaged from the exploding pus bag, as was the side of his gurney. This room was clearly going to require quarantine and a good decontamination before another patient could use it.

With my hair still wet, I gowned, gloved, masked, and bouffant capped up before reentering his room.

I looked at his colostomy site and instantly wished I hadn't. It was spewing out pus at an alarming rate. Without a bag to contain the secretions, the pus slithered down the side of his belly and formed an expanding pool of goo on the gurney.

As if the sight wasn't bad enough, the odor hit me like a Mack truck. It took a while because the smell had to pass through my surgical mask. The smell was unique, very thick and repulsive, like wet rotting flesh mixed in with diarrhea and the slightly ferric smell of blood. Definitely pretty high up on the nausea scale.

"So Raj, what do we have here … holy fucking shit!" Dr. Peters was caught off guard as she sauntered into the room expecting me to be examining our patient.

The smell hit her so hard that she turned around and came back wearing a fitted PAPR mask.

She didn't expect to see James stripped down to his boxers with half his gurney covered in egg yolk like pus. To top it off, an active efflux of more pus continued to ooze through the open wound in his abdomen, not to mention the bag full of the biohazardous substance on the floor with plenty of flecks decorating the wall.

Being the quintessential professional, Peters took it all in with one glance from afar. Then she meticulously gowned and gloved, making sure she was fully covered and protected from the potentially infectious pus, and cautiously re-entered the room to get a full report from me.

I told her what had transpired. She nodded and gently placed a hand on his abdomen.

"OH SHIT," coughed James. Apparently the abdomen was very tender, because that small amount of pressure got James' full attention. He was now wide awake.

"Where am I?" His eyes fluttering open, James frantically scanned the room with increasing panic. He was about to look down when Peters threw a sheet on his chest and introduced herself.

"You are in the hospital. My name is Dr. Peters. I'm in charge here. How are you doing?" She cleverly covered up the gooey mess all over his stomach and gurney with the sheet before James could comprehend what was going on and get even more frenzied.

"Where am I?" James managed to ask in a groggy sleep-laden voice before he again started to doze off.

"Rajen, what'd you give him so far?"

"Uhh, 2 liters of fluid and 5 mg of morphine IV."

"What was his response to the narcotics?"

"Well, he was really lethargic before, and afterwards he was a little more arousable. But his fever is still like 105°F. I guess I should have given him an antipyretic."

"So you think he's in so much pain that he's almost unconscious as a result? Very out of the box thinking. But I believe you are right on. Good call. You are also correct about his fever; I think that's adding to his lethargy significantly. If he was just a couple degrees warmer, his brain would start to literally melt, leaving him with permanent damage."

I must have lit up like a light bulb from the compliments. I was assuming that I'd done something wrong and she was going to get mad at me. Plus, I had pus all over me.

Compliments are a rare occurrence for a medical student, and to get one from the most prominent ER physician in Southern California just made my whole week. I felt like I could handle anything.

"So Dr. Mok, what else did you order for our friend here and what's our immediate plan of action?" asked Peters. Attending docs only allowed medical students to make further management decisions if they are happy with their work. Strange how medicine works in that regard; if you do good work, your reward is to get more work to do. But along with that extra work comes more autonomy and respect.

"Well, I already sent off for an extended drug panel, noticing his tachycardia, the whitish powder in his nose, and the dilated pupils. Let's see, what else … bacterial and fungal blood cultures, basic blood chemistries, liver function tests, thyroid studies, HIV, syphilis, and tuberculosis testing. I was just cutting off his clothes when I noticed the huge bag of pus attached to his abdomen. Just after I discovered its presence, it came off spontaneously and fell to the floor.

You can see the splatter everywhere. It got all over me, so I washed up and came back to finish my exam. That's when you arrived."

"Well, he's clearly well off given his Zegna slacks and Prada shirt." Peters muttered kicking aside the now useless and pus covered remnants of his wardrobe. "Glancing at the chart on my way over, I also noticed that he was found down next to a $150K car. Which, given his attire, I'm inclined to believe was his and not stolen.

"Get some more microbiology lab slips and let's send this giant bag of putrid pus for a STAT Gram stain and cultures. I think that holds the answer to why he's sick. After that, we'll have a look at his scalp; he's already soaked through that pressure dressing."

Happy at being able to leave the room for a second, I grabbed the appropriate laboratory requisition forms and a Hazmat fluid collection bag.

Returning to the scene, Peters was holding the now half empty pus bag at arm's length. She was quite relieved to see me rushing over with the collection bag in which she promptly dumped the colostomy bag. After sending that through the pneumatic tube system to the lab we reconvened at James' bedside.

Peters was unwrapping his head dressing. A suturing set was already neatly placed on a table at her side and two nurses were at attention to immediately take care of anything she might request.

"Good, you're back, Rajen. I'll need your help with his head. I had the nurses give him one gram of acetaminophen rectally. That should help with his fever. I also gave him another 20 mg of morphine to make sure he sleeps through our scalp laceration repair. I figure we can repair his head injury before thoroughly examining his abdomen. Some of your labs should be back by then as well."

Wow, it was the second time this year that I was being treated like a peer instead of a nuisance. This whole doctoring thing might actually be worth it after all.

After removing his dressing, we examined his head. There were no fractures, but he had a four inch laceration extending from the edge of his hairline on the right side directly posterior to just above his ear.

In deft movements without talking, Peters drenched the laceration in betadine and shaved off the hair on the right side of his scalp. The laceration was deep, all the way to bone in some places. It was still oozing heavily because of the highly vascular nature of the tissue there; hair requires a lot of nourishment. Which led me to wonder if bald people would bleed less.

"Dr. Mok, have you sutured before?" The question snapped me out of my reverie. I figured this would just be yet another procedure that I would observe, resulting in daydreaming instead of learning. Caught off guard by the question, I nodded in the affirmative. Medical students were notorious for claiming they had done or seen something previously in an effort to be perceived as more experienced than we really were.

Most physicians don't want to be the first to teach a student a procedure, but if they were the second, that didn't seem to be a problem. Technically I had sutured before—all those pigs in our various wet labs. She didn't *specifically* ask if I'd sutured a human before.

"Great. I'll be your assistant and you can be primary. It's a little bloody, so I'll go ahead and anesthetize the area with some lidocaine 2% with high dose epinephrine; you can take over from there." The instant she said it, one of the nurses handed her a fully loaded syringe and she began inserting the 1.5 inch needle at various points along the laceration and injecting the clear fluid. Within seconds the bleeding decreased to almost nothing, the epinephrine constricting all the blood vessels. "We must be very careful; assume he is infected with the worst communicable pathogens you can imagine, including AIDS and Hep C." She handed the syringe back to one of the nurses and started to get up.

"Alright then, he's all yours. Let's switch places and I'll hand you whatever you ask for."

Uh oh, open mouth and insert foot; that's how I felt.

With a surge of adrenaline my heart rate jumped up to match that of James' and beads of sweat soaked my brow and armpits. Thankfully the cap and gown hid my sweat stains from public view.

On cue, my Parkinson's kicked in and my hands began to tremble uncontrollably immediately after Peters handed me the needle holder with a loaded suture. Great, I probably already blew it and was going to be reprimanded any second.

"It's normal to be nervous. Don't worry, I'm here to help you, not judge you," whispered Peters.

"Thanks."

"I think you should start in the middle with a couple buried sutures to bring the edges of the laceration together. Then we can run a buried subcuticular suture to close the wound with a dissolvable suture. Normally I'd use a permanent suture, but that requires removal, but I'm not sure if he's going to follow-up."

Astonished that an *attending*, and not just any, but the famed Dr. Peters, head of ER and all things televised, was giving up her valuable time to help an insignificant med student learn to suture was more than I'd bargained for. Taking a deep breath, I slowly did exactly as she instructed.

I placed three buried stitches and the wound came together nicely.

"Ok, the easy part's done. Now we have to do the buried running stitch that is going to completely close this wound and make it look like he was never cut in the first place. I like to hold the forceps on one edge to create tension and place the first bite like this." Peters was mimicking what I should be doing just above the laceration. Then she handed me the equipment and stepped back to observe.

"Just take your time, Raj; you're doing great."

About half way through the laborious process Peters' pager went off and she slipped away leaving me alone, but giving me permission to finish.

Seconds turned into minutes and minutes into half an hour of intense concentration while I sutured the final inch of the laceration. I just finished tying off the stitch when I felt a bump on my shoulder.

"Hey hey, not bad for your first time on a human," announced Peters winking. Guess she wasn't the only one who knew I was bluffing.

We both stared at the scalp and nodded in approval. Wiping away the residual crusty dried blood we placed some Steri-strips and a piece of gauze over the cut and had the nurses clear away all the detritus that had accumulated during the procedure. The waste managed to fill up an entire garbage can; no wonder medical care costs so much. Everything is disposable, sterile, and frequently requires proper disposal.

"So Dr. Peters, what do you think …" I was cut off by somebody rushing down the corridor headed straight for us. She drew attention not so much because she was running, as that was common in the ER, but because of how she ran with an awkward hobble. My guess was she hadn't run in years.

Her name badge read Urmila Franks. While she wore a long white coat, she wasn't comfortable in the ER. Then I realized she was from microbiology.

"Dr. Peters, I just got the results of the Gram stain you sent off from the colostomy secretions. I tried calling but they said you were busy with a procedure so I came up personally. You're not going to believe what showed up."

I could start to see a smile forming on Peters' lips; she loved it. The thrill of making a diagnosis and saving this young man's life was just moments away.

"You're going to make me guess, aren't you?"

"No, that wouldn't be fair, I'll tell you: gram-negative diplococci. And not just a few, the whole sample is chalk full of them!"

Both our jaws dropped as we turned to look at James and the pus splatter that was still on the floor and wall.

Turning to me Dr. Peters was dead serious, "Rajen, I think you should go to HazMat immediately for a full decontamination. I'm going to quarantine this room. Come back when you're clean and I'll give you some Ceftriaxone prophylactically. Just go to them in the basement; I'll call and make sure they know you are arriving."

"Fucking shit," I murmured inaudibly as I took off running down the hallway to the emergency elevator. I couldn't believe that the bag of pus was really a biological bomb of actively replicating gonorrhea! And I got it all over my face, glasses, hair, and clothes.

~~~~

Decontamination, in a word, sucked.

It was nothing like what we see on television or read about in books. I walked down a dreary passageway where I was greeted by somebody who hated her job.

I was ushered into a small holding area where I met one of the ID physicians who asked if I was the one squirted by the gonorrhea bag. Word travels fast in the hospital.

I filled out some paperwork and was led to a barren room with fluorescent lights, a central bench, and a single receptacle which read "medical incineration." I stripped naked and placed all my clothes there and was instructed by the overhead speaker system to proceed into phase two. Apparently I didn't require phase one and was told I get to skip phase three, whatever those were.

The mysterious phase two was simply a shower with four spouts and four different bottles of cleansers. I washed myself in hot water and lathered up with the four cleansers, one at a time, sequentially as labeled.

After bathing, I exited and entered another barren room with a central bench. There I found a towel, boxers, and fresh scrubs. I tossed the towel into another incineration receptacle and dressed with the new scrubs. Exiting this room the ID doc met me and gave me some hospital socks and Velcro shoes, like those worn by people in the rehabilitation ward.

"Well Rajen, you're officially decontaminated. Sign here."

Signing, I handed the form back and looked at him, asking, "What do I do now?"

"Well, most people usually go home, but Peters wanted you back on duty in the ER. Real ball buster she is, huh?"

I nodded and eagerly left the HazMat unit. I never imagined I'd be treated for a STD because a bag of pus fell off some dude's abdomen and exploded all over my face. I began to re-evaluate my career as I re-entered the ER.

Peters waved me over.

"Roll up your sleeve." She wiped my skin with an alcohol wipe and jammed a needle into my deltoid.

"Argh, that burns. That the antibiotic?"

"Yea, Ceftriaxone, just in case you got infected with the clap from that little explosion."

"Great, now I can say I was treated for the clap which I got directly from some dude's colon."

Peters suppressed a giggle; medical humor sure is dark. "Worst thing is that you paid for it … tuition and all, I mean."

"I'm never going to hear the end of this, am I?"

"Nope."

"In fact, I think half the ER has been snapping candid photos of you and the room on their phones as soon as word of the gonorrhea got out."

"Great. Did you figure out how he got the infection? And why he has a colostomy?"

"Not yet, the morphine snowed him pretty good. He's just waking up now. I figured you might want to stick around to get the whole story. Oh, the good news; he's HIV and Hepatitis B and C negative, so at least we don't have to worry about you getting any of those. His toxicology was positive for cocaine, but not heroin or any other drugs."

If nothing else this year, I've definitely learned that bodily fluids can be deadly.

"Oh, I spoke with Clyde; you're off the rest of the day. Apparently they didn't want you back up there today after what happened."

"So, all it takes to get out of call is to acquire an STD?"

"Don't make it a habit." Peters smirked at me for a moment before her expression disintegrated back to business. "Well, let's get to the bottom of this James character's story and I'll buy you a drink. Just follow my lead. I don't think he'll be very forthcoming with information, but we can strong arm it out of him if we have to. I'll do most of the talking, but pay attention. Every time I grab the stethoscope around my neck, that's your cue to speak up. Just say something appropriate so we can get the hell outta that infected room."

I nodded my understanding as we donned our personal protective equipment from head to toe. After all, we were entering a chemical warzone in which James was the factory. The room had been cordoned off with two layers of heavy plastic drapes from ceiling to floor, with negative pressure ventilation.

We dressed in a full "bunny" suit of white plastic vinyl-like material covering us from feet to neck. Hats, gloves, and full face masks with eye shields rounded out the outfit. We didn't need air tight suits because Gonorrhea isn't transmissible via aerosolization.

James was now awake and alert, but he hadn't moved from his gurney. Then I realized why; he had leather restraints on both his arms and legs. Guess this whole gonorrhea explosion thing was pretty serious.

Actually, it's not all that far from chemical warfare. Hell, if he put that pus in a little squirt bottle and just sprayed it around, everybody would get gonorrhea simply by contact with mucosal surfaces of the eyes, nose, and mouth. This again reminded me of poor Cindy and her bout with the much more lethal, but less infective pathogen HIV.

Upon entering, Peters immediately started the dance of questioning to gather the information she desired. She started with attempting to build rapport.

"Hi James, how are you feeling?"

He pulled his arms causing them to tug on the restraints and rattle the gurney. "Like I'm a prisoner! You can't hold me here."

"Your fever has come down and your fluid status has improved after we administered you two units of blood and three liters of fluid. Your heart rate and other vitals are also much improved from when you arrived here in critical condition."

"Am I supposed to dance for joy? OH WAIT, I can't cause I'm restrained to this bed like a prisoner. You're doctors; last I checked your job was to fix people. Can I go now?"

"Aren't you wondering why you're here or what is going on with you?"

"Not really. Look, I was just tired and bumped my head from overworking. Now, if you don't mind, I really have to get back to work, so if you'd please … take these off." He again demonstrated his restraints by flexing both his arms and legs this time.

"James, if that's your real name, why do you have a colostomy?"

"Look, bitch! I don't have to sit here and answer your questions. I want to leave right now, and I suggest you let me out or else I'm going to sue your ass and this whole hospital."

Peters got up from her stool and stood erect to her full height of 5 feet, 7 inches, looking down at James, demonstrating that she was in charge. I figured the Dr. Nice Guy act was over.

As Dr. Peter's voice boomed out, I realized I was right.

"James, I'm a professional and deserve to be treated as such. We just saved your life; if we didn't suture your scalp you would have easily bled to death on the street. Similarly if we didn't diagnose your infection, dehydration, and profound anemia in a prompt fashion, any one of those alone could have killed you. The combination of all four without immediate treatment would have meant certain death.

"Furthermore, Rajen here could have died due to your lack of hygiene and consciousness. If he'd have known you had an infected colostomy he could have properly helped you and protected himself. Instead, he had to cut off your clothes only to find an infected colostomy bag, all because of your unconscious state."

"What, he fucking cut my clothes?! Those were worth 2G easy. You owe me for those, Nigga. And where's my watch??"

"LISTEN TO ME! You are worried about your clothes?! I just told you he saved your life and in return you almost infected him with the gonorrhea oozing out of your filthy colostomy."

There was silence in the room, but the anger on James' face was growing. He began to thrash against his restraints. There was a tapping against the plastic quarantine. Security was already gowned up and asking if they were needed. Peters told them to stand down, but be ready.

"I want to get out of here. I don't have no clap. You can talk to my lawyers; I'm out."

"James, you're not going anywhere. First off, I have placed you on a 5150 hold, meaning for the next 72 hours you have no rights. If you disrespect me or my team any further I'll call the psychiatrist on call and have you placed on a 5250 hold for two weeks. Doing so won't be a problem, as he's my friend and will do what I request without question. Furthermore, I will attest that I witnessed you intentionally throwing the contents of your colostomy at people on my staff knowing it was infected with gonorrhea. That act alone would be considered malicious intent or worse, and you'd be taken directly to jail. Thus, I suggest you calm down so we can talk honestly."

James tensed up all his limbs and thrashed against the restraints to no avail. They easily subdued his outburst. The leather wasn't even distressed by his flailing. "Fuck that shit, bitch, you bluffing, you a doctor, can't make up shit like that. I'll get your license revoked and ass thrown in jail."

Peters' resolve didn't change. She maintained her cool, detached, professional demeanor. She knew she had already won this verbal skirmish; it was just a matter of time before James realized it, too. The turning point was always the same—it was when they desperately pointed out that a doctor couldn't fabricate material. The problem was, simply put, a doctor could very easily fabricate material, and not just any material—conclusive material that held up to scrutiny in court. It was this realization that was horrifying, because James knew he'd lost. It was just a matter of when his conscious mind would realize it, as well.

Peters nonchalantly placed her hands around the stethoscope draped around her neck. Great, my turn to join in, only I didn't know what to say.

"James, I could have died today all because of you. I was just trying to help you when I got splattered by your infected excretions. But I'm not judging you; I just want to help you get better." Wow, I sounded sincere. If I kept this up I might actually one day believe myself.

I could see we were breaking his resolve. His features softened just a little, but only for a second. It was all I needed to start playing hardball and getting this case settled so I could go home.

"But you're not off the hook James. We need some answers, like why you have over $10K in cash in your briefcase? The colostomy bags contained in your briefcase can be explained, but why do you have canisters of douche and foam? And how is it you have the keys to a $150K car but no health insurance?"

I was ready to go on and drill into this bastard, but before I could begin another diatribe, Peters released the grip on the stethoscope. My role in the interrogation had come to an end. I reluctantly took a backseat and watched the events unfold.

My confrontation had the desired result, further enraging James with my insinuations.

"What the fuck, man! You say you're trying to help me, but you take my keys and go through my valise. That's illegal without a search warrant and you can add your name to the list that's getting sued buddy. I don't buy any of that bullshit of helping me, you just wanna rob me; I had $15K in there."

Peters crossed her arms, further exuding authority. This was about to get good.

"James, you clearly forgot what I had mentioned about attempting to maintain a professional demeanor and not insulting my team. Raj here is the only reason you are alive right now. We did open your belongings in an effort to obtain more of a history so we knew what we might be dealing with. It's perfectly legal in life or death situations, perhaps your need to refresh yourself on the law.

"Here's what I have learned. You are obsessed with money and respect only it and the power it brings. You work with educated individuals, but lack the appropriate education yourself. You have a problem with authority. The poor quality of the tattoo on your right shoulder indicates you've been incarcerated before, and that you were low man on the jail totem pole. The small scar near your colostomy tells me you've been shot, likely by something small such as a .22 caliber.

"You use drugs, but only high grade cocaine nowadays, probably to help you stay awake so you can work long hours. But the mild scarring on your forearms indicates a history involving heroin or methamphetamines.

"Your name isn't James, but since you came into money I'm sure your affluent and connected white clientele prefers that to Leroy Grims. It also helps you deny your relationship to Grims senior, your older brother who is known to be involved in some very public gang activity. I bet you changed your name shortly after you were admitted here through this very ER about 11 months ago.

"You might remember that you were brought in after being shot at a drug transaction that went south. You had an emergent exploratory laparotomy where the surgeons found that your colon had been perforated by the bullet. The bullet was successfully removed and you were left with a colostomy. During your hospitalization somebody came looking for you, likely to finish you off, seeing as how they failed the first time. That's when you checked yourself out AMA. Now you return, never having had your colostomy taken down and repaired. I suspect you found another use for it, which is how you came into money.

"By the way, your brother paid your last hospital bill, anonymously of course. You owe him 96 thousand dollars.

"Now, either you tell me I'm wrong, or you fill me in on what happened over the past 11 months."

James was caught as off guard, as was I. How in the hell did Peters get all that information? She must have done it when I was "decontaminating." Later I found out Higgs was able to pull this information for her while I was in the basement.

James, or Leroy, remained silent. His resolve had been fractured by Peters' recounting of his history.

"Cat got your tongue? No matter, I'll tell you what's going to happen next. You will be admitted to the hospital. We will treat your gonorrhea and get you stabilized and then you will undergo surgery to have your colostomy properly repaired."

That last part struck a nerve with Leroy; he suddenly became defensive. "You can't operate on me without my permission, and I don't want any more surgery. I'll live with my colostomy."

I couldn't fathom why somebody would *want* a colostomy. That's when it struck me; I looked at Peters in disgust. While Peters had already figured it out, I just now understood how he made his money and acquired his infection.

"Leroy, how long you been in the schlepping business?" inquired Peters.

"What?"

"Don't think I didn't put it all together. You were a mediocre gang banger and you couldn't even get a small time drug deal to go down right. Your brother protected you as best he could, but you were a nobody, probably a significant liability, in his world. Then you got your big break with that gunshot. I'm guessing you dabbled in prostitution before, but male ass doesn't make one rich these days. However, if you can offer a special service, such as a colostomy for your clients to fuck, you can enter the world of sick specialty fetishes, which pays much better. But to enter this market you had to clean up your act. That'd explain the clothes, watch, car, and valise; because most people who pay top dollar for such sick shit want somebody who can fit into their high-priced world of spoils and vices."

I didn't know if I should gag or laugh. I did both. I sounded like a monkey coughing. I'd never heard of people paying to have sex with a colostomy! Apparently the rich are always looking for new ways to unload some of their wealth. I just nodded my head in shame.

"Leroy, just to be straight, you are going to be turned over to the police as soon as I leave this room. You will go to jail. And you will have your colostomy taken down." Peters turned to leave, and as a last minute thought added, "And you will need to notify the authorities of who your clients are so that they can be treated as well. I'm sure your brother will be proud when he learns of his little bro's exploits into specialty fetish homosexual prostitution."

And with that we exited Leroy's makeshift isolation room. He had just started sobbing when we left.

I'd never have believed that in medical school I'd witness a grown man restrained to a hospital gurney sobbing like a high school girl after a break-up while oozing gonorrhea out of his abdomen.

Fact is far scarier than fiction. The kicker is he made more money per hour than most of the CEOs that he serviced.

~~~~

Having the rest of the day off meant I had nothing to do. Thus, before going home I decided to log onto the computer system to check on the most recent lab results for my patients. Pulling up my patient roster I noticed that Duane was again an 'active' patient. That could only mean he had been transferred back to the hospital from the rehabilitation unit.

Clicking on his name pulled up the tests that had recently been ordered: blood counts, urine, and blood cultures. He probably had developed a fever and was transferred to the hospital for some antibiotics.

What the hell, I figured I'd pay him a visit on my way out. That decision changed my life.

Duane was in a regular hospital room with no precautions. That was a good sign, meant he didn't have some highly contagious infection or anything.

Reviewing his chart before entering painted a completely different story. It'd been over four months from when I'd last seen Duane, since that time his wife had filed for a divorce and he'd amended his will leaving his entire estate to his daughter on her 18th birthday, almost a decade away.

Despite intensive physical and occupational therapy, Duane had regressed, he remained non-verbal, only able to grunt 'yes' and 'no' ... well, one grunt for 'yes', two for 'no'.

His paralysis had not improved, he continued to be incontinent of both bowel and bladder function. He'd had several urinary tract infections due to the constant indwelling catheters. He had non-healing decubitus sacral ulcers. His numerous skin grafts left him looking like a horrible disfigured patchwork quilt.

He'd even undergone two corneal transplants in his left eye, but both had failed resulting in so much scarring that his eyes were labeled 'inoperable' and more than ninety percent blind. The prognosis was grave; the last note stating that he'd likely be completely blind in both eyes within a few months with no hope of any future intervention.

About one month ago Duane had again met with his lawyer and changed himself to DNR/DNI status. This meant that if he was to have an acute life threatening event, he did not want any resuscitation or artificial respiration measures, including intubation, to be undertaken in an effort to save his life.

Social work notes provided even more insight into Duane's plight. After he'd removed his now ex-wife from his will, she completely stopped visiting him; her last visit was just over two months ago. She was in a relationship with an airline pilot who himself was divorced with one child, a boy similar in age to Duane's daughter. His wife was in hospice care due to end-stage breast cancer. The two met during group counseling for individuals with terminally ill spouses. They started living together shortly before her last visit to see Duane.

Duane didn't take well to his wife's moving on with him still being alive, but who can blame him?

Numerous psychiatry notes revealed that after the divorce Duane had given up on actively participating in his rehabilitation exercises, had become increasingly withdrawn, and on numerous occasions stated that death would be better than his current state of senscience.

Again, who could blame him? The guy had gone from having the American dream: gorgeous wife, beautiful daughter, great job, and excellent health to a miserable existence in which he was eighty percent paralyzed, disfigured, blind, bed-ridden, and alone. Perhaps the worst thing was that his mental faculties were intact.

The only thing left to do was actually 'talk' to Duane. Given he'd stopped writing, conversations were now carried out by Duane grunting twice if the letter of a word was between A to M and once if it was between N to Z. Then the letters were recited until he grunted once to indicate that was the desired letter.

Notepad in hand, I entered Duane's room. The sight of him caught me by surprise. He was barely a hundred pounds and had no muscle mass. His face was gaunt, his cheeks sunken in, and his eyes almost completely white due to the severe scarring of his corneas.

There were 2 IV poles with numerous bags of various liquids being infused into him through a catheter in his neck. I recognized some of the hanging IV bags: two were antibiotics, one was a blood transfusion, another contained TPN, one I presumed was just fluid, and I didn't recognize the last two.

I walked up to his right side and nudged him. His eyes fluttered open, but he made no effort to turn his head. He wasn't being rude, it was just that for Duane facing a visitor was no longer required, as he received no useful visual input. And based on the Psych evaluations, he didn't care for company any longer.

"Hi Duane, it's me, Rajen Mok. The medical student that was on your team a few months ago."

Numerous vigorous grunts.

"I presume that means you remember me?"

More grunts.

"Is it ok if we talk? I know the way you communicate and I have a notepad here."

One grunt.

And we were underway.

LIAR.

"I assume that is in reference to me?"

One grunt.

"I know, there's nothing I can do to make your situation right, it's not fair; it sucks."

Silence.

I figured I might as well continue. "I know what happened with your wife, your DNR status, and your will."

Silence.

"I'll cut to the chase. If you want, I'll help you end it, tomorrow will be your last day. I'll stay true to my offer, just in a very belated fashion. Better late than never I suppose. What's the verdict?"

One grunt. Pause. One grunt. Pause. A barely audible, "Yes."

"WAIT! You can talk?!"

His voice was very raspy and hoarse, but it was definitely present, and in English. "Yes."

He turned his head to face me, opened his scarred and opaque eyes, and just stared, unblinking. It was creepy. Many cultures believe eyes are a window to the soul; well in this case the soul was nowhere to be found. Perhaps it had already left the building. Finally a tear slid down his cheek and towards his neck where it was absorbed by the dressing around his neck catheter. Duane broke the silence, "Please … help me …"

"Help you die?"

One grunt.

"Ok, I'll be back tomorrow, late in the afternoon when the nurses are changing shifts. I promise it'll end then."

Numerous grunts. He started thrashing in his bed, well, his right side anyhow. More grunts and more thrashing.

When he finally calmed down I asked, "Is there something you want to say?"

One grunt. The activity must had worn him out.

"Ok, if you don't want to talk, I have the notepad ready."

THAT … WAS … ME … DANCING … FOR … JOY … And then he smiled, probably for the first time since I last saw him.

"I don't need to ask you if you are sure about going through with this do I?"

Two grunts.

"I'll see you tomorrow."

His grunts and thrashing were so vigorous that an alarm went off and his nurse rushed into the room.

She saw him and looked at me, and back to Duane. "I'm going to page the attending, I think he's seizing."

"No, no, I don't think that's necessary. I think he might like some music actually."

"Are you kidding me, he hasn't listened to music in months. They tried everything in rehabilitation, music, audio books, massage therapy, animals, air mattresses, mood lighting, white noise, nature sounds, you name it."

"Duane, would you like some music?"

One grunt.

"I'll be damned!" Exclaimed his nurse, and took off to get her iPOD. Hospital rooms are now fully wired with music docking stations and surround sound.

When she got back she asked, "What do you think he wants to listen to?"

"Oh, I think some dance beats would be just great."

"You got it." And she put on some hip hop.

"I'll see you tomorrow, Duane."

He was thrashing away as I left his room. I think that was the happiest dance I'd ever seen.

I headed down to the operating rooms. Most were up and running, but I saw a couple that were not in use at present because the cases were not scheduled until later in the day.

I was already in scrubs, so I just removed my nametag and put on a hat and face mask. Now I fit right in as any number of scrub clad worker bees. I saw a mop at the end of the hallway, and a plan formulated in my head.

Grabbing the mop and cleaning cart, I moved it to OR 17 which was currently not in use and pretended that I was mopping the room. I nonchalantly made my way over to the anesthesia cart where all the medications are kept.

Damn it! It was locked. There was a combination lock. I figured tons of Docs must use this cart, thus, the code must be easy. I tried the usual 1234 and 9876 combinations to no avail. Then I figured the four corners might work and BINGO, I was in.

The cart unlocked and the whole slew of anesthetic medications was at my disposal. I grabbed several vials and stuffed them in my scrub pockets, closed the cart, and meandered back to where I found the cleaning cart. I left it where I had found it and went straight to the locker room where I'd dropped off my bag.

Nobody so much as glanced at me.

Entering a toilet stall I placed all the drugs I'd procured into my bag and did a quick inventory of what I'd accumulated: Propofol, Atropine, Vecuronium, Epinephrine, and SoluMedrol. Any of those first four would be enough to do the trick.

My heart was racing; this was just too easy. I threw my bag over my shoulder and left the OR. I walked to one of the regular patient floors and into a general supply room, where I procured a 50 cc syringe and a few eighteen gauge needles.

I found a private bathroom and again found myself in a toilet stall. I quickly opened up all my vials and drew up all the contents into the 50 cc syringe. The medications filled the syringe to exactly the 50 cc mark. The lethal cocktail milky white in color … scary, it could easily be confused for an infant's formula.

I flushed the empty glass vials into the toilet one at a time and fortunately they all went down the drain without any complication, as did the needles.

Placing the filled syringe back into my bag I headed again to Duane's room. I was now acting on auto-pilot, my feet were moving, but my brain wasn't telling them were to go. There was a strange peace that had settled in. My heart rate was normal and my mind completely clear. I had no second thoughts about what I was going to do; I just didn't want to wait until tomorrow.

I found myself outside Duane's room, watching him mildly thrashing about with the music bumping. Dancing, in his own sei-zure-like way.

"Hey, Buddy, I'm baaaack!"

A few grunts.

"I moved things up. I got the goods and I figured it might be better to do it today; if I think about it too much, I might back out again."

Two staccato grunts.

"OK, here's how we'll do it. I have a syringe with enough chemicals to put away several people. I'm using some of the same stuff that did Michael Jackson in. I'll just silence you monitors, turn up the music, and slam the concoction into your TPN line. They're both the same off white color, so it won't even be noticed. You'll just go off into a sleep in a few seconds, and the medications will paralyze all your muscles and increase your BP to well over 300.

"You'll probably die of apnea, a stroke, a ruptured aneurysm, a heart attack ... hell, maybe all of the above.

"I don't think it will hurt because you'll be completely asleep first. But then again, I've never done this before. You ready?"

One grunt, then silence. This was clearly a man who'd made peace with himself and had been looking forward to this opportunity for months.

I nodded and took out the syringe and hid it under his sheets. I turned up the music. Then I silenced the alarms, buying me 90 seconds of quiet before they'd begin to blare their myriad of warnings. As soon as I did that, I connected the 50 cc syringe and slammed it into his IV over the course of about eight seconds.

Unhooking the syringe, I walked out of his room without looking back and headed straight for the exit and to my car, dumping the empty syringe in one of the random trash cans on my way to the parking structure.

~~~~

I came to work the next day to round at 5:45 am. The ICU was exactly as I remembered it the day before. I logged onto a computer and pulled up my patient list and the only thing I noticed was that Duane was no longer listed as 'active.'

I clicked on his name and saw that some labs were drawn shortly after I'd left the hospital yesterday. There were several critical lab values. Curiosity overcoming me, I just had to walk by his room.

As I walked by, I saw that his room was empty with a well-made bed ready for its next occupant. I glanced at the patient board at the central nursing station and the only difference was that instead of his name by the number of the room he'd occupied yesterday, it said 'DECEASED.'

Nobody paid me any attention or questioned my presence on the floor. I was just another medical student going about my day's duties.

Appendix 1:
Acronyms

5150: An involuntary 72 hour psychiatric hold.

A & 0: Alert and Oriented (out of a possible of 4: person, place, time, and event).

ACGME: Accreditation Council for Graduate Medical Education.

AMA: Against Medical Advice.

Ampho: Amphotericin B.

AMS: Altered Mental Status.

ANC: Absolute Neutrophil Count.

BFF: Best Friend Forever.

BMI: Body Mass Index.

BP: Blood Pressure.

BS: BullShit.

CD4: Cluster of Differentiation 4 (a glycoprotein found on the surface of Helper T Cells).

CMV: CytoMegaloVirus.

CNA: Certified Nurse's Assistant.

CP: Cerebral Palsy.

CPR: Cardio-Pulmonary Respiration.

Crypto: Cryptococcus (a genus of fungus).

CSF: CerebroSpinal Fluid.

C-spine: Cervical Spine.

CT: Computed Tomography.

CYA: Cover Your Ass.

DIC: Disseminated Intravascular Coagulation.

DNA: DeoxyriboNucleic Acid.

DNR: Do Not Resuscitate.

DOA: Dead On Arrival.

ECHO: ECHOcardiogram (ultrasound of heard).

EKG: Electrocardiogram.

EMS: Emergency Medical Services.

ENT: Ear, Nose, and Throat.

ER: Emergency Room.

ET: EndoTracheal.

FACS: Fellow of the American College of Surgeons.

FLK: Funny Looking Kid.

GHB: Gamma HydroxyButyric acid (also, Rohypnol).

GOMER: Get Out of My ER.

H & P: History and Physical.

HAART: Highly Active Anti-Retroviral Therapy.

HIV: Human Immunodeficiency Virus.

ICU: Intensive Care Unit.

IM: Intra-Muscular.

IV: Intra-Venous.

IVIG: Intra-Venous ImmunoGlobulin.

JD: John Doe or Jane Doe.

LP: Lumbar Puncture.

MA: Medical Assistant.

Mg: Milligrams.

MI: Myocardial Infarction.

MIA: Missing In Action.

MILF: Mother I'd Like to Fuck.

MRI: Magnetic Resonance Imaging.

MRSA: Methacillin Resistant Staphylococcus Aureus.

N95: A type of face mask corresponding to NIOSH (National Institute for Occupational Safety and Health) standards.

NPO: Nulla Per Os (nothing by mouth).

NYU: New York University.

OR: Operating Room.

PACU: Post Anesthesia Care Unit.

PC: Politically Correct.

PCA: Patient Controlled Analgesia.

PCP: Phencyclidine (Angel Dust).

PET: Positron Emission Tomography.

PICC: Peripherally Inserted Central Catheter.

PO: Per Os (by mouth).

RBC: Red Blood Cell.

RNA: RiboNucleic Acid.

SAT: Standardized Achievement Test.

SIRS: Systemic Inflammatory Response Syndrome.

STAT: STATim (Latin for immediately).

STD: Sexually Transmitted Disease.

SUV: Sport Utility Vehicle.

TEN: Toxic Epidermal Necrolysis.

Tox: Toxicology.

UCSF: University of California, San Franscisco.

V-Fib: Ventricullar Fibrillation.

VIP: Very Important Person.

Appendix 2:
Definitions

Amphotericin B: An extremely toxic antifungal agent used to treat only the most severe human fungal infections.

Anemia: Low blood counts or concentration (measured as hemoglobin or hematocrit).

Apenic: Not breathing.

Atropine: A neurotransmitter that decreases parasympathetic activity, dilates pupils, and in high doses causes severe abnormal cardiac rhythms which can be fatal.

Autoimmune Hemolytic Aanemia: When a person's body attacks its own red blood cells.

Bacteremia: Systemic infection by a foreign bacteria, usually severe and in the circulatory system.

Bactrim: A sulfa containing antibiotic, commonly used.

Bell's Reflex: A primitive reflex in which eyes roll upwards to keep the corneas covered and hydrated (often making eye examinations very difficult).

Bicarbonate: HCO3-, used to buffer pH in biologic systems.

Boba: Tapioca balls used in 'pearl milk teas.'

Bolused: To administer a large amount of fluid rapidly (in medicine usually one liter IV given within a few minutes counts as a bolus).

Cachexia: Severe malnourishment, loss of body mass that cannot be reversed nutritionally.

Calculi: Mineral deposits that can form a blockage in the urinary system.

Cannula: A tube for insertion into a vessel, duct, or cavity (vein, eye, nose, stomach, etc …).

Catheterization: A tube inserted someplace it doesn't belong (heart, bladder, etc …).

Central Nervous System: Brain and spinal cord.

Cerebral: Brain.

Code Blue (a.k.a—code): Called when a non-DNR patients either stops breathing or beating his/her heart (extreme emergency).

Code White: An acute heart attack in which intervention, usually by cardiac catheterization and stenting is required with the hour.

Colic: Severe pain or other symptoms of distress (occurs in babies and with kidney stones).

Colostomy: A procedure in which the intestine is sutured to the abdominal wall creating an opening known as a stoma (yes, fecal matter is collected into a bag taped around this opening).

Cricothyroid: A joint in the neck connecting the cricoid cartilage and the thyroid cartilage, placing pressure here can make the view of intubation easier.

Cryptococcal meningitis: Fungal infection of the membranes covering the brain and spinal cord.

Cryptococcus: These fungi grow in culture as yeasts and are usually aerosolized from dirt, infection in non-HIV individuals is rare.

Cyanotic: Blue, usually due to lack of adequate oxygenation.

Decubitus: The most dependent part of a patient when they are lying down, prolonged periods in the same position can cause ulcers in these dependent positions which are difficult to treat.

Delirium Tremens: A severe form of alcohol withdrawal that involves sudden and severe mental or nervous system changes. Failure to treat can result in death.

Diaphoresis: Sweat.

Diaphragm: Primary muscle of inspiration, separating the chest from the abdominal cavity.

Diazepam: Valium.

Doppler Effect: The frequency of sound of an approaching object is higher than when the same object recedes (very common as an ambulance approaches and passes).

Dyscrasias: Nonspecific term that refers to any disease or disorder, but it usually refers to blood diseases.

Ecstasy: MDMA (3,4-methylenedioxymethamphetamine) party drug that makes people more sexual, high doses can cause severe hyperpyrexia.

Emboli: Any detached, traveling intravascular mass (can cause a stroke).

Emesis: Vomiting.

Endotracheal: Inside the trachea, a tube here is used for artificial ventilation during anesthesia.

Epidermal: Outermost layers of the skin.

Erythema: Redness.

Eschar: A piece of dead tissue that is usually black.

Excoriated: Damage or remove part of the surface of the skin.

Exenterate: To remove the eye and associated skin, muscle, and superficial bone.

Exsanguinate: To lose a severe amount of blood.

Extubation: Remove an endotracheal tube (one used for artificial respirations during anesthesia or on a ventilator).

Formalin: Used as a disinfectant and for preservation of biological specimens.

French: Used to size catheters in medicine, dividing the French by 3 gives the diameter equivalent in millimeters.

Fulminant: Intense and severe to the point of lethality.

Genetic Immunoglobulin Abnormalities: Abnormalities with the body's ability to make antibodies to fend off infections (numerous varieties).

Gentamicin: A very toxic antibiotic.

Grand Mal: Big seizure.

Hadrian's Wall: An ancient defensive wall built in Great Britian.

Hand: Unit of measurement equal to 4 inches.

Hematocrit: The volume percentage of red blood cells in blood.

Hematoma: A blood filled cyst.

Hematuria: Blood in urine.

Hemoglobin: Iron-containing protein in red blood cells that carries oxygen.

Hemostats: Metal clamps used in surgery to stop vessels from bleeding.

Hemothorax: Blood in the thoracic cavity where it doesn't belong.

Heparin: Very potent blood thinner.

Hepatitis C: Virus that infects the liver and can cause cirrhosis and failure, no vaccine available, much more infections than HIV.

Herniation: When tissue protrudes through an abnormal bodily opening.

Hydronephrosis: Kidney obstruction causing it to enlarge.

Hypovolemia: Inadequate fluid in the circulatory system (dehydration).

Immuno-compromised: Weakened immune system (HIV/AIDS, high dose steroids, etc …).

Infiltrated (IV): When an IV fluid leaks into soft tissues instead of the vein in which it was placed.

Intravitreal: To place something into the vitreous (back) cavity of the eyeball.

Intubate: To place a breathing tube into a person's trachea.

Kaposi's Sarcoma: Cancerous tumor of connective tissue associated with AIDS.

Kocher maneuver: A surgical maneuver to expose structures in the retroperitoneum behind the duodenum and pancreas.

Kuru: An incurable degenerative neurological disorder caused by a prion (linked to cannibalism).

Laparotomy: A surgical procedure involving a large incision through the abdominal wall to gain access into the abdominal cavity.

Lipo-dystrophic: A medical condition characterized by abnormal or degenerative conditions of the body's adipose tissue, sometimes in odd distribution patterns.

Liver bomb: A sick liver patient that is likely to require intensive care and take weeks or months before they leave the hospital, every interns worst nightmare (also known as a rock on the service).

Manometer: An instrument used to measure pressure.

Metastasis: Typically a cancer that has spread to other parts of the body from its origin.

Microsporidial: Eukaryotic spore forming obligate intracellular parasites.

Micturate: Fancy word for urinate.

Midline shift: When a bleed or other pressure (tumore) causes one side of the brain to shift past the midline an onto the other side.

Myiasis: Infection by maggots.

Naso-gastric: A tube/cannula going through the nose into the stomach.

Naso-tracheal tube: A tube/cannula going from the nose into the trachea (used to help a patient breathe or undergo artificial respirations).

Necrolysis (or Toxic Epidermal Necrolysis): It is characterized by the detachment of the top layer of skin (epidermis) from the lower layers of the skin (dermis) all over the body.

Nephrotoxic: Damaging to the kidneys.

Nissen fundoplication: A surgical procedure to treat gastroesophageal reflux disease (GERD).

Non-rebreather: A mask providing high concentrations of oxygen.

Normal saline: 0.9% saline solution, usually for IV use.

Nosocomial: Infection caught from the hospital (usually bad).

Onychomycosis: Fungal nail infection.

Orbital: The bony cavity which surrounds the eyeball.

Oxycontin: Very strong narcotic, high abuse potential.

Palliative: Relieving or soothing the symptoms of a disease or disorder without effecting a cure.

Palpation: To feel or touch something.

Parenteral: Introduction of nutrition, a medication, or other substance into the body via a route other than the gastro-intestinal tract (usually tough an IV).

Parkinson's: A brain disorder that leads to tremors and difficulty with walking, movement, and coordination.

Percocet: A strong oral narcotic drug, often abused.

Pharynx: Part of the throat situated immediately behind the mouth and nasal cavity, and superior to the esophagus (where tonsils are located).

Pimps: Questions asked to lower level trainees, known as "pimping."

Pleurisy: Inflammation of the lining of the lungs and chest.

Pneumocystis jirovecii: Yeast-like fungus causing lung infection in those with AIDS.

Pneumothorax: Is the collection of air in the space around the lungs (i.e.—collapsed lung).

Prosthesis: Fake limb, eye, etc …

Pustular: Inflammatory skin condition with rupturing pus filled cysts.

Renal: Kidney.

Resect: To cut our or remove surgically.

Retinitis: Infection or inflammation of the retina.

Retractor: Something used in surgery to hold tissues out of the operative or surgical field.

Scrubbing: The act of washing before entering the operating room prior to surgery.

Shaken Baby Syndrome: When a small child is shaken and found to have brain and retinal bleeding, usually in conjunction with broken bones.

Sodium amytal: Commonly used as 'truth serum.' Only moderately successful.

Spinous processes: The bumps one can feel if they run their hand down their spine. Attachment sites for muscles.

Spleenectomy: Removal of spleen.

Squamous cell: A type of cancer, usually confined to the skin.

Staph: A type of bacteria that is very common and getting resistant to many drugs.

Sternal: Center of the chest where the ribs join.

Stone: Unit of measurement equal to 14 lbs.

Subdural: Space in between the skull and the dura matter.

Thoracic: Upper back.

Thrombosis: A blood clot.

Thrush: Fungus (usually Candida) that occurs in the mouth.

Toradol: Non-steroidal anti-inflammatory medication that is very strong.

Trach: Short of tracheostomy.

Tracheostomy: Usually an emergency procedure used to create an opening in the neck to bypass an obstructed airway.

Troponin: Laboratory used to check for a heart attack.

Tuberculosis: Infection that typically occurs in underdeveloped countries and affects the lungs.

Viral load: Number of actively replicating viruses during acute infection.

Whipple: A type of major surgery used to treat/cure pancreatic cancer.

Xanax: More potent but shorter acting Valium.

Yankauer: Type of suction used in surgery.

Zosyn: A powerful broad spectrum antibiotic.